Dear Reader,

Sometimes an idea just won't let go of you for years.
The initial seed of this novel was the title that eventually
turned into **The Frugal Wizard's Handbook for Surviving
Medieval England**. At first there was no story to go with
that title, but I wrote it down and kept coming back to it,
wondering what that book could possibly be about.
Something else I thought about off and on for years was
the classic concept of a man waking up in another time
and another place, with no idea how he got there.
It was when those two ideas came together, and I placed
a book with that title into that man's hands, that this novel
was born. I hope you'll have as much fun with it as I did!

Brandon Sanderson

THE FRUGAL WIZARD'S
HANDBOOK FOR SURVIVING MEDIEVAL ENGLAND

BY CECIL G. BAGSWORTH III

Cecil G. Bagsworth III

FICTION BY BRANDON SANDERSON®

THE STORMLIGHT ARCHIVE®
The Way of Kings
Words of Radiance
Oathbringer
Rhythm of War

NOVELLAS
Edgedancer
Dawnshard

THE MISTBORN® SAGA

THE ORIGINAL TRILOGY
Mistborn: The Final Empire
The Well of Ascension
The Hero of Ages

THE WAX & WAYNE SERIES
The Alloy of Law
Shadows of Self
The Bands of Mourning
The Lost Metal

THE RECKONERS®
Steelheart
Mitosis: A Reckoners Story
Firefight
Calamity
Lux (with Steven Michael Bohls)

SKYWARD
Skyward
Starsight
Cytonic
Defiant

NOVELLA
Defending Elysium

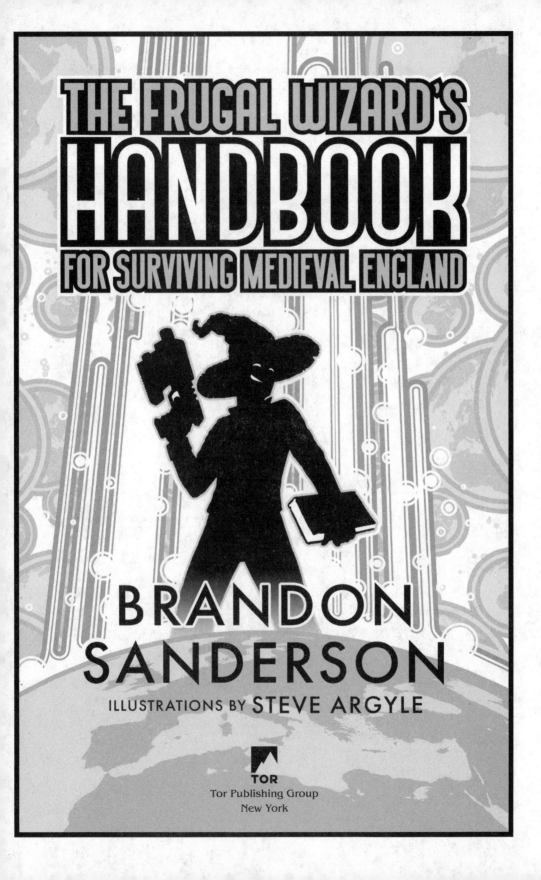

THE FRUGAL WIZARD'S
HANDBOOK
FOR SURVIVING MEDIEVAL ENGLAND

BRANDON SANDERSON

ILLUSTRATIONS BY STEVE ARGYLE

TOR
Tor Publishing Group
New York

THE FRUGAL WIZARD'S HANDBOOK FOR SURVIVING MEDIEVAL ENGLAND

Copyright © 2023 by Dragonsteel, LLC

Mistborn®, The Stormlight Archive®, Reckoners®, Cosmere®, and Brandon Sanderson® are registered trademarks of Dragonsteel, LLC.

Illustrations by Steve Argyle
Copyright © 2023 by Dragonsteel, LLC

A Tor Book
Published by Tom Doherty Associates / Tor Publishing Group
120 Broadway
New York, NY 10271

www.torpublishinggroup.com

Tor® is a registered trademark of Macmillan Publishing Group, LLC.

The Library of Congress Cataloging-in-Publication Data is available upon request.

ISBN 978-1-250-89968-2 (trade paperback)

Our books may be purchased in bulk for promotional, educational, or business use. Please contact your local bookseller or the Macmillan Corporate and Premium Sales Department at 1-800-221-7945, extension 5442, or by email at MacmillanSpecialMarkets@macmillan.com.

First Tor Paperback Edition: 2024

Printed in the United States of America

0 9 8 7 6 5 4 3 2 1

For Matt Bushman

Who is our wonderful family skop, always ready with a song, though never a boast. So I will do it for him.

CONTENTS

ACKNOWLEDGMENTS

Not all the wizardry involved in this volume was mine. In fact, a whole ton of people helped make this book a reality. In particular, though, I want to single out three. The first is the amazing Steve Argyle—a great friend and brilliant artist. I basically handed this book to Steve and said, "This is yours to play with—do whatever you would like to make it awesome." And man, even with my high expectations, his art blew me away. If you're listening to the audiobook, I suggest you stop by my website to see the art Steve did, because it's incredible.

The second special note is for Dr. Michael Livingston. Probably best known by my readers for his scholarly work about Robert Jordan and The Wheel of Time (check out his volume *Origins of The Wheel of Time* for an in-depth look at the story behind the story), he also has written some fantasy stories of his own, which I recommend you check out! He's a medievalist and professor of history, and he gave me a great in-depth read to help correct some of the inaccuracies in the volume. If that weren't enough, he rewrote all of my attempts at Anglo-Saxon poetry to be more accurate, and

ACKNOWLEDGMENTS

his poems are far, far superior. I'm indebted to him for the time he spent on this project.

Third is, of course, my wonderful wife—first reader for all of these "secret project" books and the person for whom I wrote them. It is because of her encouragement and excitement that you have these books!

A lot of the rest of the folks working on this project are members of my company, Dragonsteel. In the Art Department, ᛁᛌᚠᚠᛌ Stewart art directed with support from Rachael Lynn Buchanan, Jennifer Neal, Priscilla Spencer, Ben McSweeney, and Hayley Lazo. Bill Wearne is our go-to printing expert who helped put this all together. These books took a lot of extra art and printing work, so I appreciate all of them for their help.

Editorial is headed by the inland Peter Ahlstrom, and Kristy S. Gilbert was lead editor for this project. Also rendering invaluable editorial services were Karen Ahlstrom and Betsey Ahlstrom. Kristy Kugler did the copyedit.

The Operations Department is overseen by Matt Hatch. His team includes Emma Tan-Stoker, Jane Horne, Kathleen Dorsey Sanderson, Makena Saluone, Hazel Cummings, and Becky Wilson.

Publicity and Marketing is headed by Adam Horne, and his team includes Jeremy Palmer, Taylor D. Hatch, and Octavia Escamilla. Their work on the Kickstarter was a big part of why it went so well. I believe this is Taylor and Octavia's first appearance in an acknowledgments! Nice work, both of you.

Fulfillment and Events is headed by Kara Stewart. Her people are the ones who are in charge of shipping out hundreds of thousands of copies of books to you all, and they worked extra hard this year getting everything sent out. Many thanks to them for their hard work! This team includes Christi Jacobsen, Lex Willhite, Kellyn Neumann, Mem Grange, Michael Bateman, Joy Allen, Katy Ives, Richard Rubert, Brett

ACKNOWLEDGMENTS

Moore, Ally Reep, Sean VanBuskirk, Isabel Chrisman, Owen Knowlton, Alex Lyon, Jacob Chrisman, Matt Hampton, Camilla Cutler, and Quinton Martin.

Thanks to our friends at Kickstarter, Margot Atwell and Oriana Leckert; our friends at BackerKit, Anna Gallagher, Palmer Johnson, and Antonio Rosales; and our ever-vigilant friends at Inventor's Guide, Matt Alexander and Mike Kannely.

At the JABberwocky literary agency, Joshua Bilmes, Susan Velazquez, and Christina Zobel have done an excellent job placing this book at publishers worldwide. For the trade release at Tor in the US, I would like to thank Devi Pillai, Tessa Villanueva, Lucille Rettino, Eileen Lawrence, Alexis Saarela, Rafal Gibek, Peter Lutjen, Greg Collins, and Hayley Jozwiak. In the UK I'd like to thank Gillian Redfearn, Emad Akhtar, and Brendan Durkin at Gollancz, as well as my UK agents, John Berlyne and Stevie Finegan at the Zeno Agency.

Alpha readers for this book (who read an actual print copy!) included Brad Neumann, Kellyn Neumann, Lex Willhite, Jennifer Neal, Christi Jacobsen, Ally Reep, and Tyson Meyer.

Beta readers were Drew McCaffrey, Brian T. Hill, João Menezes Morais, Richard Fife, Joy Allen, Glen Vogelaar, Megan Kanne, Bob Kluttz, Paige Vest, Jayden King, Deana Covel Whitney, Chana Oshira Block, Christina Goodman, Heather Clinger, Zaya Clinger, and Chris Cottingham.

Gamma readers included Brian T. Hill, Joshua Harkey, Tim Challener, Ross Newberry, Rob West, Jessica Ashcraft, Chris McGrath, Evgeni "Argent" Kirilov, Glen Vogelaar, Frankie Jerome, Shannon Nelson, Ted Herman, Drew McCaffrey, Kalyani Poluri, Bob Kluttz, Christina Goodman, Rosemary Williams, Jayden King, Ian McNatt, Anthony, Lyndsey Luther, and Kendra Alexander.

PART ONE

The White Room

1

I came alert, fists raised, an electric jolt of adrenaline surging through me. I spun, light on my feet, looking for someone to punch, sweat streaming down the sides of my face.

I was in a field.

A sunny field, with a forest nearby.

What the hell?

What the *ever-loving* hell?

Heart thumping like a bass beat, I tried to make sense of things. Something sounded behind me and I spun, hands back up at guard.

It was only a bird. This was just a field. Ridged and furrowed, with undulating lines in the earth. There was a burned-out section around me, marked by charred stalks of grain and smoldering ash. I searched my memory for clues and found it blank, like a white room ready for paint.

Empty. I was empty. Except for . . . a vague dislike of swimming?

At the moment, that was the sum total of what I could remember about myself. No name. No background. Just a latent fear of large bodies of water.

I raised a hand to my head and glanced around, trying to make sense of my emptiness. The plants growing outside the burnt area were a few inches tall. My inability to distinguish the variety indicated I probably wasn't a farmer.

The strange burn marks made a circle, maybe ten feet in diameter, with me in the center. Looking closer, I noticed that the plants under my feet *hadn't* been burned. I glanced behind me, and found an unburned portion in a distinct human shape. My shape. A person stencil.

Maybe I was fireproof? Perhaps I had augments to that effect. I appeared to be male, of average height and muscular build. I wore a pair of sturdy laced boots, a long shirt, a brown tunic on top of that, and a vibrant cloak over *that*. So I probably wasn't going to get cold any time soon. Under the tunic . . .

Blue jeans?

With a tunic and cloak? That was odd.

Oh *hell*. Was I a cosplayer? And why could I remember that word, but not my own name?

Right, so I'd gone out into a field to take pictures for the local Renaissance faire or whatever. I'd brought along pyrotechnics to make for a cooler shot, and I'd accidentally blown myself up. That seemed plausible enough.

So where was my camera? My phone? My car keys?

My pockets turned out to be empty except for a ballpoint pen. I stepped away from the me-stencil, my feet crunching on the crispy remains of the former plants. The air smelled of smoke and sulfur.

I quickly searched the area, but I didn't find anything of note. Dirt, vegetation. No pile of belongings; I was beginning to doubt my photoshoot theory. Maybe I was simply a weirdo who liked to dress in old-timey clothing to . . . go explode in fields?

You know, as one does.

In the distance, I saw a dirt road leading to a cluster of antiquated wooden buildings with thatched roofs and few windows, with a taller structure beyond them. They were partially obscured by a hill, so I couldn't tell much else about them. I shook my head and let out a lengthy sigh. I had to—

Wait. What was that on the ground?

I rushed over and plucked a fluttering piece of paper from between two larger plant stalks. How had I missed this? The edge was burned, and it had only a few lines of text on it.

The Frugal Wizard's Handbook for Surviving Medieval England
Fourth Edition
By Cecil G. Bagsworth III

I read the words three times, then glanced at the old-timey buildings again. I wasn't a cosplayer. I was visiting some kind of *theme park*. Was that more or less nerdy?

Now that I knew what to look for, I spotted another loose piece of paper over near the woods. Maybe it would have a map on it—or at least list where I could find a first aid station. I'd obviously hit my head or something.

This page was burned worse than the other one. Two chunks of the text were legible: one on the front side, one on the back.

can be traumatic, though don't worry! As part of your package, a suitable location will be chosen for you to recuperate upon arrival. In addition, it is suggested that you use the handy notation page at the back of the book to record pertinent information about your life.

The transfer process can leave the mind muddied—a few facts about one's life can jog loose other details. Don't stress the initial disorientation. It is a common side effect, and all you need to do is

What a perfectly awful place to cut off. I flipped the page over.

seem that the offerings of more expensive packages, sold by so-called premium companies, might be more useful in helping you recuperate. Servants, a luxury manor, and medical staff. Though we can accommodate such requests, don't fear if you can't afford them! The Frugal Wizard™ doesn't need to be so extravagant. Indeed, such services might make things too easy! (See the study done by Bagsworth et al., page 87.)

Yes, the Frugal Wizard™ is capable and confident on their own, and does not need coddling. Read on to learn all the tips and secrets you will need for

All right, so I'd bought some kind of travel package. One that was . . . really hard on the body, for some reason? A thought flickered at the edge of my consciousness.

I'd chosen this. I *wanted* to be here.

For a moment, I felt close to answering the more important questions. Then it was gone. I was back to staring at a white room inside my brain.

Regardless, I hadn't arrived at a "suitable location" to recuperate. I'd woken up in the middle of a burning field. The review almost wrote itself. *An ideal experience, if you happen to be a pyromaniac cow. One star.*

Wait.

Voices in the distance.

My body moved before I registered the sounds. In seconds I'd slipped into the forest and put my back to a tree trunk. I reached to my side by reflex for . . .

Hell. Was I reaching for a *gun*? I wore nothing of the sort, and was also uncomfortable at how quickly—and silently—I'd dodged for cover.

It didn't *necessarily* mean anything nefarious. Maybe I was a champion hide-and-seek player. Paintball hide-and-seek?

I'd been thinking about finding help, so I should have been happy to be noticed. But some instinct kept me hidden behind the tree, my breathing slow and deliberate. Whoever I was, I had experience with this sort of thing.

I was close enough to hear when the people arrived.

"What is it, Ealstan?" a timid man's voice said—speaking perfect, modern English, albeit with a vaguely European accent. "Landswight?"

"This was no act of a wight," a stronger male voice said.

"Logna's flames, maybe?" a woman's voice said. "Look at the outline of that figure. And there were all those incantations scattered about . . ."

"It looks like someone was burned alive," the first voice said. "That clap of thunder on a bright, sunny day . . . maybe fire from heaven consumed him."

The deeper voice grunted. I resisted the urge to peek. *Not yet,* my instincts whispered.

"Call everyone together," the firm voice eventually said. "We'll put out sacrifices tonight. Hild . . . that skop. Did she leave yet?"

"Earlier today, I think," the woman said.

"Send a boy to chase her down and beg her return. We may need a binding. Or worse, a loosening."

"She's going to like that," the woman said.

Another grunt. The crops rustled as the people retreated. I finally peeked around the side of the tree and picked out the three people walking toward the distant buildings. Two men and a woman in archaic clothing. Tunics and loose, baggy trousers on the men— weren't they supposed to wear hose? I could swear I'd seen that in a museum. Their clothing was dyed in faded earth tones, though the taller of the two men wore an orange cloak—a color so vibrant, I had trouble believing it was period authentic.

The woman had on a sleeveless brown dress over a slightly longer white dress with long sleeves. Other than the colorful cloak, they looked the part of old-school peasants—at least, better than I did, with my jeans. Another point in favor of this being a theme park?

Yet, wouldn't workers in a theme park speak with old-timey British affectations? "Thees" and "thous" and "mi'lords" and the like. But would they keep up the act when nobody was around?

I needed more information. I noted another person running up to them, carrying something. Scraps of burned paper. Most of the pages of my book must have blown toward the town, and someone had gathered them up.

All right. Mission accepted.

I *needed* those pages.

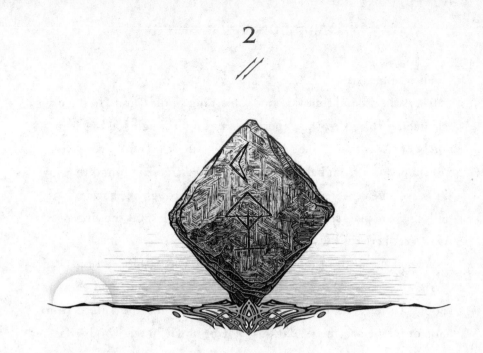

2

Part of me wanted to stalk out and demand answers. Play the role of irate customer, make them break character.

Yet . . . Something about all this . . .

A part of me was convinced that they *weren't* actors. That—insanely—this was all authentic, and I should stay hidden.

Damn. That sounded ridiculous, didn't it?

Nevertheless, my gut said I was a person who trusted his gut. So I stayed put, watching covertly from the shadows as the sunlight waned. I waited a little too long, because eventually, the place went dark.

Basement from a horror movie dark. Clouds moved in, obscuring the stars—and there was apparently no moon tonight. Plus, I didn't see a single light in the town. I'd expected some torches or bonfires.

I patted the tree I'd been hiding behind. "Thanks for the cover," I whispered. "You're a good tree. Tall, thick—and most importantly—wooden. Four and a half stars. Would hide behind you again. Half a point off for lack of refreshments."

Then I paused.

It was the second time I'd done something similar, and I found myself itching to record the experience and my thoughts about it in a notebook. Was that a clue to who I was? Some kind of . . . reviewer?

I slipped out from behind the highly rated tree and found that my skills as a sneak were exceptional. I moved through the rows of partially grown plants, barely making a sound, despite the darkness. Awesome. Perhaps I was a *ninja*.

Beyond the field, I found the road, which was fashioned of packed earth. I headed toward the town, glad that the clouds had thinned enough to let a little starlight through. It turned the village from "horror movie basement" dark to "horror movie in the woods" dark. An improvement, maybe?

I wasn't accustomed to such primal darkness. The shadows were deeper than any I'd ever seen, as if strengthened by the knowledge that I couldn't control them with the flip of a switch.

I reached the village and moved among the silent homes. There couldn't be more than twenty buildings here. All with wooden walls and thatched, triangular roofs. (Two stars. Probably has terrible wifi.)

I heard a river somewhere in the near distance, and there was a large lump of darkness farther on. I found the river—wide, but shallow—on the other side of the village. Here, I knelt and scooped up some water to drink. My medical nanites would neutralize any bacteria before they gave me too much trouble.

I froze in place, hands halfway to my mouth.

Medical . . . nanites?

Yes, tiny machines inside my body that performed basic health-care functions. They'd stop toxins, prevent disease, and break down what I ate to provide ideal nutrition and calories. In a pinch, they could provide emergency wound-healing functions. Last time I'd been shot, I'd been back on my feet within the hour—but my nanites had been knocked completely out for a good two days.

Hot damn! A piece of the puzzle. Did I have any other augments? I couldn't remember, but I did know I'd need more food than an average person. Specifically, I needed high-calorie food, or . . . carbon? Technically, anything organic would work. But some sources were better than others.

I glanced back at the town. A child had started crying, and the solitary wails creeped me out.

Controlling my nerves, I slipped along the river until I reached a wooden bridge and crossed it. The large shadowy lump turned out to be a fortification of upright logs, driven down into the ground with sharpened ends toward the sky, about eight feet tall.

The wall looked sturdy enough, though I'd have expected something taller and made of stone. Castle-like. A wooden palisade left me a tad disappointed. I withheld my review, though. Maybe it was period accurate.

This had to be where I'd find the more important people in the town—like the man with the deep, authoritative voice.

I scouted around the entire outside of the fortification—it was only large enough to enclose a few buildings—but the gate was closed and there was a big pit dug all the way round. There was also an elevated wooden platform at one corner, inside the wall. A guard post. I'd never make it inside without drawing attention if I tried to jump the pit and climb the fence.

Therefore, I used my entire life's experience—roughly half a day so far—to devise a plan. I hid behind a nearby tree with a view of the gates, then waited for them to open.

(Tree report: Three stars. Uncomfortable root network. Not for an inexperienced hider. See my other reviews of trees in the area for more options.)

I was contemplating demoting another half star from the tree when I heard something approaching quickly along the road. For a brief moment, my heart leaped. A car?

No. Beating hooves. Two horses with riders emerged from the gloom, illuminated by starlight, traveling way faster than I thought safe to do at night. The riders stopped by the gate and called to those inside. I was too far away to hear the exchange, but the double gate wobbled open soon after.

I couldn't tell much about the two hooded riders as they trotted through the gates. A few lights inside illuminated two larger structures—one made of stone, the other made of the same wood-and-thatch of the village.

There was apparently something odd about the visitors, for most of the people inside—including the guards—gathered around them. Leaving nobody watching the gates.

I took my opportunity, slinking forward through the darkness. My sneaking skills got me through the gates without being spotted. My instinct for how to stick to the shadows, how to not present a profile, and how to move without making noise made me concerned about where I'd gotten these skills. That, and the fact that I kept wanting to rest my hand on a nonexistent gun. They didn't seem the type of abilities that belonged to a law-abiding citizen who spent his days reviewing trees.

I crouched beside some barrels, taking stock of what I could see. In the center of the courtyard was a large black stone with a jagged top, taller than it was wide. Like a small version of the Washington Monument with the top broken off. On the far side of the courtyard was a small stable. There, the two riders had dismounted and handed their horses to a groom.

A boy ran for the stone building. It seemed to be of much finer construction than the others. Perhaps it was the lord's manor? And maybe the wooden one was a meeting hall?

Curiously, a series of dishes with lit candles at the sides were set in front of the stone building. Bowls of fruit, some saucers filled with cream, and . . .

And a single, singed piece of paper.

The boy soon returned and gestured for the two riders to follow him. The three entered the wooden building I'd guessed was the meeting hall, and I thought I heard the word "refreshment" as they entered. Perhaps I should have been interested in those men, but my attention turned wholly to that sheet of paper. Was it from my book? Why leave it out in front of the building like that?

This was all so bizarre. Was I part of some ridiculous social experiment? A reality television game?

I forced myself to wait a few tense minutes until, as I'd expected, a man in an orange cloak left the manor, accompanied by two men carrying long, one-handed axes and round, wooden shields. No armor that I could see. They had a vaguely Viking look to them.

"Oswald," one of them shouted toward the wooden watchtower. "Close the gate."

As the lord and his two men entered the hall, a younger soldier came scrambling down from the tower. He grinned to the others and bowed a little too much to the lord, then crossed over and began to swing the gates closed.

It was time to make my move. Like the old saying goes. Carp diem. Seize the fish. I was out and scuttling across the courtyard before I had time to think. My body seemed to know that while I couldn't miss my opportunity, I shouldn't sprint. That would make too much noise. Feeling exposed, I swiftly walked past the large black stone, then past the bowls and the candles, where I snatched the paper.

Within seconds, I had found cover beside the meeting hall. My heart was thundering. I took a few long, quiet breaths to calm myself, then glanced at my paper.

Right. Darkness. Horror movie. All that. Well, there was a window a little farther along. The shutter was latched, but light seeped out. I crept over, then held my paper close to the cracks.

It was filled with printed words, matching the other pages I'd found. But this one was barely singed. It read:

Your Own Dimension

The intricacies of dimensional travel are unimportant, and we recommend you not trouble yourself with them. We here at Frugal Wizard Inc.® have done the hard part for you. All you need to do is pick the package you want, and we will deliver one pristine, Earth-lite™ dimension to you.

I stopped reading, the words blurring as my eyes unfocused. Another tiny puzzle piece snapped into place.

This wasn't a theme park, a strange social experiment, or a game.

This was another dimension.

And I *owned* it.

YOUR OWN DIMENSION

The intricacies of dimensional travel are unimportant, and we recommend you not trouble yourself with them. We here at Frugal Wizard Inc.® have done the hard part for you. All you need to do is pick the package you want, and we will deliver one pristine, Earth-lite™ dimension to you.

That said, a little history never hurt anyone. Unless you end up getting stabbed by a knight! (That's a little interdimensional humor. Our dimensions are perfectly safe.[1])

_____

1. Legal Disclaimer: This statement is made for entertainment purposes only. The interdimensional traveler takes any and all responsibility for all

Though interdimensional travel was discovered in 2084, the technology was only recently declassified and deregulated. This allows not only recreational dimensional tourism, but the opportunity of a lifetime! As an Interdimensional Wizard™ you are part of a bold new coterie of explorers. Like the ancient homesteaders who rushed to claim land in the American West, you may stake your own claim on a unique dimension!

Frugal Wizard Inc.® has obtained a band of the 305th spectrum of category-two medieval-derivative dimensions. That fancy lingo simply means our dimensions are similar to one another, and are two categories removed from Earth itself. Things will be familiar, but not *too* familiar! We want it to remain exciting, after all.

We spend all our time poring through the dimensions, selecting only the most favorable for wizard habitation. Act now, before all the good dimensions are claimed![2]

---

killings, maimings, injuries, dismemberments, and impalements that might happen to them in their respective dimensions. In the event of a dispute, you agree to arbitration, to be adjudicated in the dimension of our choice.

2. Legal Disclaimer: This statement is made for entertainment purposes only. Dimensions are, technically, infinite and we cannot "run out."

3

Yes, I owned it.

I owned England. I owned this planet. I owned this *entire universe*. On paper, at least.

I wasn't sure about all the specifics—my memory was still performing at a decided zero-out-of-five-stars level. But I knew people could *buy* dimensions. Well, technically, you bought exclusive access—managed by an unbreakable quantum passcode only you could unlock—and the legal right to do whatever you wanted in that dimension. I mean, in some of these places, the laws of *physics* (as understood in our dimension) didn't apply. So why would the UN General Constitution?

Whatever the reasoning, this place was my playground the size of a planet.

But . . . what did that make me? Tourist? History buff? Would-be world-emperor? What had been my motives for coming to this place? And why had I woken up in a field, rather than in some pre-prepared stronghold or some . . . I don't know . . . science place?

Well, I definitely hadn't been an academic. But I knew something had gone wrong.

As I considered the implications, voices inside the hall reminded me to pay better attention to my surroundings. I was unarmed and confused. If I were to saunter in, explain that I technically owned all of this, and ask them to kindly obey me . . . I suspected they'd saunter over to me, explain that the sword they'd rammed into my gut didn't care what I claimed, and ask me to kindly avoid bleeding on the rug.

Could I impress them with my fantastical futuristic knowledge? Did I have any of that? I racked my brain, but it seemed my futuristic knowledge equated to a handful of movie quotes. I also knew that computers would exist someday. They involved circuits. And, uh, processors.

I had medical nanites, but that would be difficult to show off in an impressive, "Look, I'm a god" sort of way. My most consistent "superpower" was the ability to get coughed on a lot without getting sick. I could heal from a larger wound, but while the nanites rebuilt themselves, I would be exposed if someone decided I should replicate the feat. None of that felt like a good peasant-quelling mechanism.

Maybe I could get bitten by a snake or something, and not die? Where did one find a snake?

I had to find the rest of the book. Maybe it would include some kind of help line.

I made my way carefully around the back of the building, approaching a closed window closer to the voices.

". . . I would certainly not wish to offend the earl," a deep voice was saying. I recognized it—Mister Orange-cloak, the local lord. "But this is most unusual. We have a skop in town. Perhaps she could—"

Another voice said something, quieter, but threatening.

"Now?" Orange-cloak said. "You want to visit the site . . . now?"

Footsteps followed, and they left the building. Great. I'd missed the entire conversation.

I snuck around the side of the building, hoping to catch something relevant as they left.

"If this man you're seeking is nearby," the lord said, "we shall find him. But I must warn you . . . it looked very much like he had been struck down by an act of a god."

The visitors didn't reply. Together, they strode out the freshly opened front gates, and the lord—distinctly annoyed—followed with wide strides, shaking his head.

Wait.

They were looking for me?

They were *looking* for *me*.

Relief surged through me. Something had gone wrong during the transfer to this dimension, so the people who maintained this had obviously sent rescuers. I *wasn't* the only one who could get to this dimension. Maybe I'd left them with the key and permission to come help.

I raised my hand, preparing to call to them, when I heard a sound.

I reached for my nonexistent gun yet again as I spun and found two people crouching behind me. They'd been creeping up through the shadows behind the hall. The person in the back—a twenty-something woman—pointed at me with a panicked expression.

I immediately fell into a fighting stance. Hands in front of me, feet ready for action. Huh.

The younger man in front of the woman carried a knife, which he immediately swung—and which I blocked, by instinct, with my forearm.

And . . . it didn't hurt.

Why on Earth didn't that hurt?

The young man had hit me hard with a blade, and I'd *taken* it like an utter champion, not even a nick on me. I *did* have other augments! Platings under my skin? I was a fighter! I could . . .

I heard shouts in my memory.

Flashes of light. From a time before.

I felt pain, deep shame. It choked me, a black vine wrapped around my lungs.

I put a hand to my head, trying to banish these phantoms from my memory while simultaneously latching on to them as something *real* from who I had been. What was *wrong* with me?

The man swung again. I felt a deep, nearly uncontrollable panic, and was slower to block.

I'd fallen . . . I'd . . .

The man's blade connected with my exposed wrist, and his eyes widened as his knife failed to cut me. He backed up a step. I stumbled, overwhelmed by the fragments of memories.

Flashing lights. Angry voices. I . . .

I blinked and glanced to the side. The woman had found a wooden board somewhere. She swung it, and I didn't respond this time. I was too unnerved. But theoretically, my platings would protect me from—

The board connected with my face, and I felt a flash of agony before my nanites cut out my pain receptors. I briefly saw stars, but at least I was unconscious by the time I hit the ground, so the terrible memories stopped assaulting me.

Have I Time Traveled?

 No, you have not. This might seem counterintuitive, as you're probably living in your own castle at the moment, commanding legions of peasants while you engage in a Better than True Life Experience™, such as inventing electricity, writing Shakespeare's plays, or attempting to speedrun the conquest of France.

While your surroundings might *seem* medieval, your Personal Wizard Dimension™ has seen roughly the same number of centuries as ours has. However, our specially cultivated dimensions have moved slower through their technological and social development. Therefore, you *do* get a semi-accurate experience reminiscent of medieval England, but you *haven't* time traveled.

Still confused? Think of Nebraska. Nebraska is a landlocked state in the center of the United States of America. Because of its general lack of importance—and its distance from trendy population centers—it lags a few years behind the coasts in fashion, music, and distribution of collectible card games.

You might feel like you've time traveled when visiting Nebraska, but careful scientific experiments using synchronized timepieces have proven no time dilation is in effect. (See Luddow, Sing, and Coffman, "Nebraska really is just like that" in *Journal of Relativistic Studies*, Volume 57, June 2072.)

Just as Nebraska is a few years behind everyone else, your Personal Wizard Dimension™ is behind our dimension by half a millennium or so. You have, essentially, purchased your very own, unique Super-Nebraska™.

4

When I woke up, the young woman and man were standing on the ceiling.

Or . . . wait, I was upside down. Yeah, that made more sense.

My head had a faint pulsing at the base of my skull—without my nanites, there would have been some serious throbbing from that plank-to-face contact—and my hands and legs had been bound tightly. Was I tied to the wall? Yeah, they'd hung me from the ceiling beam, then tied my hands behind me. I wondered what they'd wrapped the rope around.

It was an innovative interrogation technique, so I gave it a point for originality, but . . . wouldn't a chair be more effective? It was an old standby for a reason. (Three stars. Watch more spy movies and report back.)

As soon as I opened my eyes, the woman stepped forward. She had blond hair in tight curls that barely reached her collar, and wore a black sleeveless dress over a white dress that was longer through the sleeves and hem. It had some nice maroon embroidery on the neck, but the white ropes wrapping her waist had a frayed look, giving it an intentional, handmade air.

She narrowed her eyes.

Right then. How to get out of this? The shame and fear I'd felt before had faded completely, replaced with embarrassment. I obviously had physical augments, but I'd stood there and let a woman plank me in the face. Unprofessional.

"You've made a terrible mistake," I told her.

She didn't respond, instead cocking her head.

"I'm a very powerful being," I told her. "You have angered me."

The young man hid behind her, peeking out at me. He seemed unremarkable—a shorter fellow with similar blond curls and a slight build. Upon closer inspection, he looked younger than I'd assumed. Perhaps only fifteen or sixteen.

"Sefawynn," he hissed, "I don't think the inversion is doing anything. He still has his powers!"

"Has he eaten you yet, Wyrm?" the woman asked.

"No."

"Then the inversion is working," she said.

"It's not working," I said. "I'm gathering my powers as we speak. Release me now, or I'll bring fire and destruction upon your house."

The woman narrowed her eyes further, then raised both hands, fingers up and thumbs out toward one another. Then she spoke.

"I live the last light   of lovings long-lost.
Care-keeper I am   and ken my kindred."

As she finished, both of them leaned closer, as if to see the effect on me.

"Poetry?" I said. "That was nice."

The youth squeezed the woman's arm. "Try a stronger boast."

She nodded, and made the same sign with her hands before speaking again.

"I banished the beast   of Bastion's Barrow.
Song-sounder I am   and sing out strongest."

I frowned, and both of them shied back.

"Not even a flinch," the youth whispered. "That's bad, isn't it, Sefawynn?"

"I don't know," she said, folding her arms. "I've never loosed an aelv before." She tapped her index finger against her arm. "Fetch the little father, but do it quietly, so the visitors don't hear you."

The boy nodded, then paused.

"I'll be fine," the woman said without looking at him. "The inversion has rendered him helpless."

"But he said—"

"Once again, Wyrm," she said, "have you been eaten?"

He looked down, as if he needed to check.

"If the aelv's powers weren't bound," she said, "we wouldn't be standing here. We'd either be controlled by him, or we'd be puddles of human juice, mashed to the floor. Go fetch the little father. I'll be fine."

The youth bobbed a nod, then hurried out the door. I revised my assessment of his age downward again. Perhaps he was big for his age.

"Could you at least put me right-side up?" I said to the woman. "I'm starting to feel light-headed."

She studied me, and didn't respond.

"So . . ." I said. "You keep calling me an . . . eelev? I'm not rightly aware of what that is. Maybe you could fill a guy in?"

No response.

"That younger fellow is your brother?" I asked. "And you're the lord's daughter?" They had to be—both she and the boy were dressed better than the others in this town. But why did she call the lord "little" father?

Yeah, she wasn't saying anything.

"You saw the boy's weapon bounce off my arm," I said. "I'm warning you. I'm a powerful person, and I'm growing upset."

Her eyes were like steel, her face completely expressionless. Zero stars. Would rather have a conversation with a corpse. It wouldn't glare at me the entire time. Would probably listen better too.

I turned my attention to my augments. Obviously I had improvement on my forearms. Those were called . . . platings. That's it. I had a microfilament mesh under my skin, backed up by structural nanites and bone reinforcements. Basically, it would take an industrial-strength laser or a military-grade weapon to cut through my flesh—as long as my nanites continued to function. Another augmented person could punch me senseless with enough time, but I'd be invulnerable to a bunch of medieval peasants.

As I thought of it, I instinctually called up a visual overlay display. It listed my augments and their status. Hot damn! I had platings from the tips of my fingers all the way up to my shoulders and across my back. Another set ran along my legs, from my thighs down to my feet. Both sets also worked for force redistribution and gave me some strength advantages, mostly in gripping ability.

Those were extremely expensive augments. It wasn't uncommon to start plating a few body parts, then move on to others. Most people would go for the head and the chest first. That made the most sense.

However, my nanite-healed concussion indicated I hadn't done that. I frowned at the menu. I *did* have skull and chest platings—but they were listed as *nonfunctional*. What the hell?

I had the vague impression that I hadn't paid for the augments, that I worked for a living and didn't have that kind of money. So maybe . . . whoever had purchased my augments hadn't finished installing my head and chest platings? But why were my arm, leg, and back platings functional?

My memory provided no answers, so I tried to untie myself. Unfortunately, the knots were good, and my enhanced grip strength wouldn't help if I couldn't reach the ropes. None of the muscles in my chest seemed to be augmented, as a little exploratory flexing didn't lead to me ripping free or anything. I probably looked silly, though.

Eventually, the door opened, and the oil lamps on the table sputtered as two figures entered. One was the youth from earlier—Wyrm, she'd called him? The other was Orange-cloak. Muscular, and a good six-foot-four, this fellow towered over the woman. His beard was streaked with grey, as was his hair, and he looked to be in his midforties. But man, he looked like he could have gotten into a boxing match with a boulder, and won.

Weren't people in the past supposed to be much shorter than modern people or something?

"I'll be frank, Little Father," said the young woman—what had her name been? "I have no idea what to do with this one."

"What is he?" the lord asked, eyes narrowing as he studied my jeans—now fully on display, with the bottom of my tunic flopping down to the tie about my waist.

"Not a landswight," she said, "since we can all see him fully. But look. He's clean-shaven as any woman, with shorn hair, feminine hands—"

"Hey!" I said.

"—and not a particularly muscular build—"

"I'm considered quite athletic among my people."

"—plus pale skin and delicate features through the face," she finished. "Also note the perfect teeth and pristine nails. I know the lore, Little Father. This man matches the descriptions of an aelv perfectly."

"Not a god, then," the lord said, relaxing.

"Plenty dangerous," the woman said. "Perhaps more so. A god would want something natural of us. An aelv . . ."

"He took one of the offerings, Little Father," the youth said. "The incantation. He didn't care for the food or drink."

"Written word," the lord said, stepping closer to me. "Did you bring it to our realm, aelv, or did its arrival draw you? What can we do to appease and loose you?"

"Cut me free," I said in my most intimidating voice, "and apologize for the treatment I've suffered."

The lord smiled. I'd been prepared to see a mouth full of dingy, rotting teeth. I'd been wrong about that guess as well, as he seemed to have all of his teeth—and while they weren't pristine white, they weren't rotting either. They weren't exactly straight, but for a guy living in a time before dentists, his smile wasn't half bad. (Two and a half stars. Won't break the camera.)

"Cut you free?" the lord said. "You think I've never heard a ballad before, aelv?"

"It was worth a try," I said. "Very well. I shall require a berry that has never seen the sun, two stones polished by a frog, and one leaf of nightshade—in return I shall leave your quaint village with a blessing and return to my people."

The lord glanced at the woman, who shrugged.

"I'll . . . see what can be done," the lord told me.

"Or," I said, "you could tell those two men looking for me that I'm here? Then you could turn me over to them . . . ?"

"Ha!" the lord said. "You are very cunning! But as you aren't red-haired, nor do you have the features of a foreigner, I don't believe they want you."

Wait.

The men *weren't* looking for me?

The lord turned to the woman. "I need to attend the earl's messengers before they find my absence strange," the man said to her. "Something *is* odd about them, about this entire day. Will you stay here, or join me?"

"I'll stay," she said. "Take my brother; send him with word if anything else unusual happens."

Orange-cloak nodded to her and left, the younger man trailing after him. I found his interaction with the woman curious. She wasn't bowing or scraping nearly as much as I might have assumed. Barely a mi'lord mentioned.

I really should throw away everything I thought I'd known about the past.

The woman was still watching me. Great. Was this going to be another "conversation" with a wall?

"Look," I said, "can we—"

"Let's cut the lies, stranger," she interrupted. "I know what you really are."

5

Y ou . . . do?" I said.

"This is a good village," she said, "with a strong and diligent thegn. Yet, they don't have much. Why upon the lands
would you pick *here* to run your scam?"

Scam?

"Oil with a stencil to create the burned-out figure," she continued, "which I'll admit is ingenious. Scattered pages of text is nothing
new, though I'm shocked you were brazen enough to take one from
an offering. But the demands you made of the thegn? Ridiculous."

Ah . . . She thought I was a grifter, come to bilk the locals. It was an
apt description of a dimensional tourist.

"Next time," she added, "flinch at my boasts. I find it incredible
that you could put so much preparation into your scam, but do so little
research. You look exactly like an aelv—even shaved your *beard*—but
you couldn't do a little playacting? How can you be so incompetent yet
capable at the same time?"

Play along, my instincts said. *You can ride this.*

"The hit to my head," I said to her. "Did you have to swing so hard? When I woke up, I barely remembered what I'd had for breakfast, let alone what my plan was."

She grunted, arms still folded, golden curls wobbling as she shook her head at me. "You can't be alone. Those messengers have your accent."

"Yeah," I said. "They'd have told your father how to get rid of my haunting. Then I'd appear in the night, give him a scare, to encourage him along."

"Why do you think Ealstan is my father?" she asked.

"You called him . . ."

"Little father? Thegn? Lord of the local lands?" Her frown deepened. "You speak words, yet you don't understand them. My brother and I are only passing through this area. We were brought back because they needed a skop."

"Oh," I said. "Um . . . hit to the head . . ."

She sighed. "Why Stenford? Wellbury is right down the road, and they've many times the resources."

"I'm known there," I said. "Look, we don't need much. Just a little to get us on our way. We wanted your lord to get all frightened because he'd seen an eelev, then pay us to leave." I gave an upside-down shrug. "My friends aren't going to be happy I got caught, by the way."

She rubbed her forehead with thumb and forefinger, eyes closed. "Why do they have your description wrong?"

"I was supposed to put on a disguise," I said. "To look more exotic. Look, we've got an easy out. You give me another boast or two in front of the lord. I'll act however you tell me. Then you can hand me off to my friends, and we won't demand anything. Everybody walks away happy."

"Huh," she said.

"What?"

"That's not an unreasonable ask."

"I promise you, I just wanted a warm meal," I said. "We're off for bigger winnings elsewhere, and were running low on supplies."

She nodded, as if she expected something similar.

And damn. I . . . I was building quite the unflattering picture of who I'd been. Sneaking. Combat augments. Practiced at grifting . . .

But if I had been a thief, why did my stomach immediately turn at the idea? Why did my instincts resist it so strongly? Surely if that was me, it would feel right to acknowledge it.

Instead, a piece of me was *screaming. No,* it said. *That's not who you are.*

"Look," I said to her. "What was your name again?"

"Sefawynn," she said.

"Right. Sefawynn, you're obviously not the type who wants to see a guy get hanged because he's hungry. Let's do this the easy way. I'll even let you know how I did the arm trick, if you want."

"I know your type," she said. "Far too well. I know you'll take whatever you can get. That you'll turn on me in a second. But *don't* try it, all right? I understand you better than you think I do."

"Sure, all right," I said. "After this, I'll stay far away from this village and anyone in it—you have my word."

"For what that's worth."

I shrugged again. "It's either that, or you try to convince the little father I'm a liar—then I do my best scary eelef imitation, and we see who wins. But in that scenario, someone *also* has to lose."

"Aelv," she said. "Ae-lv. At least say it right."

"Aylev," I tried.

"Closer." She walked up to me, slipping a knife from her pocket. Hey, she had a pocket in her dress. Funny to find someone living in the Middle Ages who had one of those, when Jen had always complained that *her* dresses didn't have any.

Wait. Who was Jen?

Sefawynn tensed as she cut my hands free, prepared for a fight. I slowly brought my hands in front of me, then rubbed my wrists in a nonthreatening way.

"Thanks," I said.

"Brace yourself," she said, then untied the rope holding my feet.

I used my hands to do just that, then tucked and rolled to my feet, kicking free of the ropes. *See that,* I thought. *Athletic.* I didn't bolt for the door. My best bet at getting free was still to have her turn me in to those messengers.

Except, they hadn't described me. But she'd said our accents were similar? Hell, I *really* needed more information.

"Don't suppose," I said, "you have the rest of my 'incantations' stashed around here? Those were kind of hard to get ahold of."

"You shouldn't be playing with the written word," she said. "You'll attract the attention of the gods."

"I'll risk it."

She shook her head at my apparent foolishness. "Honestly, I wasn't sure what to do with them. Burning them would draw Logna's ire for certain, but merely having them will draw Woden's. So I'll fetch them for you. And then you must carry the wyrd away with you and your foolish aers."

Whole lot of gibberish there, but I nodded to her in thanks. The papers were my best bet at learning about this place. I was practically a baby in my knowledge of the Middle Ages. Jen would laugh at me for . . .

Oh.

Jen was dead.

6

It was strange to feel a sudden sense of loss and pain for a person whose face I couldn't remember. But it was there, a knot—no, a suddenly audible *scream*—inside of me.

The pain felt fresh and raw, like a bruise before it went blue. I'd lost Jen. Somehow, I'd *lost* her.

I stumbled, putting one hand on the nearby wooden pillar. I put the other to my head. Jen. Hot damn . . . this had been *her* dream. This place, this was what I had left of her.

Isn't it incredible? her voice drifted into my mind. *Generations upon generations—thousands upon thousands of years' worth—of people have lived, but they're all the same as us. Teleport someone from Ancient Egypt to the modern era, and they'd be indistinguishable. Same passions. Same cleverness. Same biases, if about different things.*

You'll see. Someday, when we can afford it, you'll see . . .

I didn't remember much more than that at the moment. Just some words, a voice. And the pain. Too personal to joke about. Too real to belong to me.

Sefawynn stepped closer, watching me with suspicion. Yeah, this looked like a classic weakness feint, and she likely worried I'd make a play for the knife. Instead, I forced out a wan smile.

"Sorry," I said. "Hanging upside down did *not* help this headache. Did you have to swing so hard?"

She rolled her eyes.

"Did you roll your eyes at me?" I demanded.

"Oh look," she said, doing it again. "Cobwebs near the ceiling."

"You're lucky you caught me by surprise," I told her. "I can be very dangerous in a fight."

"Careful," she said. "The spiders in the eaves look for empty, unused spots to build their webs. Keep talking, and they'll investigate the vacuous cavern between your ears, aelv." She gave me a flat stare.

I folded my arms. "What's the plan?"

"We'll tell the lord I used your ancient name to bind you. If he asks, tell him the craeft has forced you to do my bidding, and I am banishing you."

"Crayft," I said. "Got it."

"Craeft," she said.

"Crayft."

"Your accent . . ." she said with a shake of her head. "You're Waelish, aren't you?"

"Welsh?" I said, figuring that one out. "Uh, yeah. Totally. And this place is . . ."

"Weswara," she said. "Home of the Weswarans? You can't think I'll believe you don't know that."

Weswara? My British history wasn't the greatest, granted, but . . . shouldn't I have heard of this place?

"Come along then," she said. "We'd best talk to Lord Ealstan before your friends end up saying something that ruins our plan."

I followed as she picked up a lamp—one of those old-school ones that look like a gravy boat—and blew out the others. We'd been in a side chamber of the meeting hall, pretty close to where I'd been dropped.

We entered the main courtyard, which was empty for the moment—though candles still illuminated the bowls of berries and milk in front of the lord's manor. I had to guess this was a folk superstition. A way to appease these "landswights" I'd heard people mention.

"So," I said, "you're a poet. Who performs boasts and ballads? A . . . skop? Is that the term?"

"No need to act so amazed," she said, eyes forward as we walked to the front of the manor, where the young tower guard now stood at the door with axe and shield.

"Uh, hey," he said to her. "Um . . . I'll just see . . . if you can go in?"

She nodded. I glanced over my shoulder, extra wary. Face-board me once, shame on you. Face-board me twice, and . . .

Wait.

The candles were still there, as were the dishes. But their contents were *gone*.

Sefawynn noticed my alarm, because she spun, hand going to her pocket. "What?" she hissed.

"The berries and milk," I said, pointing. "They've vanished."

"Unsurprising," she said, relaxing. "The wights have been staying near you. If you're nice, I'll try a loosing for you. I think one of them may be upset about the page you stole."

"It was mine!"

"Not after it was offered to them, it wasn't," she said. "I did warn you about inscriptions . . ."

I scanned the courtyard. Though it seemed empty, those shadows could hide plenty. As I'd proven by, uh, getting caught.

This has to be some kind of sham, I thought.

I wasn't given much time to think about it, as the good-natured guard returned. He eagerly held the door open for us, and even bowed as Sefawynn entered. Poets were given respect here, it seemed. Miss Bushman, my middle school English teacher, would have been proud.

Another bit remembered! Grinning, I followed Sefawynn into a small entryway. A pair of oil lamps hung from chains from the ceiling, and we trod over a bright orange-and-red rug on the floor. Sefawynn walked forward with her hand sheltering the flame on the lip of her lamp.

She turned left and led me into a large open room with a firebox in the center and a cauldron above it. It had a high ceiling—the structures here didn't seem to have second floors—and the walls were decorated with shields and spears.

Near the fire, Lord Ealstan and a tall woman—I assumed his wife—spoke with the two messengers. They were facing him, but I could see them in profile.

It was the first time I'd seen their faces. I stopped. I *knew* them. That one on the left—the tall brute whose chin and forehead were trying to outdo one another—was Ulric Stromfin.

A man who absolutely, one hundred percent, *no question about it,* wanted me dead.

FAQ:

Why Do Some Things About My Dimension Contradict the Historical Record?

WHOSOEVER
PULLETH OUT
THIS SPORK

No alternate dimension matches ours exactly. Each represents some level of deviation from what happened in our dimension.

That said, some deviate further than others. The dimensions that most closely resemble ours (category one dimensions) are reserved for historical study by the government. (Yes, there are a few "theme park" dimensions set aside for guided tours. In these, you can see what things were authentically like in the Middle Ages. But why would you want to visit such a place when you could—for not much more money—own an entire dimension yourself?)

At Frugal Wizard Inc.®, we specifically chose a band of dimensions that offer an Earth-lite™ experience. Our dimensions are close enough to true history to offer some thrilling, anticipated experiences—like jousting, knights, castles, and the Spanish Inquisition![1] However, there's enough novelty that you'll never find them stuffy like a history book.

While it is unlikely that historical individuals from our history will exist in your dimension, there will be new monarchs to meet. You might not be able to meet Richard the Second, but you can make Tom the Second your vassal! You'll visit kingdoms with new names and borders. You will see battles that never occurred on Earth! Local customs in our dimensions often deviate in fascinating ways from the Earth historical record.[2]

The Frugal Wizard™ isn't only a shrewd businessperson, he, she, or they are also an explorer, excited by the idea of dimensions that provide a challenge!

---

1. Specific time periods in the Middle Ages are not guaranteed for those purchasing Wizard Wildcard™ dimensions. Our band runs from the equivalent of the early AD 600s to around 1350. In addition, some Earth-lite™ dimensions have significant cultural deviations on Great Britain—such as ones where the Romans dominated the entire island, or ones where they never arrived. If you desire a specific time period or experience, be certain to purchase a Fully Guaranteed Dimension™.

2. Ladies! And gentlemen who are into that sort of thing! And everyone else who never gets mentioned in declarations like this! Investigate our unique Celtic True Matriarchy™ dimensions for an experience where women wear the pants! (Legal Note: Nobody tends to wear pants in these dimensions.) Face paint lessons included!

7

Ulric Stromfin. Current head of the Seattle branch of the Fabian Augments cartel.

Augments were expensive. Most people didn't have any, other than the basic medical nanites, which were administered universally at birth to those whose parents agreed. To get anything else, you needed a whole lot of cash. The cartel was great at finding desperate people and locking them into *very* illegal contracts. The type that were never written down, but got you killed if you broke them. Want to join the unrestricted enhancement martial arts league, take a chance at stardom? The cartel could fund your journey. Need advanced medical nanites for your wife who's dying of a rare disease? The cartel could help. And then there were the illegal augments. Things like stealth or weapons enhancements. In return, you incurred some big debts. The "spend your life paying them off" type. There were entire legions of thieves who were obligated to share their takes with the cartel.

The amount I knew about this from seeing one man's face pretty much confirmed what I was. A mobster, or at best a thief. Maybe I was from a rival cartel. I couldn't think of any other reason I'd know so much about the way they worked—and be so certain Ulric wanted me dead.

For now, I moved by instinct, grabbing Sefawynn by the arm and putting my hand over her mouth, then towing her back out into the entryway. The motion snuffed out her lamp and dropped oil to the floor.

I pushed her against the wall right beside the doorway and waited, tense. Had I been spotted? When no cry followed us, I glanced at Sefawynn to find her eyes wide and . . . Wow, look at that. She'd placed the tip of her knife against the side of my throat. Girl was handy with a weapon.

It said a lot about Ulric that even with that knife kissing my skin, I was *far* more worried about him than I was about her. "That man isn't who I thought he was, and I can't let him see me," I whispered. "That's why I grabbed you. I'll let you go now, but *please* don't draw his attention."

I carefully slipped my hand off her mouth. She eyed me, but didn't move the knife. I breathed slowly, and caught the scent of herbs— mint, sage, maybe rosemary. Weren't people from the Middle Ages supposed to stink? I thought they bathed, like, once a fortnight or something.

Finally, she removed the knife, eyes narrow. "I thought they were your friends," she whispered.

"I didn't see their faces earlier," I said. "Those *aren't* my friends."

"Who are they?"

"The taller one is Ulric," I said. "He's a thief, but not like me. He's the boss of a cartel. Uh, the leader of a group of thieves?"

"Like a bandit chief?"

"Sure. Or maybe even more important. Listen, that man is *dangerous*. He's not a 'pretend to be an aelef' kind of thief. He's a 'let them find the bodies; I don't care' kind of thief."

"We need to tell the thegn," she said.

"No, we need to *hide*."

"My brother is in there."

Was he? I'd been distracted by Ulric. And . . . what was the other one's name? The shorter, leaner man next to him—with the face like a shovel and a set of boxer's augments. That was . . .

Quinn. Quinn Jericho. Ulric's enforcer and right-hand man. I didn't remember either of them having a beard, but wearing those, they fit in with every other man I'd seen here.

Why were they here? And searching for someone who wasn't me?

"Your brother will be fine," I whispered. "But *we* won't if those men spot me. Hide me until they leave."

I was beginning to think I'd pushed her trust too far, but she nodded her head to the right. We slunk into a small room nearby—an armory. At least, there were a bunch of axes and swords in here, in a rack. The only lighting came from the lamps in the entryway—and that dimmed as Sefawynn pulled the door shut, leaving it open only a crack.

We'd moved none too soon, for not two minutes passed before Ulric and Quinn stepped into the entry hall, trailed by the thegn and his wife—then by three servants, including Sefawynn's brother. The skop and I huddled by the door, watching through the slit.

"Word will be sent," Lord Ealstan said, "if this man with red hair is seen."

"Or if any more strange happenings occur," Ulric said. "I don't want to hear about another flaming outline discovered in your field secondhand, Thegn."

"You forget your place," Ealstan said. "I will send word to the earl. You personally do not need to be informed of anything."

Ulric paused by the door, which swung open as the young guard outside—having apparently heard the exchange—opened it for him.

Leave, I thought at Ulric. *You came here imitating a messenger. You can't get mad when someone treats you like one.*

"I don't care for your tone, Thegn," Ulric said instead, lowering the hood of his cloak as he turned. "I am . . . trusted of the earl. I share his authority."

"Alwin might trust you, stranger," Ealstan said. "And if he does, that is well for you. But *you* have no authority here. Go and tell him what you've seen, and carry with you my words of promise. If the land-swights are unsettled, as your message warns, we shall uncover the cause."

"Indeed, indeed," Ulric said, inspecting the entryway. "New times are coming, Thegn. New . . . ways of doing things. Does that excite you?"

Hell. I knew that tone to Ulric's voice. I'd even heard those exact words from him before.

I reached for one of the swords.

"New times?" Ealstan's wife said. "Those come whether we want them to or not. And we shall bear them as we bear the changing of seasons—which bring friends and foes, men and spirits."

"And if those changing seasons bring me?" Ulric said. "Someone who is neither?"

"Neither friend nor foe?"

"Neither man," he said, "nor spirit." He reached into his cloak and brought out a Torrington 11940, a military-grade pistol with force ejectors and—most likely—spread rounds with an anti-nanite payload. A gun like that could bring down someone with the toughest augments.

The smiling guard at the door didn't have a chance.

I looked away as the shot went off. That kind of firepower could punch through an inch of steel—it turned skulls into confetti. The *bang* was flagrantly loud. Ulric preferred not to use suppressors, even though they came standard, and at no detriment to a gun's firepower.

A faint rushing sound in my ears indicated my medical nanites were moving to protect me from further dangerous sounds. When I looked back, a pair of booted feet in the doorway was all I could see of the dead warrior. Smoke hung in the air. That wasn't standard either. Ulric wanted this weapon to leave an impression—and I realized why as I glanced at the locals. Lord Ealstan had stepped in front of his wife, but his eyes were wide, his jaw slack. The guards behind him seemed stunned, weapons drooping in their fingers.

"I kill any I choose," Ulric said. "New times, as I said. Would you like further evidence, Thegn?"

"No," Ealstan said.

Ulric pointed the gun at one of the guards behind Ealstan.

"No, *lord*," Ealstan said.

"Excellent," Ulric said. "I look forward to working with you. Your people have a tradition, I believe. Bearn-gisel? Did I say that right?"

"Yes," Ealstan whispered.

"Excellent," Ulric said, nodding to Quinn. He pushed aside the lord and lady and grabbed . . .

Sefawynn's brother?

Aw, hell. They must have noted the kid's nicer clothing, heard him call Ealstan "little father," and put two and two together, arriving at five, same as I had. I didn't know what "bearn-gisel" meant—but judging by the way Sefawynn stood with her knife out, it wasn't good.

Quinn pulled the boy over to Ulric.

He's taking a hostage, I realized. *To keep the local lord in line.* That was cruel.

Sefawynn grabbed the door, ready to storm out. I seized her arm, and she spun toward me. Her stare *dared* me to stop her.

I dared, feeling an almost debilitating panic. Once they shot her, they'd probably search the room to see if anyone else was hiding inside.

I shook my head at her frantically. *No,* I mouthed. *NO.*

"Stay in line, Thegn," Ulric said, "and you can visit your son at Wellbury. The reeve has proven agreeable to my visits. I'm certain your boy will be cared for with . . . special attention."

Sefawynn pulled against my grip, and for a moment, I thought about bursting out and tackling Ulric myself. If he was surprised to see me and I could get that gun away from him . . .

But my platings were only half functional. I'd be risking my life for nothing. I squeezed Sefawynn's shoulder, silently pleading with her. Please, no.

Ulric and Quinn left, towing the boy along as they called for their horses.

Sefawynn slipped to her knees and began trembling. Crying. Nobody moved—not until hooves in the night announced the two "messengers" leaving. Back into the darkness that had spawned them.

8

The first one to break the spell was Ealstan's wife. The tall
woman knelt by the body, shaking her head.

"Fetch Hairud," she ordered. "I'll speak to her, then Oswald's mother, and tell them both of his heroism—and his passing.
I will prepare an urn for his burial and place him in our barrow. He
died in our defense."

"Yes, Rowena," a guard said, running off.

I let out a long, relieved breath. That had been way too close. Still, I
was alive. (Five stars. Hiding place sufficient, despite the lack of trees.)

Lord Ealstan *punched* the wall, shaking the entire structure.
"What *was* that? What did he *do*? Someone fetch the skop! She needs
to know of her brother's . . ." He trailed off, looking toward our
door, perhaps hearing Sefawynn's moan at his mention of the boy.

I pushed open the door and held up my hands, stepping around Sefawynn. Ealstan muttered a curse and went down on one knee, bowing his head. His wife and the guard immediately followed.

"Honored spirit," Ealstan said. "My imprisonment of you brought this evil upon us. Please, take no more of my people. I shall find your quest objects, and more. Please. Have *mercy*."

"I . . ." What did I say? I glanced out the door, then quickly away. The poor guard looked like he'd been hit by a cannon. Ulric wasn't . . . a subtle man.

The sight nauseated me, which . . . was a good sign, right? It meant I wasn't as awful as someone like Ulric.

No, you're not, I thought. *But you are a coward. And selfish. That's your first thought upon seeing a dead body? Happiness that you find it nauseating?*

"He's no spirit, nor lord," Sefawynn said, shoving past me. "Nor is he an aelv." She looked a mess, her eyes red, and she held her dagger in a death grip. "If he were any of those, he'd have been able to help. Lord Ealstan, I must impose upon you for your fastest horse."

"Skop," he said, still kneeling, bowing his head. "I . . . I should not have let him take your brother. You shall have no boasts of this household. I am sorry."

"You are no fool, Little Father," she said. "You could not fight whatever that was. The only one who could have stopped it was . . . was me. But I did not speak. A horse. Now, please."

"What are you going to do?" I asked.

"I will give chase until they stop," she said, still clutching her knife in a white-knuckled grip, "then confront the monster and try to bind it or loose it. If it is an aelv or spirit, I might succeed. If it is a god . . ."

"He's not a god," I said. "Ulric's a regular person—though *I* once thought he might be part ape or something. But if you go after him, you're gonna get killed . . ."

I trailed off as she glared at me with reddened eyes. Yeah, okay. I didn't need to be told what she thought of me at that moment. Fat lot of thanks for saving her life, but I got it. That wasn't how you felt when you'd just seen your brother get kidnapped.

"I'll see a horse prepared," Ealstan said, climbing to his feet, waving for his guard and his wife to do likewise. "But take time to think and plan, skop. The creature is taking your brother to Wellbury, so you will find him in Wealdsig's house. So long as the lad holds his tongue, he should be safe."

"Please," said Rowena. "At least let us prepare supplies. And send you with guards."

"I must not be seen approaching," Sefawynn said. "Perhaps one guard to aid me would be allowable. Supplies would be good. I will retreat to your founder's wēoh to meditate, if I may. I will need boasts. Powerful boasts."

"Of course," Ealstan said, waving for the second guard to escort her. The guard took a lantern and guided her out into the darkness.

Rowena saw to the body, working with a practical familiarity with death as she placed a shield over the top half of the corpse, which had been blown off. Then she gathered some servants—all women—to help her care for the body.

Everyone—the lord included—gave me a wide berth.

Sefawynn was as good as dead. She'd chase after Ulric and recite poetry at him. The only question was how long he'd laugh before he shot her. That wasn't my fault, though. I mean, landing here *had* drawn Ulric's attention, so *that* was my fault. But I didn't even remember starting this journey. Maybe I'd been forced into the dimension or something.

The justifications felt hollow. After hiding in the armory, after feeling that sense of panic, I knew exactly what I was.

"Hey," I said as a servant rushed past carrying a piece of Oswald wrapped in cloth. "I had some, um, incantations with me when I first arrived here. Any idea where those might be kept?"

She pointed a nervous finger to the room with the firebox. She scuttled away before I could ask anything else, so I wandered in. It was remarkable how little the room smelled of smoke. Toward the back of the room, I found a larder with various meats and fruits in baskets.

The pages from my book were dumped in the corner in a singed, torn, and disorderly mess. Some of the pages were crumpled and folded.

"Couldn't you have at least stacked them nicely?" I muttered, digging around until I found an unlit lamp. I lit it with a stick from the fire, then grabbed a short stool and headed to the larder.

As much as my instincts said I should get out of here, I was too curious. This pile of ramshackle papers might hold the secrets to who I was—and they'd certainly tell me something about *when* I was.

I sat down and blinked three times to call up my nanite control protocol. Glad I remembered that much, at least. The visual overlay warned me that basic wakefulness had been maintained for over forty-eight hours and that I would need to sleep in another day or so. Apparently being knocked out didn't count. I wasn't too worried—you could go five or six days without needing an override command, which I had anyway.

I reached for the pile of papers on the floor, then immediately sprang to my feet. The papers were now stacked in a neat arrangement.

I looked around, but both the larder and great room were empty, besides myself.

Maybe . . . maybe I needed sleep more than the warning had indicated. It had been a long, *long* day. Heart thumping in my chest, I forced myself to sit back down.

When I glanced at the stack of papers this time, the few pages that had been folded before were now *un*folded and sitting on top of the stack.

"Oh, come *on*!" I snapped.

I snatched up the stack and set it in my lap. If someone was trying to frighten me off, they wouldn't succeed.

Now that I had the pages, though, I found them daunting. Still, I forced myself to continue. Using the page numbers, I grouped them into stacks of ten—and the prankster left me alone.

I wanted it all in order before I tried to make sense of it. But as I worked, I found a page that stood out. It was a series of printed questions from the back of the book, judging from the page number in the three hundreds. Lines after the questions indicated the owner should write answers.

To help with the transfer, I realized. *To jog your memory once you arrive.*

At the very top of the page was a simple, clean question: *What is your name?*

Below it, handwritten in blue ink, was the name John West.

Oh, *hell*. That was *my name*.

And beneath that: *What was your profession before you became an Interdimensional Wizard™?*

That part of the page was burned, but I could make out a completely unexpected word.

Cop.

That awakened a vague set of memories. The academy. Wearing a uniform. Hot damn. I wasn't a thief.

I was a specialist detective in the Seattle Police Department: Anti-Cartel and Illegal Augments Division.

FAQ:

FAQ: What Can I Expect from My Dimension?

A:▷ Frugal Wizard Inc.® sells only the highest-quality dimensions. All of our standard packages—including our Wizard Wildcard™ tier—come with three guarantees.

Before we continue, we should explain how dimensions are investigated in the first place. (More info on page 85.)

The apparatus to choose specific dimensions is, unfortunately, imprecise. Imagine that the total spectrum of available dimensions is like the electromagnetic spectrum of visible light. Technically, there are infinite colors—as each minute change along the spectrum is distinctive.

Our technology can determine a band of dimensions that share similar attributes—imagine this like the "blue" colors on the spectrum.

Narrowing in on the color wheel might get you a range of "deep blue" colors. Likewise, further narrowing of the dimensional band would find you a group of dimensions where their current time seems very like our medieval history.

Let's say you narrow your examination specifically to Blue #000099 on the color spectrum. This correlates to the specific band of dimensions we've bought. (The 305th spectrum of category two, medieval-derivative dimensions.)

At that point, however—just like our eyes might have trouble distinguishing between different shades of Blue #000099—our technology can't isolate different individual places within the 305th spectrum of category two, medieval-derivative dimensions. Basically, we randomly pick one of the infinite dimensions within this band, investigate it, and record its attributes—then offer it up for sale depending on its suitability.

Because of the variables involved, and in order to ensure your satisfaction, we make three specific baseline guarantees. If your dimension does not have at least these three properties, you can return it for a full refund or a replacement dimension. (Note: Premium packages can be purchased with additional guarantees. See page 192!)

GUARANTEE ONE

Your dimension will have an island of Great Britain populated by a society of humans who work steel, but have not yet discovered gunpowder. They will have a functional society and culture that roughly equates to the Late Classical, Early Medieval, or Late Medieval (pre-gunpowder) Earth time period.[1]

GUARANTEE TWO

The people on Great Britain will speak a language that is intelligible to modern English speakers. We chose our dimensional band specifically for this reason!

---

1. A limited number of gunpowder-era, late-medieval dimensions are available in premium packages. See page 189. Arr, matey!

There's a lot of dry, scientific, historian mumbo jumbo theorizing on what probably occurred to allow this linguistic feat. Short version: We think a large migration of Norman refugees came to Great Britain sometime in the distant past, deeply influencing local linguistics. The end result is astounding. You have to hear it to believe it! Yes, you *will* be able to understand them![2,3]

GUARANTEE THREE

Neither the people of the British Isles nor mainland Europe will currently be suffering a global pandemic. This guarantee is good for five years from the purchase of your package. Note: We strongly recommend that Interdimensional Wizards™ keep their personal medical nanites updated in the weeks leading to their departure. It will not only protect you from

---

2. British accents and/or "medieval-sounding" word usage guarantees are available as add-ons to our premium packages. Note that even in the best of cases, some unexpected jargon or terms may exist. This is a feature, not a bug! It adds to the originality of your Personal Wizard Dimension™.

3. Dimensions with intelligible variations on Old English, Latin, Gaelic, Middle English, and various Celtic, Germanic, and Brittonic languages are available for a reduced price. We also occasionally have dimensions available where the inhabitants of Great Britain speak languages intelligible to modern speakers of Italian, Spanish, French, or other Romance languages. See the current list on our website. Warning: These sell out quickly!

local diseases, it will make certain you don't bring anything harmful into your realm.[4,5]

---

4. Legal Note: Our Plague-free Guarantee™ is void for all customers who refuse to use personal medical nanites. Enter your dimension at your own risk. Maybe bring a prefitted casket.

5. Are you a kind soul or a medical buff who wants to purchase a dimension that *IS* undergoing a massive global pandemic? Ever wished to single-handedly cure the Black Death? See our Fantastic Packages section for more info on how you can! See page 191. Pandemic dimensions are available at a steeply reduced price, depending on the severity of the pandemic. Warning: These dimensions tend to have limited lifespans.

9

I was a cop.

That explained *so much*. I knew how to sneak because I was a frontline investigator of underworld activities. I knew about cartel tactics because I'd studied them, infiltrated them, planned how to take them down. I had augments provided through the department. Ulric wanted me dead because he knew what I was. And I'd come into this dimension because the cartel was here.

I still didn't remember many details about my life, but the sense of overwhelming relief I felt after discovering this information was all the proof I needed. I'd hoped, deep down, that I wasn't a criminal. This was *right*. This was *me*.

My name was John West, and dammit, I was a *hero*.

So what did I do about it?

Well, something *had* to have gone wrong with my investigation. I was too unprepared to believe otherwise. I was partially in period costume, partially not. I didn't have a safe place to set up while I recovered—and if I'd so much as glanced through my book before leaving, I'd have known that was a good idea. Hell, I didn't even have a gun.

So it stood to reason that I'd either been rushed, surprised, or somehow hadn't expected to end up here so soon. To date, my performance was an *obvious* one star. Could be worse, but only as a result of gross incompetence.

To alleviate my ignorance, I tried reading some of the book. It was over three hundred pages long, and I'd recovered at least half of it. Honestly, the early chapters weren't very helpful. It was more of a marketing brochure than an actual handbook—but maybe the real information was later on. I mean, who'd make a three-hundred-page sales pitch?

I tucked the pages under my arm for now and took stock of my situation. I wasn't in any shape to continue my mission. But when had that ever stopped me? As far as I knew, never. Besides, what else was I going to do? Hide? Ulric had an innocent young man in his clutches. Hell, he had an *entire dimension* in his clutches.

I needed to find a way back to my own dimension so I could get backup. I had no idea *how* to get out, but I was willing to bet Ulric and his cronies did. Following him quietly and gathering intel was the right move.

Today, I'd been a coward. Maybe it had been the right call tactically, but it sure as hell *felt* wrong. So now, I was going to do what felt right.

I went looking for Sefawynn. In the courtyard, I found Lord Ealstan preparing two horses with saddles and supplies near the large obsidian stone. The gate was open. Through it, I could see a flickering light in the near distance.

"Sefawynn?" I asked Ealstan, gesturing toward the light.

"Yes," he replied.

I felt safer in the darkness than I had in the courtyard, but I didn't let those instincts fool me into thinking I was a criminal this time. The flickering light proved to be a lantern set on a bench in the center of a small ring of grass surrounded by some triangular stones in a regular pattern. They were maybe five feet high, not big Stonehenge-type stones, and the points sloped up to the right. Sefawynn sat on the bench, eyes closed, face tipped up toward the sky.

Was she praying? I decided not to interrupt her. Instead, I leaned against one of the stones and brought up my nanite protocols again. Three menus deep—controlling the search with blinks or taps of my fingers against my leg—I found the specific augment controls. Now I could read details about what I had.

Forearm plating with reinforcement and a hand-to-hand package, read one heading. A second heading was more interesting. *Plating of vitals.* I clicked eagerly, entering the submenu.

The status simply read *Offline.* That made no sense. The system must be malfunctioning. Unfortunately, a few tentative stabs at my chest with a stick proved that the listing was right. Wonderful. Perhaps the explosion had messed it up. I pulled up another menu and selected, *Bring Online.*

The display read: *Password required.*

That was ridiculous. Why would it require a *password* to turn on my augments? I let my fingers—tapping on my leg—input a few passwords that came easily, but none of them worked.

I clicked on *troubleshooting,* but that tried to bring up a web page. Delightful. There was no offline manual or documentation, which I guess I understood. There were very few places on Earth's surface that didn't have omnipresent wireless these days. Whoever designed the system hadn't counted on the owner teleporting to ancient England.

I also didn't have any local files stored in the nanites or a wetware hard drive. At least I remembered the reason for that. Local, on-body data wasn't secure enough. Department protocol would have been to keep everything remote.

Still, the fact that I hadn't downloaded any useful databases was more proof that I'd gone into this mission haphazardly. I backed out to the main menu and hit a secret command function.

I didn't even know quite how I'd done it. But it pulled up a new heading. *Stealth augments.*

Oh, wow.

Now we were talking!

I immediately turned on night vision, brightening the area around me considerably. Not quite to daylight levels, but it was colorized.

Along with the night vision—and an eyesight zoom of 3x—I had a few other small augments. A sensitivity and stability upgrade for my fingers. That would be for picking locks and other delicate work. A couple of surveillance upgrades to let me wirelessly hack systems— probably not terribly useful in the Middle Ages, but who knew? I could turn up my hearing—that was a good one. I also had a skin mod that gave me some simple camouflage—basically, I could turn the skin on the plated regions of my body a dark green or a few other colors.

Last, I had a vocal mod. Oooh . . . now *that* might be fun. With it, I should be able to imitate other people's voices, add some interesting effects, and absolutely *kill* at karaoke. Which I'd have to invent, along with electricity and, well, pop music. But it was nice to know I had the option. (Four stars for the hidden superpowers. My day—and night—had just gotten a lot brighter.)

I reviewed the stealth augment controls so I wouldn't have to access the menu to activate them—honestly, I wasn't certain I *could* get back to this menu—then exited out.

Sefawynn was looking at me.

"You look happy," she said.

"I've done some searching inside myself," I said. "Sefawynn, I want to help you get your brother back."

She considered me, then finally spoke. "I don't know that I want the help of someone I cannot trust. You haven't even told me your name."

"I understand," I said. "You're right to mistrust me. I haven't been completely honest with you."

"Really?" she said, then deliberately rolled her eyes. "Oh look, stars. How lovely."

"I'm serious this time, Sefawynn," I said. "You think I am a charlatan, a grifter. But I'm not. It's important that you understand." I paused for effect. "I am a *wizard*."

YOU ARE A WIZARD

The following is an excerpt from *My Lives: An Autobiography of Cecil G. Bagsworth III, The First Interdimensional Wizard™*. (Frugal Wizard™ Press, 2102, $39.99. Signed editions available to Frugal Fans™ subscription club members.)

I took my first trip to the Middle Ages in 2085, as part of the government's initial expeditions into alternate dimensions. My expertise in the field, and my accomplishments in the Micronization War, led them to seek me in specific. I jumped wholeheartedly into the endeavor, as has ever been my nature.

After winning my first jousting tournament, earning the trust of the king, and using a primitive battery to demonstrate an electric light to the abbot, I realized something important.

I was a wizard.

Many societies have curiously similar lore surrounding what are sometimes called "wise men" or "cunning women." Whether it be the Swedish *de kloka*, the Welsh *dyn hysbys*, or the biblical magi, European and Middle Eastern folklore is fascinated by the scholar-healer-philosopher.

We get the word "wizard" itself from the same root as "wisdom." While modern pop culture has co-opted the term to evoke the image of long beards, pointy hats, and the occasional bescarred boy with a wand, in ancient times it wasn't so much the magic that identified these individuals. It was *knowledge*. Yes, this knowledge is often attached to the arcane or unseen in the stories—but what is magic but a science not yet discovered?

In the life you now live, you might think yourself unaccomplished, stuck in a rut. You might mourn at how little you've accomplished. But in the scope of the history of humankind, you are a *god*. The knowledge you hold from a simple high school education is vast compared to the comprehensive knowledge of some of the weightiest minds in history. You carry technological marvels that could literally topple kingdoms in your pocket, or perhaps embedded in your own body.

Have you ever wanted to make a real impact in life? Change the world—not in a pedantic "plant a tree" sense, but in a literal "usher in the Renaissance" sense? Rule kingdoms? Save millions of lives? Alter the course of history? Or simply be renowned for your incalculable knowledge?

The more I've studied history, the more I've realized that grand achievements aren't so much about aptitude as about *timing*. Just as nature abhors a vacuum, history *will* fill important roles with the people it has available.

We credit the Wright brothers with being the first to fly—but the truth is, a dozen others were on their heels. Someone would have done it if they hadn't.

Your physics class might have taught you that Einstein invented $E=mc^2$—but conduct a surface-level investigation, and you'll find the idea of mass–energy equivalence was built upon the backs of dozens of scientists all working simultaneously. Einstein was simply the best with pithy notations.

In short, The Beatles didn't invent modern rock. Modern rock invented The Beatles.

Your life isn't unremarkable. You are merely living in the wrong time. Find your Perfect Dimension™. Embrace your destiny—whether it be to bring Promethean light or exert relentless domination—and travel the dimensions.

Become a wizard.

10

A what?" Sefawynn said, cocking her head.

"I'm a wizard," I said. "You know. Someone who does magic?"

"I don't know either of those words."

Right. What had the book said? "I'm a wise man. A scholar-philosopher . . . uh . . . topiary critic. You've got to have a word for this, right?"

"A runian?" she asked. "Someone who writes?"

"Sure, that and more," I said. "A person who knows things. Strange things, dangerous things. Like Merlin."

"You mean . . . Myrddin?"

"Yes! Him!"

"Gods," she said. "You *are* Waelish."

"Okay, look, I can prove it." I held up my arms, then commanded them to turn red—like blood. That would be properly dramatic.

Only . . . Hell. What had that shortcut command been again?

"Look," Sefawynn said. "A shooting star. And a constellation that looks like a bear. How fascinating."

"Wait a sec," I said.

She ignored me—grabbing her lantern and stalking out into the darkness. I hurried to keep up while trying to remember how to activate the hidden menu.

"I can see in the dark," I said to her. "Don't you find *that* impressive? I can—" I grunted, colliding with a shrub. Simultaneously walking, looking through menus, and attempting to prove how mystical I was did *not* work well.

I extricated myself from the shrub to find her standing with her lantern raised, eying me. "See in the dark, eh?"

"I needed some berries," I said. "Wizard business."

"Sure." She turned and continued stalking back toward the lord's keep.

A few seconds later I found the hidden menu and held up my forearms—which were now a stark crimson. "Ha!" I said.

"Madder root dye," she said, barely glancing back at my arms. "I've seen that done a dozen times. What's next? Turning your staff into a snake with sleight of hand? Using a fake knife to pretend your skin is iron? Oh wait. You tried that one already."

"It was your brother's knife," I said.

"Still trying to figure out how you swapped them," she said, not slowing down.

"Look," I said, striding after her, "can you *stand still* for a moment? Do you realize how frustrating it is to try to talk to you?"

"I'm sorry!" she snapped, spinning on me. "I'm sorry you feel disbelieved when you *already admitted you were a charlatan*! I'm sorry for not believing your *third* grift of the night! I'm sorry this is all so werging hard on you! You must be having a werging difficult day! *How unrelentingly awful for you!*"

I pulled up short, feeling her ire almost like a physical force. She breathed several rasping breaths, eyes wide, before she turned and resumed her march.

"I'm sorry about your brother," I called after her. "I want to help you, Sefawynn."

She stopped again, but didn't turn. "Wyrm and I are poor. There won't be anything of value in it for you."

"I don't need payment," I said. "But I know the men who did this. You saw what they can do. I understand their weapons. I can help you counter them. And I intend to go after them either way—so we might as well go together."

She glanced back at me, judging me. Measuring me.

"Plus," I added, "I'm pretty damn good with a lie now and then. You could use that."

"Good?" She gestured to my hands. "You call that good?"

"Hey, you believed I was an aeluf at first, didn't you? I'm new to your lands, but I think I did pretty well, all things considered. You don't know as much about me as you think you do." I snapped my fingers and returned my arms to their regular skin tone.

This, at last, gave her pause. She stepped toward me, raising the lantern. "It's *aelv*. And that was impressive," she admitted.

"Well, I—"

"Don't tell me how you did it," she said. "I'll figure it out." She studied me again, then waved the lantern. "Come on then."

With a grin, I hurried to keep up. I could have found my way to this other city on my own—but I had no doubt that it would be way, *way* easier to track down Ulric with a local guiding the way. Plus, it might have the added benefit of helping keep Sefawynn alive.

I'd let her brother get captured. Now that I knew who I truly was, I *was* going to make up for it. Preferably in a way that ended with Ulric locked in a cell back in Seattle PD high-enhancement holding.

"You have a name?" she asked.

"Runian is fine," I said. Better that I didn't spread my real name around—if Ulric left cronies watching for people from our dimension, a name like John West was going to be a *tad* obvious.

"You realize that's like naming a smith, 'Smith.'"

"I've met several people named just that," I said. "It works for me." I felt at my face. "Should I let the beard grow, to be less conspicuous?"

She eyed me.

"Not going to work?" I said.

"It will take more than some scruff to make you inconspicuous." She glanced at my hands.

"I do *not* have feminine hands," I said to her.

"You say that like it's an insult," she said. "Some of us think women are more than just men who didn't quite grow big enough."

Damn. "I respect women," I said. "I regularly wear a pink ribbon in October to advance breast cancer awareness."

Why on Earth did I remember *that*? It was even less useful than the whole swimming thing.

"You are an exceptionally strange person," she told me as we reached the wooden wall around Ealstan's keep. "I suggest you remain clean-shaven. You will stand out no matter what, but this look makes it seem intentional. Ethereal. People will think twice about molesting you. Perhaps. Either way, they will likely stare at you long enough for me to escape."

Well then, I'd leave the medical nanites with their current clean-shaven instructions. Inside the courtyard, Ealstan had three horses ready. One appeared to be a smaller pack animal. Maybe it was a mule? I knew as much about horses as I currently knew about myself.

"Little Father," she said. "This one has insisted on joining my journey." She nodded toward me.

"Is this so?" he said, looking to me.

"I've been having a glorious time on this visit!" I said to him. "You mortals and your antics! I was *so* going to enjoy watching you scramble for the trinkets I demanded! Such fun!

"But alas, that monster who killed your soldier has stolen a thunder weapon of my people. I have been tasked by my father, prince of the aelefs, to recapture it and punish the mortal for his foolishness. I regretfully must abandon our game and see to familial duty."

I glanced at Sefawynn, expecting to find her rolling her eyes again. Instead, she gave me a little shrug of, *Eh, it will do.* Maybe even a, *Not bad. Three stars for the effort.* Or was I stretching?

I snapped my fingers and turned my hands red again. "For vengeance," I explained as Ealstan's eyes went wide. "This is the message my father sent. You need not fear my glamours and tricks any longer."

Behind Ealstan, Sefawynn wobbled her hand in front of her. *Maybe pushing it,* that seemed to say. But what did she know? I had the little father right impressed, particularly after I snapped my fingers and turned my hands back, then gave him a shushing gesture and a wink.

With a shout, he had another horse saddled and trotted up. A big white thing with suspicious eyes. Hell. I was going to have to ride it, wasn't I? I doubted it came with built-in suspension or Bluetooth speakers.

"Where is our soldier, Little Father?" Sefawynn asked.

"You deserve our best," he replied, then waved to his wife—who stepped out of the manor carrying a shield and an axe. He kissed her, then strapped the weapons to his saddle.

"You?" Sefawynn said. "Little Father, I can't let you—"

"The boy was taken from before my hearth," he said. "And the strangers ride for the earl. It is my duty as thegn, and as your host, to deal with these men. I would accompany you, skop, and earn my boasts again."

She bowed her head. "As you wish, then."

Huh. Well, I'd get to keep practicing my elf act. I packed the pages of my book into a fold in the saddle that looked like it was for carrying things. As I worked, I noticed Sefawynn walking over to the large stone in the center of the courtyard. She rested her hand on it, then traced what appeared to be carvings in the surface.

Were those . . . runes? Yeah, they were. The kind you saw in fantasy games. I recognized a few of them. Huh. Were they . . . glowing softly?

Nah, that must be a trick of the light. I nodded toward it. "What is that?"

Ealstan grimaced. "Must you mock us, aelv?"

"I . . . Well, it *is* my nature."

"Our runestone has a proud history," Ealstan said. "It binds and pacifies our wights, even now. Mock me, if you must, but not it. Please."

Okay, then. Sefawynn returned and nodded to Ealstan. He, in turn, pointed toward the distant horizon—where dawn was breaking.

"I give you lead in this journey, skop, but I suggest we leave now, as first light blesses our path."

Both expertly mounted their horses. I stood next to mine. So . . . foot in the . . . foot thing . . . then heave? The horse regarded me as I tried to figure it out.

"Don't look at me like that," I grumbled. "Vehicles aren't supposed to stare back at you."

"Aelv," the thegn called. "Is there a problem?"

"I've ridden on the Wild Hunt," I responded, "and once crossed the sky on a rainbow made solid. But those both involved aelef mounts—which handle like the wind. This beast does not seem to . . . respect me."

"You must earn respect!" the thegn said. "Use a strong hand. The animal must know you lead it!"

"Yeah, okay," I said, then managed—with effort—to get into the saddle. "Maybe today, we'll settle for not making it laugh at me, human."

"She will follow where I go, honored aelv," the lord said, stifling a laugh. So much for my air of mystery. "Hold the reins, but do not pull tightly unless you want her to stop—and do not yank unless you wish to see rainbows again."

"Right . . ." I said.

Ealstan looked to the skop and she nodded, leading us out as light began to shine.

Well, I thought I'd done fairly well for myself during my first day in the Middle Ages. I'd made friends. (Well, companions.) I'd found out who I was. (My name, at least.) I'd even figured out why I was here. (Stop the guys with the industrial-sized chins.)

I decided to improve my rating. Two and a half stars: Not bad for a dude without a beard. That was a big improvement over how things had been going at the start.

Hopefully, the next step would include remembering why the hell I was here without backup, weapons, or proper equipment.

THE END OF PART ONE

PART TWO

How to Be a Wizard
Without Even Trying

11

R eading on horseback was not as easy as I'd have preferred, particularly when dealing with a loose-leaf book. But after stopping three times to grab pages I'd dropped, I managed to get the hang of it. Lord Ealstan kept glancing at me—I think he assumed I was dropping the pages as some kind of trick. He seemed to be losing some of his fear of me and replacing it with befuddled amusement.

Well, I'd worry about impressing him later. For now, I dug into the pages, searching for answers to a question that seemed pretty important. When the hell was I?

This didn't seem anything like the medieval England I'd seen in movies. Where were the knights in full armor? The maidens waving handkerchiefs and wearing dunce caps? The jesters? And . . . meat pies? I guess I didn't know a lot about the time period.

A few careful questions told me that Ealstan had never heard of a fortress made entirely of stone, and thought my descriptions of castles were fanciful.

"That sounds so empty," he said, our horses thumping along the beaten dirt roadway. "What would you do with all the space? You'd hardly ever see your family. It does sound very strong, though."

"I've heard of something like that," Sefawynn said from in front of us. "In stories of the Black Bear's lands . . ."

That name quieted Ealstan. Or maybe it was the fatigue. The two of them hadn't gotten any sleep the night before, and didn't have medical nanites to keep them perky.

"We should move faster," Sefawynn said from in front.

"We'll injure the horses if we push too hard, skop," Ealstan said. "Let us maintain an even pace. Those two men will have stopped to sleep along the way. As we have not, we should be able to reach Wellbury first. We can find out what is *truly* going on from the reeve and lay a trap for the kidnappers when they arrive."

It was a reasonable plan. How do you deal with someone who has mystical powers? Get backup, and jump him with the element of surprise. Unfortunately, they wouldn't stop to sleep.

"I . . . don't think we can beat them to Wellbury, Ealstan," I said. "Ulric and Quinn won't need sleep. And, depending on the time they've had to prepare, their horses might . . . uh . . . not be mortal, despite their appearance."

If *I'd* been planning to come to the Middle Ages while keeping a somewhat low profile, I'd have brought along some enhanced horses. Hell, I'd have probably brought a hovercycle or two, just in case.

"No need of sleep?" Ealstan said. "You said they were common men."

"Who have stolen some of the powers of the aelefs," I said. "I suspect Ulric bears the Amulet of Vigor, which can grant a mortal a constitution somewhat like an aelef."

"So, you do not need sleep?" Ealstan asked.

"I enter a trance once every week or so," I said. "To contemplate—and be renewed by—the beauty of my homeland. It seems much like sleeping to a mortal, as your kind cannot distinguish between something effulgent, like a renewal, and something crass, like simply falling unconscious."

Ealstan took this with thoughtful consideration, but Sefawynn let her horse drop back beside mine, trading places with Ealstan.

"Root chicory," she whispered to me.

"Excuse me?" I asked.

"I once helped a woman whose children couldn't sleep," she said, glancing to make sure Ealstan couldn't hear. "Though she blamed wights, the children were chewing on root chicory—which keeps a person awake. That's how you're doing it."

"A true artist never reveals his secrets," I said. "Have you figured out the arms yet?"

"Working on it," she said, then grew more solemn. "Why do you say their horses aren't mortal?"

"There are certain things you can feed your horses to make them run a long time without needing rest," I said. "It is a secret of the runians."

She studied me through narrowed eyes, likely trying to figure out if I was leading her on.

"I'm not trying to grift you, Sefawynn," I told her. "It's as close to the truth as I can explain it. Please trust me on that."

She shook her head, but turned her eyes forward—and damn, she looked tired all of a sudden. Slumped shoulders, red eyes. Yet she pushed on, saying nothing.

"We'll find him," I promised. "I *will* get Wyrm back for you."

She looked at me again, but this time nodded slowly. And . . . hell,

I'd gotten off topic somehow. Hadn't I been trying to figure out what time period I was in?

Jen would have known instantly. As I riffled through the pages, I missed her. She'd gone on that trip to Europe and died. Gone in an instant. Like wet paint on a canvas left in the rain. Her family had never liked me. I'd found out about her death via a *text*. There hadn't even been a funeral.

She'd always wanted to travel to one of these dimensions, and now I was here. In part because of her . . .

Information was returning to me in a trickle. For instance, I was starting to remember a lot about my childhood, growing up in Tacoma. There was also a big part of my life falling into place in my midtwenties: the police academy. There were still plenty of blank spots, though. Why had I started the academy relatively late? What had I been doing in the years since?

I was in this dimension to stop Ulric, wasn't I? How did that reconcile with what I remembered of Jen? Part of me felt I'd come here to fulfill her dream, now that she couldn't. Which was it? A police operation, or a way to pay homage to a dead loved one? Was it both, somehow?

Either way, I eventually found a bit of useful information in the book.

If you've opted for a Wizard Wildcard™ dimension, you might find yourself a little lost at first! Literally anything can occur in alternate dimensions, but certain hallmarks are much, much more likely. (Others are so ridiculously implausible that they—despite being technically possible—are statistically impossible. See FAQ: Can I Have a Dimension Full of Talking Bananas?)

It's fully possible that you'll end up in a dimension that doesn't align to the historical record, though we try to weed these out and sell them as unique experiences. Before you panic, use these easy dividing lines to determine what era you might be in. (Remember, though we treat medieval Britain as a single time period, the Middle Ages were quite varied! They included many distinct cultures, technological revolutions, and eras.)

Do you see castles, knights, and banners? Congratulations! You've found a High Middle Ages dimension. Go have a joust.

I wouldn't be reading this if I'd seen castles or knights. I shook my head and kept looking.

Do the people in your dimension talk about Caesar, have soldiers who dress in red, and really like building forts? You might be in the Roman Period! They lived in Britain for a while—and in many dimensions, they conquered the entire island! In some dimensions, Britain becomes the center of the Roman Empire after Rome falls to invaders. Turn to page 184 for more info.

Did they really think I wouldn't notice if the people around me were *Roman?* How dumb did the authors assume I was? Though . . . considering how much trouble I'd had so far, I decided not to continue that line of reasoning.

Do the people in your dimension wear blue face paint when at war? Do they use little or no metal in their daily lives? Do they really like knot patterns in their art, or haul big stones around for seemingly no reason? You might be in a Celtic-dominated dimension! These are the native people of Britain, and in most dimensions, aren't as technologically advanced as you might find in a Roman or High Middle Ages dimension. Turn to page 184 for more information!

That seemed like a possibility. They did seem fond of stones—at least, they'd piled them around their religious grove—and they certainly didn't feel technologically advanced. But their swords looked like they were made of iron to me. I kept reading.

Do the people of your dimension resemble Vikings? Do they have a decent grasp of warfare, using armor and shields, but not advanced things like full plate armor? Do they worship gods that sound like the Norse ones, only with silly names? You might be in an Anglo-Saxon dimension!

"Hey Sefawynn," I said. "What were the names of the gods you all worship again?"

She glanced at me. "How do you know so much, yet so little, all at once?"

"Humor me," I said.

"We live beneath the eye of Woden," she said, "to whom this land belongs. He who claims all words and arranged all worlds. We are, in his wisdom, blessed by his hand."

"Blessed?" Ealstan said. "Cursed, you mean."

"Do not blaspheme," she snapped at him. "Woden demands sacrifice. If we persist long enough, he will see our tenacity, and will turn the season again in our favor."

Curious. "And there are other gods?" I asked.

"Logna," Ealstan said, "mother of monsters, stealer of words. Tiw, the warrior—and Thunor, Woden's son. Friag, wife of Woden and mother of Thunor, first created writing, and she died in the war against the Black Bear. Woden then forbade us writing."

Those names *did* have a familiar ring to them. Woden was, maybe, Odin? And Thunor was . . . Thor? Hot damn. The book had included something useful!

"Where did your ancestors come from?" I asked.

"We fled across the seas," Sefawynn said, "escaping the rampages of the Hordamen. We claimed this land, pushing back the treasonous Waelish, who initially offered us land—but then tried to rob us. Again, how could you not know—"

I was barely listening, as I'd gone back to reading.

"Anglo-Saxons" is a general term used to refer to varied Germanic tribes (with additional Scandinavian cultural roots) who settled Britain in the fifth century on Earth. Turn to page 186 for more info!

I searched eagerly, and . . .

I was missing page 186. Of course I was. The only thing I had was a concluding paragraph on page 188.

warlike people who, nonetheless, had a deep and important impact on British society. Indeed, the name England comes from the tribe known as the Angles!

In our experience, the actual Angles (Aengli in their language) or Saxons (or Seaxe) don't appear in many dimensions. Indeed, during the actual historical period, they used their specific tribe names—like the Gewisse or the Mierce—rather than the name Anglo-Saxons.

Don't worry if these names are unfamiliar in your dimension. That's common! Indeed, you will find tribes with their own heritage, customs,

and beliefs! If you are uncertain, watch for stories of Viking-like people who landed and drove back the local Britons. (The Anglo-Saxons
called foreigners "waelisc" in their language. That's the origin of the
modern name of the Welsh.)

I was happy to finally have an answer on *something*. A quick look
at the earlier page mentioned that the era after the Anglo-Saxon one was
the Norman Era. In these dimensions, it seemed there had been an infusion of Norman language to Britain in the past, but the places still
tended to follow our history—with a second Norman invasion later on.

The Norman Era, at least, I knew something about. That's when
the French—or early French-like people—sailed over and conquered
Britain in something like AD 1066. Judging by that, I was somewhere
between AD 500 and 1066.

So, no castles or, um, trebuchets? What I *did* know seemed to come
from the eras after this one. That left me without as many preconcep-
tions to get wrong, right?

Man. Jen would have loved this.

I spent the next few hours of the ride thinking of some way I could
show off to my companions. Other than the hand trick, the only
obvious thing I could do with my augments was change my voice—
though my instincts said I should keep that power hidden. It wasn't
the type of advantage you revealed to perform a party trick.

Surely there was some other way I could impress a couple of un-
educated, backwater Anglo-Saxons? I had a modern education, the
advantage of hindsight, and an understanding of the scientific method.
Hell, I could read and write, which alone seemed rare in this place. I
was a wizard.

However, when I dug out my pen and wrote Sefawynn's name, she grew pale and hissed at me. "Do not tempt Woden's ire! Incantations will destroy us. You might have Ealstan fooled, but do not go so far as to deceive yourself!"

So, yeah. Not very useful there. Surely there was something else I could do. I was a modern man! Gunpowder, electricity, antibiotics!

And did I know how to *make* gunpowder, electricity, or antibiotics? Didn't that last one involve . . . mold? And gunpowder had bat pee in it or something? Damn. This wasn't my dimensional-travel-induced amnesia. I hadn't ever *had* to generate electricity, and the things I'd learned about penicillin had fled my mind.

I realized that a modern education—vaunted as it was—depended on two things. First, specialization. Modern technology was too complicated to be an individual activity. Second, reference material. The real purpose of school was to teach us how to learn. I had little doubt I could create gunpowder if I had access to a simple Wikipedia article. I understood the process of experimentation, but I hadn't memorized the sum total of human knowledge. Why would I when a quick internet search could call it up?

That was all well and good until you got trapped in the past. Definitely a flaw in the system. (Modern internet: three and a half stars. Poor reception in the Middle Ages. Please patch now, devs.)

As I rode, I found myself sketching in the margins of the page about Anglo-Saxons. Now that I had the hang of staying on horseback, I barely had to hold the reins. The animal did its own thing and followed the others. That left me time to try to think of a few things I *could* create on my own.

"Hey Ealstan," I said, still doodling, "you ever heard of a shield wall?"

"Where warriors work in concert?" he said. "Using spear and

shield to form a line against the enemy? It is a common war tactic, aelv. Why do you ask?"

"Just trying to figure some things out," I said. "What about water-wheels? You people have waterwheels?"

"To grind grain?" he said, sounding amused. "Yes. We have one at Stenford. Did you not see it?"

"Was busy trying to find mortals to prank," I said. "By the way, when you go home, do *not* look under your bed." Let's see, the simple tools, maybe? They had the wheel, and levers would be obvious. "What about pulleys? You people have pulleys to lift things?"

"Of course we do," he said, laughing. "How in Logna's name do you think we built the fort wall?"

Damn. I really *didn't* know anything useful to them, did I? Why couldn't I have been sent to caveman times? I could have wowed *them* with my ability to make fire out of two sticks.

. . . I could do that, couldn't I? You . . . rubbed one against the other? Really fast? Or something?

Damn. I'd have probably been eaten by a saber-toothed wombat or something. I was best off being thankful for the fact that—

Sefawynn suddenly gasped. "What, in Tiw's holy name, is *that*?" She was riding beside me again, and pointed at my hands.

"The writing?" I said. "Yes, I know. Incantations and—"

"No!" she said. "What you've done beside it?"

I looked at the quick sketch I'd done of her face. Nothing all that good, just a simple line drawing . . .

With a modern understanding of perspective. Crosshatching to shade. A basic artist's knowledge of the underlying musculature and the way shadows fell.

Hot damn! Maybe my education hadn't been *completely* useless.

FAQ:

Can I Have a Dimension Full of Talking Bananas?

A:▷ No.

12

S efawynn called to Ealstan, who circled back to join us. He took the drawing and inspected it, then looked at Sefawynn, then back at the page. "Gods," he whispered. "The likeness is uncanny!"

It wasn't even that good. Ballpoint pen on margin of guidebook wasn't exactly my preferred medium. But they were *amazed*.

As we'd been riding for several hours, they decided to take a break. We dismounted and settled in a little hollow beside the road. Sefawynn got out some cured meat and bread for a meal. Ealstan, in the meantime, respectfully asked if he could watch me draw.

I found a larger section of blank paper at the end of a chapter, then did a quick sketch of him. As I did, I thought about what—if any—art these people had seen in their lives. Maybe some pottery with paintings on them. Perhaps some scroll- or knotwork in stone or metal ornaments. The designs might be incredibly detailed and intricate, but even the most talented artists in the old days had worked in a style akin to modern stick figures. It wasn't until the Renaissance that you really started to see studies in anatomy and perspective leading to realistic paintings and drawings.

As I drew, Ealstan hovered over my shoulder. Even Sefawynn scooted closer to watch. As the sketch came together, Ealstan put his hand to his mouth, eyes growing wide.

"It's *me*," he whispered. "Aelv, your skill is otherworldly . . ."

I smiled, engaging my hand-steadying augments to give me more of an edge. Still, what I created wasn't terribly impressive by modern standards. I wondered what Ealstan would think if he knew I'd washed out of art school? I—

I was an art school washout! *That's* what I'd spent my late teens and early twenties doing! The hole in my memory between high school and enrolling in the police academy shrank. I'd tried to be *an artist*.

I'd quit three years in, after determining my art would never rival that of the other students. I'd been an imposter. It was foolish to think I could create anything of lasting value.

But I'd . . . used my art somehow . . . in the academy?

"Aelv," Lord Ealstan said, "this image doesn't give you power over my soul, does it?"

It was tempting to . . .

No, be good.

"No, Ealstan," I said, finishing the sketch—my pen was running out of ink. "It's just a drawing; nothing mystical about it. In fact, among artists of my kind, this isn't all that good."

"The other artists must work with godly skill, then," Ealstan said. "I have never in my life seen anything like what you have done there. And so quickly!" He shook his head.

Nearby, Sefawynn had taken a small ceramic plate from her satchel.

She set it on the ground and put three small berries on it. Beside that, she placed three straps of leather.

"Skop," Ealstan said. "We are far beyond the bounds of the holding, let alone our hearth. These are open lands, with no homes nearby."

"I know," she said. "This is a test." She looked to where we'd hitched the horses, who were contentedly munching on some grass beside the road. Judging by other chewed patches, this was a common resting spot for travelers. "I'm going to wash up. If you're ready to continue on before I return, give me a shout."

As she left, Ealstan nodded, then unhooked his axe and fished out a whetstone to do some sharpening. Sitting around and relaxing didn't seem to interest either of them. The axe was smaller than I thought it'd be, based on similar ones I'd seen in video games. It had a long, straight handle, and a thin—if somewhat elongated—axe head.

Ealstan noticed me studying him as he settled down on a log and began sharpening his weapon, each motion making a long metallic scrape. "Might I beg information of you, aelv?" he asked me. "These men we hunt . . . can they be killed by a normal axe?"

"Technically, yes," I said. "But it would be extremely difficult. Their skin resists blows, and cannot be pierced or cut. The only way to defeat them would be to keep hitting them until the . . . um, craeft that protects them is worn down. Once their systems overload, you can kill them."

He nodded, thoughtful. "Weak points? What about the eyes?"

"They'll resist almost as well," I said. "Really, Lord Ealstan, you *shouldn't* try to fight either Ulric or Quinn."

"They do not use bows, do they?" he asked.

"They have something worse. Aelev weapons we call guns."

"But no bows?"

"No."

"Good," he said. "I hate bows. They stop you before you can engage in a true fight."

"Guns are the same," I said. "You saw what happened to your soldier. Ulric can give copies of this weapon to his minions, and they will be able to kill by just pointing the end at a person and activating the weapon. There's a substance inside the gun like captive thunder—when you add fire, it explodes and sends out a bit of metal."

He nodded in thought. "Like a sling, but more powerful."

"Yes, actually," I said, surprised he'd made the connection.

"So theoretically, I could . . ." he trailed off, then bowed his head to me. "I apologize, aelv. I should not contemplate stealing a dweorgar weapon."

"No, that's not the problem," I said. "If you *could* get Ulric's gun and make it function, that would be a fantastic idea. I wouldn't be offended at all. Problem is, it wouldn't work." How did I explain modern biometric-controlled weapons? The guns Ulric's team used would be coded to them individually, and wouldn't fire for anyone else.

"The weapons know their owners," I explained to Ealstan. "They're not smart like a person, but they can identify the hand holding them. There's a little bit of metal called a trigger, you pull that to engage the weapon—but it will only work for its owner. I'm sorry."

"I understand, honored aelv," he said, then drew his whetstone along his axe in a slow, careful way. I could imagine that motion being ominous from someone else, but Ealstan had a workmanlike way of doing it. And he'd purposefully pointed the blade away from me.

I chewed on some dried meat—didn't know what kind—and a little carbon indicator at the corner of my eye lit up. My nanites wanted more, of course. I'd have to find some charcoal or something. Maybe at the evening fire.

"How far is it to this city, Wellbury?" I asked.

"Pretty far," Ealstan said. "It will take the rest of the day to get there."

I blinked. "One day. It's only *one day* away?"

"Yes," he said. "Beyond that, another day's ride, is Maelport—the earl's seat. He is ruler of these lands."

"Which extend how far?"

"Another few days to the north," Ealstan said, pointing, "beyond Stenford. And another day south of Maelport. Ten villages, each with a thegn like me. Two reeves, like Wealdsig. One earl."

"And the king?"

"We do not have one; that is a thing of the Waelish, and their Black Bear. It turned out poorly for them. 'Bretwalda' is the proper term here."

Man, an earldom that was only about a five-day walk across? That would be less than a hundred miles. Not a terribly large kingdom, but I supposed things worked on a different scale in these times.

Ealstan continued to draw his stone across the axe with an even, meditative motion.

"If you don't mind me saying so, Lord Ealstan," I said, "you are not what I imagined."

"What do you mean, honored aelv?" he asked.

"I expected someone of your position to be more . . . demanding, I guess. More self-absorbed? You're lord of an entire village, yet you came on this mission yourself."

"I'm a thegn, honored aelv," he said. When he noticed I didn't seem to register that word, he continued. "I'm an attendant of the earl and caretaker of this region. Yes, I own land, but being thegn of a village is an honor beyond that. I do what I can to live up to it, though I worry these days . . ." He shook his head.

"Worry?" I asked.

"It is a frailty of mortals," he explained. "Hordamen press against our runestones, and there is the Black Bear and his dark beasts and . . ." He took a deep breath. "And I am growing old, aelv. I was too slow and weak to protect Oswald or the skop's brother. It is . . . not my only recent failing. It will get worse as I grow older, and the earl shows less and less concern for the outer villages."

"Old?" I asked with surprise. "Pardon, Ealstan, but . . . you don't look that old to me. Maybe forty?"

"Forty-two," he said. "It is not old for many, perhaps. My grand-mother reached past a century! And clear of mind the entire time. But she did not swing an axe. Nor did she carry the defense of a village upon her shoulders."

I supposed if you depended on unaugmented physical strength to protect that which you loved . . . your forties *would* be a difficult time. Most athletes still retired before then, medical advances not-withstanding.

"Are you . . . required to fight often?" I asked.

"My duty is to land and lord," he said. "I go whenever either needs me. The earl sometimes demands my axe, and lately, he speaks of trying to become bretwalda. He squabbles with the other earls. I would not call him foolish, but his attention would best be turned elsewhere.

"Our coasts fall to raids. Barely a week goes by that we don't find some sign of the Hordamen. And then there are the encroachments from the Bear's realm. Our village has been attacked six separate times during my time as thegn, and we quite nearly fell each time."

Despite his imposing height and arms, Ealstan suddenly seemed very small. "Last raid we suffered was a little over a year ago now," he continued softly. "We lost six people. I . . . lost both of my sons. I could have prevented two of those deaths, had I been stronger. It was the first moment I understood that time was beginning to claim me. It must be wonderful to have weapons that can kill so easily, to keep the danger from those you love . . ."

"It is not as nice as you think," I said. "It allows very dangerous people to kill with few repercussions." I thought a moment longer. "That man who died, Oswald. Did you know him well?"

"He was my brother's son," Ealstan explained.

"Such a close relation!"

He looked right at me, brow furrowed. "Aelv . . . *everyone* in the village is a close relation. My family has worked those lands for generations. Ever since the crossing, hundreds of years gone now."

Oh.

Right. Small town, not much social mobility, and a requirement to farm every season to survive. This man wasn't worried about losing his strength because he'd fail his lord. He was worried about losing it because it could quite literally cost him his family.

"You mentioned raids," I said. "Are there . . . bandits in these lands too?"

"Sometimes," he said. "More often, rogue Hordamen, left by their ships. Or refugees from other parts of the land, turned desperate. Those, we can sometimes take in."

"Prison for the rest, I suppose," I said.

"I do not know this word."

"A place you put the guilty?"

"Until I judge them? We use a pit."

"And after?"

"After?" he said, genuinely confused. "If guilty, they would be dead. If innocent, they'd be returned to their hearth."

"And the smaller crimes?"

"A lashing or such," he said, frowning. "Is it different in your realm?"

"Very different," I said. "We do not hurt the guilty, but many we lock away for a very long time."

"I do not mean disrespect," he said, "but that seems like it would hurt me very much indeed."

"It's . . . complicated," I said. But I supposed his life was complicated too. Trying to keep up your strength and skills, knowing that at any moment, raiders or soldiers could emerge from the forest and try to kill you all. Knowing each man at your side was a close family member. Some of whom were going to die . . .

Damn.

Sefawynn returned a short time later, her blonde hair wet and plastered to her head, and she was wearing a different dress. She set down her satchel, and I saw the sleeve of her other dress poking out. So by "wash up," she'd apparently meant "take a bath." Was there a river nearby? I turned up my augmented hearing, and then clearly picked out the sounds of water . . . But no, that was waves. We were on the coast.

Could I ask them to draw a map of the land? I started to sketch England for them, but the ink ran out, and I barely managed a few lines. Well . . . hadn't I seen a map on one of the pages of my book? Would they be willing to look at it if I covered up the other writing?

"Ha!" Sefawynn said, holding up the pieces of leather, which were now braided together in an intricate pattern.

I glanced at the bowl beside the straps. The berries were gone. Ealstan hadn't been nearby, and I hadn't touched them, so Sefawynn must have palmed them. But why? What was the point?

"What does it mean?" Ealstan asked. "A free landswight, far from runestones? Is it bound to a nearby wood, perhaps?"

"Not free," she said, pointing at me. "It self-bound to him. A cofold, based on my read of it."

Ealstan leaned forward, hand on his axe. "What wyrd is this? Good or ill?"

"I can't tell yet," she said, studying me. "But it did the task, which indicates good wyrd. I will watch."

I considered it all with bafflement, their words loud in my ears from the augmented hearing. Was this ritual or religious observation for my benefit, or simply their unique custom?

I opened my mouth to ask, but my enhanced ears picked something up in the distance. "Did you hear that?" I asked, standing up and looking in the direction.

"What?" Ealstan asked.

"Horns," I said, frowning. "From that way."

"What . . . kind of horns?" Ealstan asked.

"Long and low," I said. "Three sharp notes."

Ealstan looked to Sefawynn. "Please," he said. "It is a delay, but I need to at least see."

She drew her lips to a line, but nodded curtly. In seconds, I'd been forced onto my horse and we'd left the road, heading toward the coast. I tried to get an explanation, but the sound of the hooves—and my desire to stay in the saddle—interrupted me.

I soon got my answer. At Ealstan's urging, we dismounted and approached the shallow cliffside at a crouch—looking out over the water some forty feet below. Waves crashed against the rocks. Sailing parallel to the coast and frighteningly close were three ships.

Even I could recognize Viking longships. And based on the postures of my companions—and the way Ealstan cursed softly—this was *not* a welcome sight.

All Right, WHY Can't I Have a Dimension Full of Talking Bananas?

We often get requests like this. "I'd like a dimension where humans can fly!" or "Please find me a dimension without frogs; they freak me out." Or "I'd like a dimension where the sky is plaid!"

Such questions display a fundamental misunderstanding of both alternate dimensions *and* probability. The prevailing dimensional theory is based around the idea of "branching points." Each dimension *shared* our dimension's history up until some branching point, where a single event caused their futures to deviate—sometimes in tiny ways, sometimes in fundamental ways.

The scale of the differences between a given dimension and our own depends on two factors. First, when did the branching point occur? If it was long, long ago, then significant differences are likely, though not guaranteed. (Parallel evolution happens!) Second, what caused the branching point? If it was the result of a huge event (such as an asteroid hitting a dimension's Earth in the 2020s when it missed ours), then the changes could be significant, even if the branching point was recent.

Dimensions near each other on the dimensional spectrum tend to have similar attributes. Imagine the whole thing like a tree. The trunk is our dimension, and each "branch" is formed by a deviation. Then those branches branch smaller to other subtle changes that tend to share the qualities of their parent branch.

At Frugal Wizard Inc.®, we have purchased a branch of this tree where Britain tends to be inhabited with medieval-era people speaking languages we can understand. But dimensional distribution works on a bell curve. Let's say we cataloged a thousand dimensions and rated them by how similar they are to our own. Then we graphed that data with the x-axis indicating similarity to our own dimension, while the y-axis indicates the number of dimensions we found of that level of similarity.

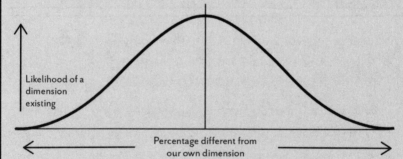

As you can see, at the leftmost part of the graph, you'd find the dimensions most similar to our own. These are fairly rare in our band of dimensions. (Note that in some dimensional bands, the center of the curve can be moved left or right.) In the center of the graph, you'll find what we call Earth-lite™ dimensions. Those are somewhat similar to ours, but with interesting cultural deviations. Statistically, most of the dimensions in our band will fall into this portion of the bell curve.

The important part comes in noting the right end of the graph. It extends into infinity, and therefore it is *technically* possible to find dimensions that are *incredibly* different from our own, even in our proprietary band. However, statistically, we could search for thousands of years and never find a dimension with talking bananas. That's because sapient bananas simply aren't very likely.

The unfortunate truth is that while, *technically,* dimensions can contain anything, the more unusual or bizarre something is, the more unlikely it is that anyone will ever *find* such a dimension.[1]

Scientists have, to date, found a few precious dimensions where Neanderthals became the dominant species of human. But nobody has ever found one where any non-human species (not even different ape-derived ones, sorry, Charlton!) evolved to dominate Earth. And sapient elephants are millions upon millions of times more likely than sapient bananas.

We have, however, found thousands of barren Earths destroyed by asteroids or other catastrophes. Because unlike sapient bananas, cataclysmic failure is incredibly likely.

But never fear! Cultural changes (like Greeks who speak Latin) are far more plausible, and we find those all the time. Furthermore, the Middle Ages are so different from the modern experience that you're sure to find plenty to delight and amaze you.

---

1. Legal Note: Please be advised that if your dimension features an "extraordinary attribute" (as defined by paragraph 10.ii of your contract) that was missed in our initial survey, congratulations! You will be given a finder's fee of $100,000! (To be paid after your mandatory, non-negotiable relinquishment of the beacon and codes to that dimension.) Please read your contract carefully, and direct any questions about this amazing opportunity to our legal team.

13

Yeah, those were definitely Viking ships. I zoomed in on the lead ship with my eye magnifications. Sinuous draconic figurehead at the front, a dozen or so dudes rowing on each side behind. They looked a lot like the people I'd seen so far, with their colorful clothing and very little armor, save one domineering figure in a chain shirt. No horns on his helm.

I'd expected them to be grungy, but they weren't. In fact, they were remarkably well-kempt, with longer hair—blond, for the most part—that seemed brushed, their beards groomed. They looked like men who enjoyed spa days and bought the nice conditioner.

There was an ethereal-looking woman on each ship as well, their long hair trailing in the wind. Four stars for the intimidation factor. How do they keep their locks from tangling?

I looked to Ealstan, who had gone pale. "Those people are dangerous, I take it?"

"Murderers," he whispered. "Raiders without mercy. They laugh when they kill, aelv—and laugh harder when they carry away the ones you love. They burn villages and leave men to die, their stomachs slashed open and their entrails spilled, haunted by the knowledge that their families are in the hands of butchers."

"Vikings," I said.

"I do not know this term," Ealstan said. "We call them Hordamen."

"Do you know the land they come from?" I asked. "Denmark? Norway? Sweden, maybe?" I was still trying to sort through what was similar to my dimension and what was different.

"No," Ealstan said. "They come from Hordaland in the east, across the ocean."

"I know Norweg," Sefawynn said. "That was once a kingdom in the region. And Dansic, another land nearby. The Hordamen enslaved them all. All but the Geats, who hold bravely, because of their rune-stones." She narrowed her eyes. "Only three ships. Maybe . . . maybe they are scouting the coast, rather than coming to raid?"

"Hordamen *always* come to raid," Ealstan said. "They hunger for runestones, skop. Like a glutton who cannot stop eating." He gripped his sword. "They head north . . ."

North. Toward Stenford. The village couldn't be very far inland. Well within raiding distance, I'd guess, considering the visible pain on Ealstan's face.

"Go to them, Little Father," Sefawynn said. "If those Hordamen land . . ."

"Our runestone still works," Ealstan said. "Mostly. Unless they brought skops."

"Skops like Sefawynn?" I asked. "What does that have to do with anything?"

"Hordaman skops are powerful," Ealstan explained. "Their boasts intimidate the landswights, negating the power of our stones. Neahtun was raided and burned to the ground not three months back, and their stone was stronger than ours."

"There's a woman on each of those boats," I said, pointing.

"You can see that?" he asked, amazed.

"Yeah," I said. "They're standing at the front."

As we watched, the ships turned toward the land just up north, finding a convenient beach where they could disembark.

"Are the men armed?" Sefawynn asked.

"Yeah," I said, dialing in my vision. "There's one guy on each ship in mail. Everyone else is holding a sword and shield. The women are going with them."

Ealstan stood up, as if to run for his horse. But he looked at Sefawynn, and paused.

"An evil man has a weapon of the aelvs," Ealstan said. "I . . . should go to the earl. He must be warned, and he would ask me to forget Stenford in the face of this greater peril. But I fear I am not strong enough." He seemed on the brink of tears. "I cannot leave Rowena and the people alone."

"Go, Ealstan," Sefawynn said. "It is the right choice."

"If you save your brother," he said, "will you continue on and tell the earl what has happened? And ask him to send someone . . . to bury our bodies?"

"Wait," I said. "Ealstan, you act like the fight is already over!"

He looked sorrowful. "Once, the earl's ships patrolled these shores, fought them back . . . Now, Woden abandons us, and my village cannot stand alone against three ships. That is some *seventy* Hordamen, aelv. There are no longer hearthmen enough in the region to call on for help. Not after the attacks from the Bear's men."

"So . . . you're going to go die?" I said, standing up.

"What else *can* I do?" Then his eyes went wide, and he bowed down on one knee before me. "Aelv. I know you came to torment and trick us. But if we die to these raiders, there will be nobody for you to sport with. Please. Can you do something to stop these raiders?"

I froze, stunned.

"He cannot help you, Ealstan," Sefawynn said softly. "I wish . . . I wish my boasts could. But . . ." She looked away.

Ealstan nodded, stood, and turned toward the horses. I stood there, numb and . . . terrified. That wasn't right. I was a cop, wasn't I?

But what could I do against an entire army of bloodthirsty Vikings? I'd *said* I was a wizard, but my knowledge was basically useless. I had a whole lot of stealth augments, but again: This was an *army* of *Vikings*.

And yet, the way Ealstan's shoulders slumped, the tone of Sefawynn's voice when she'd said I couldn't help, the memories, raw yet vague, of getting the news of Jen's death in a far-off place . . .

"Ealstan," I called.

He stopped, looking hopeful.

"Will they speak our language?" I asked him.

"If not, their skops can translate," he said. "They will have learned our tongue, to be understood as they boast to our wights."

"Good," I said. "I need madder root, a feather, and a good place from which to observe those Vikings for a few minutes . . ."

A short time later, I sat by the cliff, drawing pictures of the distant Vikings on the shore. They had sent a few men to fetch fresh water from the river. Guess they wanted to be well hydrated for their murderous rampage.

Sketching with a quill and madder root ink wasn't the easiest thing in the world, and it didn't help that my subjects kept moving. But I had a vague recollection of training to draw without a nib, and I soon realized that my optical augments let me take pictures.

I was going to run out of semiblank pages to use at this rate, but it *did* work. As I drew, I focused on my own emotions.

And my growing terror.

It didn't make sense. I was a cop, a detective who infiltrated cartels. I'd obviously been in many dangerous situations. So why did I need to activate my finger-stabilizers to keep from trembling?

As I thought about it, I realized I didn't *remember* being in danger. I might have been in a hundred firefights, but the experience of those moments was lost to me in my current state. Of *course* I was nervous. I was essentially a new recruit.

The way I'd caught Wyrm's knife on my arm indicated I had ingrained combat instincts. If this went poorly, my body would know what to do, even if my brain did not.

Ealstan hovered nervously at my side, axe in hand, like a heavily armed puppy. To his credit, he didn't rush me. He *trusted* me. That felt both gratifying and terrifying.

"The horses," I said to him as I drew. "You said they know their way home?"

"Indeed, honored aelv," he said. "Turn them loose, and they'd follow the road to Stenford."

"Maybe we could send warning that way," I said. "In case this doesn't work, and we all end up as slaves."

"They do not take men as slaves," he said. "They would—"

"I don't need to know the details, thanks. But as none of us want to ride back, it might be a good idea to send a note on the pack animal."

"A . . . note?"

"Written message," I said. "I could write it for you, so that you wouldn't have to . . ."

He was looking at me blankly. Right. Who would read said note?

Footsteps in the brush announced Sefawynn's return. She'd fetched a waterskin from the saddlebags. She eyed me kneeling among the bushes with my improvised quill pen, bowl of red ink, and ream of singed papers. But she didn't say anything.

I dug out the last of the sheets I'd found with space at the bottom. Then I zoomed in, took a quick shot of the third Viking leader, and started my final sketch.

"Someone among you knew how to write once," I said. "There were letters on that stone in your village."

"Yes, Logna stole writing from Woden, and she gave it to our fore-fathers," Ealstan said. "They created the runestones with it—binding and empowering the wights within the boundaries of our villages."

"So, like, your runestones . . ." How did I put this? "These stones trap fairies and force them to obey you?"

"I do not know this 'fairies' word," Ealstan said. "But when the landswights are within the boundaries of a runestone, they are offered peace. They have a choice; a binding does not *force* them. It . . . encourages them to settle down, to pick a home to serve. The stone empowers them with the ability to protect and defend. But if they are not treated well with offerings, they may still become a bog."

"That's bad?"

"Pardon, honored aelv," he said. "But do not wights often serve in your realm? One has bound itself to you as an individual, a thing I have never seen. Surely you know all this already."

"A god knows your heart before you give him offerings and prayers," I said. "Still, the mortal must say the words and make the actions. Do not question, Ealstan. I judge your knowledge."

"Of course, honored aelv," he said. "Yes, bogs are bad. Destructive bearers of an awful wyrd. In earlier times, the runestones would drive them away, once they changed. But now they're weakening, and Woden forbids us to restore them. None of us could anyway. So it is good we have the skops to do service for us."

He nodded to Sefawynn, who nodded back.

"Why would Woden forbid writing now?" I asked. "What does he gain?"

Ealstan glanced at Sefawynn, who settled on a stone nearby and leaned forward, hands out. "Woden tests us," she said. "He demands sacrifice. Loyalty. Penance. You see, Friag—the great heroine, the wife of Woden—fell during the final battle against the Black Bear.

"At first, our war with the Waelish had been of little concern to the gods. Just another petty dispute between mortals. But then, the Waelish king—the Bear himself—turned to the darkness in desperation. The land grew black from his touch. The landswights corrupted, and the barghests came forth out of shadow and flame to his call.

"The gods stood with men to resist him. Unfortunately, the Black Bear sought out the great wolf, Fenris, once bound by Tiw. Forced to heel to the Bear's dictates, Fenris brought with him the implements of metodgodas, the end of gods.

"Not willing to risk the end of the world, the gods retreated. And yet, when men called out in pain and death and desperation, Friag returned to battle."

She paused, and I looked up. "Well?" I demanded, surprised by how hooked I'd gotten on the story. "What happened?"

Sefawynn smiled. "Boasts," she whispered. "The finest boasts that men have ever heard—furious boasts that drove back the *Black Bear* himself. Her power and confidence *bound* him to his land as if *he* were a wight. That day, Friag saved all of humankind—not only those of our land, but the Waelish, the Hordamen, the distant Ériuians, and the men of the far lands, though they know it not.

"But Fenris, that wolf who would consume the world, remained unbound. Weakened by her conflict with the Bear, Friag was consumed. With her dying breath, she bound the wolf to the hill of the Black Bear, to slumber until the final death of the gods.

"This was to be Tiw's fate," Sefawynn said, leaning forward, as if sharing a secret. "It was his hand the wolf had taken, and his blood it had tasted. Friag's sacrifice changed everything that would be—wyrd gone mad—and in so doing, created *hope* in the world.

"But Woden did not want hope—he wanted love. The runes were Friag's. She had crafted them, taught them to the gods, and granted their wisdom. But men would write no more. Woden forbade writing as punishment for the loss of the goddess. Now, Woden's sons punish any mortals who desecrate her memory. Only Logna—ever tricky and calculating—dares disobey.

"The skops are Friag's heritage. We do what she no longer can, directing the wyrd and protecting the land from bogs. And we remember, for no longer can the runes do it for us."

"Some say the skops serve Logna," Ealstan added.

"Nonsense," she said. "We wait for Woden's forgiveness. After enough sacrifice, it *will* come. I promise it, Ealstan. Perhaps . . . once the skops are again worthy . . ."

Sefawynn's story hadn't been half bad, I'd admit. If you didn't have movies to watch, I supposed you could do worse than listening to her over the hearth at night. (Four and a half stars. Might be better with puppets.)

For Ealstan's benefit, I nodded and said, "You mortals remember much, but there are things you do not. Curious . . ."

Ealstan looked out past the trees to the beach, breaking the spell of the story. "We must hurry. Their scouts have returned."

"I'm nearly done," I said.

"Then I will see to the horses," he said. "Your earlier suggestion was a good one, honored aelv. If our plan here goes poorly, I can send Black, the packhorse, home with my seal on a strap—bloodied, with an axe mark on it. Rowena will assume I sent it as a warning with my dying breath. They will prepare for invasion." He nodded to me. "You proved your wisdom again."

He marched off, and damn me if I didn't feel a little bolstered by his compliment. I mean, he was an off-brand Viking with more boldness than brains, but I liked the guy. He felt genuine in a way I didn't think I'd often known in my dimension.

Sefawynn got off her rock and looked over my drawings. As before, she found them remarkable. If only my teachers in art school could see me now—and be forced to acknowledge that I was literally the best artist in the entire world.

"That was a fine story," I said to her.

"It's one we tell children," she said. "And you didn't know it. You aren't Waelish at all. You're from the distant lands, aren't you?"

"More distant than you know."

"This is a dangerous plan, Runian," she whispered. "I doubt you've done a grift with stakes like these before."

"I'm not a grifter."

"You can't honestly expect me to believe you're an aelv prince with craeft-made weapons and power over nature itself."

I met her eyes. And for some reason, I couldn't lie. I didn't *want* to lie. "I am a regular human," I said, "with a few special advantages."

"So this *is* a grift. You're going to fake your way into making those Hordamen leave."

"I suppose," I said. "But I'm not lying to *you*, Sefawynn. I haven't told you the precise truth, but that's because you wouldn't *understand*. I'm a wizard—a runian. That's the best way I can explain it."

She looked down at the sketches as I finished the last of them. Then finally she said, "How can I help?"

I paused. "Really?"

"Don't sound so surprised," she said. "Ealstan is right. The raids are getting worse, and the thegns grow weak. If you're going to try this, I want you to succeed. We could save hundreds of lives."

"Any way you can help me seem authentically an aelev?" I asked.

"Aelv," she said.

"Aelv," I repeated.

"Good," she said. "You have the look, and your accent—though amusing at times—actually helps. The painted hand trick and the drawing might be enough." She thought a moment. "We could imitate a reverse binding. That's where a faeigerman overpowers a skop by use of her true name. It's in the stories, and they'll know about it."

"Great. How do I do that?"

"Order me around a lot," she said. "And call me 'thrael,' an old word for slave. I can do the rest."

I nodded, wafting the final sketch gently to dry it. She'd lent me one of her ceramic offering dishes to hold the ink, and I handed it to her. "Keep this, if you have something to store it in. If we survive, I might need to sketch again." I forcibly calmed my nerves about what was coming next. *You're a hero. Even if you don't remember it.* "If this goes poorly . . ."

"I know," she said. "Nobody will be left to rescue Wyrm. So don't let it go poorly. All right?"

"All right." I nodded firmly. "Time to do this. Carp diem."

". . . Carp what?"

"Seize the fish," I said. "You know, like the old saying 'carpe diem,' except it's funny because . . . Never mind."

14

Apparently, the traditional way to greet Hordamen was to run away screaming. So I was amused at their bafflement as we marched right up to them. It was like how a wolf pack might react to a trio of overconfident bunnies.

"Alakazam BIOS discography Philadelphia à la disco," I said, stopping right in front of the invaders, hands on my hips. "Nitrogen! I.E. polyester Garfunkle'n Garfield!"

Don't judge me. It sounded like a perfectly mystical and unknowable language to *them*.

Sefawynn bobbed her head, cowering down. "The great aelv," she "translated" for me, "demands to know your intentions for his lands." Then she glanced to me, cringing.

The Hordamen muttered to one another in their own language, then sent someone running toward the ships. We'd stopped right at the edge of the sandy beach, where the guards had been standing.

It didn't take long for the three ship captains to arrive, led by the fellow with the chainmail shirt I'd spotted at the front of the lead boat. His trousers were a deep red, and that hair—the man could have been a shampoo model.

He glanced at Ealstan—who stood behind me like a retainer—then looked me up and down. The leader didn't seem intimidated, though the other Hordamen kept their distance and didn't attack us—a good sign.

Sefawynn was obviously right about the way I looked. My face— clean-shaven beyond the ability of a normal razor—mixed with my build, my way of carrying myself, and the lack of weapons . . . it confused them. Made them wary. I didn't look like any man they'd met before.

"You're an álfr?" the man asked in thickly accented English.

"Californication?" I said. "Bromance, vlog, podcast?"

Sefawynn bobbed into another bow. "Yes, my lord," she said. "This Hordaman is their leader, of a station to speak to you directly."

"Very well," I said, hoping my American accent sounded as exotic to the Vikings as it did to the Anglo-Saxons. "You. Leader of the Hordamen. What do you seek with this land?"

"What do you think?" the leader said, smiling. The two other captains stood to his left and right, content to let this one take the lead. He nodded to some of the guards, who moved to encircle us— causing Ealstan to mutter softly, hand on his sheathed axe.

My heart hammered in my chest. What was I doing? This was *insane.*

You'll be fine, I told myself. *You can handle a bunch of primitives barely out of the Stone Age.*

"I haven't finished with these people. They amuse me," I told the leader. "Turn around and leave this land."

"You think I'll be frightened because you chopped off your beard?"

the captain said. "You are no álfr. I have *met* the álfr. You are a weak man from a weak land."

"If that is so," I told him, trying to keep my voice steady, "then you won't mind if I take your soul."

"Gorm," the captain said, pointing, "take the skop and put her with the captive. Give the men a taste of—"

"Thank you," I said loudly, slipping one of the pictures from the inside pocket of my cloak. "I will use your soul well. Tell me. What are your parents' names?"

"No, my lord," Sefawynn said, tugging on my sleeve. "That is too cruel, even for them."

"Silence, thrael!" I bellowed at her. "Or I shall Nintendo you!"

She cowered, whimpering. Damn, she was good. She was a completely different person—no hint of her former confidence.

One of the Viking women stepped closer, looking at my drawing. She hissed softly, dancing back. She spoke in their own language to the captain.

"Careful, lord," Sefawynn whispered in translation for my benefit. "He has a strange wyrd, and I think a landswight follows him. Of its own choice."

What made them all say that? At least the picture had the desired effect. Vikings froze in place as I turned around, holding up the picture of their captain. I did a full rotation, then with a flick of my thumb, I fanned the pages out—revealing two more pictures depicting the other captains.

This agitated them. One of them yanked out his sword and stalked toward me. This man had tan hair in tight, delicate braids. He gestured toward me with his sword, arguing with the Viking woman in their own language.

"He wants to destroy the picture," Sefawynn whispered, still maintaining her subservient act. "He thinks it will free his soul, but the woman disagrees. She's a skald, their word for skop."

"So, kill her and they'll leave?" I asked.

"Perhaps. After murdering us in retribution. I should not like to try it."

Right then, on with the plan. "You'd like them back?" I said to the captains, stepping forward and holding up the pictures. I proffered the picture to the man with the tan braids. "Strike it," I said, "and kill your soul."

The Viking woman translated for him softly.

"My soul is my own," the leader said.

"Then you shouldn't have offered them so freely!"

"We offered nothing!" the golden-haired captain shouted.

"Which is coincidentally what these souls are worth," I said lightly. I stepped forward, enjoying the way they shied away. "You should know we aelvs always get the better of a bargain. And here you claimed to know us."

The captain glared at me.

"This is our deal," I said. "If you leave and do not return, you may keep these. Protect them well, and you may know blessings from this—for while your souls are imprisoned by these incantations, they are also kept safe."

It was Sefawynn's suggestion. In their society, an elf's offer should have both advantages and disadvantages. The three captains and the skald argued softly, while the rest of the Vikings kept their distance around us, shuffling and muttering. A few of them covered their faces with cloths, perhaps to stop me from taking their souls.

I'd only had time to draw these three, though. I'd miss the pages, but I'd already read them. More marketing fluff.

"Did you hear what he said earlier?" Sefawynn whispered. "They've taken someone already."

I glanced at the ships, moored just beyond the beach, and enhanced my vision. There was a man tied up near the back of the center ship, lying like a sandbag. I hated to think what might happen to the poor fellow.

But my attention was drawn away from him as the discussion between the three captains devolved into an argument. The two lesser captains stalked up to me. In turn, each nodded, then—watching me like you would a cobra—snatched his picture and retreated.

The skald remained with the head captain, who had stopped smiling. He ignored his fleeing companions and the large groups of men with them. Those loyal to the leader remained. He stood there, arms folded, eyes narrow.

I'd seen that expression on someone's face before—that unconvinced posture. He knew I was trying to dupe them.

My nerves were starting to get the better of me. What was I doing? Facing down a Viking raiding party? I tried to tell myself I was only scared because I didn't have my memories.

It wasn't working. I covered my nervousness by focusing on the next part of my plan. I handed the final picture to Sefawynn, then nodded for Ealstan to back up. He did so while trying to keep an eye on all of the Hordamen at once.

Calm, I told myself. I only had to deal with the captain—and the golden-haired skald at his side.

"You doubt my power," I said to the captain.

"I am thinking," he replied, "that up close, our souls look very much like drawings in madder root dye, not blood, as it might have seemed. And I've raided far to the south, where men make drawings on parchment to tell stories." He squinted at the picture Sefawynn was still holding up. "It *does* look like me . . . One who could make such strange drawings would be valuable. Very valuable. As a slave . . ."

I held up my hands, sleeves pulled back to the elbows, and made them turn red—as if blood was running up from the elbows, covering my forearms, hands, then fingertips. I made fists, then spoke to him.

In his own voice.

"Do not test my patience," I said. "The longer you deny my gracious offer, the stronger my hold over your soul will become."

He scrambled back, eyes wide. Ealstan's jaw dropped. Even Sefawynn seemed impressed. After how she'd taken my red-arms trick, it was satisfying to see her flabbergasted stare.

I smiled, then added a reverb to the vocal modulation. "I am Runian Von-Internet of Cascadia! Aelv prince and keeper of souls!" I reached a hand toward him, and made the fingertips turn stark white—the coloration moving up along the skin. "I claim you! And each of your soldiers!"

This caused a stir among them as the skald translated. The captain glanced to his soldiers—even if he didn't believe, *they* did. He wouldn't get far in his raiding if all of his men fled.

"Fine!" the captain said, seizing an axe from the soldier at his side. He pointed it at me. "Stop! As you wish, álfr!"

"My demands increase," I shouted, pointing. "I require an offering for your insolence! The captive in your ship. You will give him unto me!"

"I will give you nothing!" the captain said. "But . . . neither will I

122

fight you over him. Come take him, if you must. But you will leave my image in his place."

With that, the captain turned and stalked toward his ship. He was trailed by his skald and some of his men—though many remained behind, not wanting to interfere with me.

I glanced at Ealstan and Sefawynn. He was grinning outright, but she looked toward the boat, and the captive.

"They assume you won't do it," she whispered to me. "Because of your kind's aversion to water. He's trying to save face by escaping one of your demands, but he doesn't dare refuse directly after what you showed him." She glanced at me. "It was . . . a remarkable display."

I glanced at the Viking ship. Aversion to water, eh? That was . . . uncomfortably close to the truth.

Still, I was a hero, right? I had to do this. Had to prove to my uncertain nerves that I wasn't a coward.

Setting my jaw, I waved the other two forward, marching through the center of the Vikings, who made way for me and wouldn't meet my eyes. I climbed the gangplank after the captain and stopped at the top, awed.

On one hand, the ship wasn't much—a big canoe with places for men to sit and row. But I was standing on a real Viking ship, smelling the sea air and the faint scent of sweat. Up to this point, my experiences in this dimension had mostly included scrambling to stay alive.

In that moment, it sank in. I was standing in a place scholars and historians throughout time would have practically killed to visit. I paused, not wanting the experience to be *entirely* wasted on me.

The captain examined me carefully. This was another test, wasn't it? I made a show of wavering, as if the water affected me—but then hopped down and took a deep breath.

I met his eyes. "You thought a prince like myself would be stopped by mere water?" I forced out a reverb-enhanced laugh I didn't feel. The captain looked away and gestured to the captive.

It was a man with an olive skin tone. In fact, with his curly black beard and white, robe-like clothing, he didn't feel British to me at all. Middle Eastern, perhaps? I was shocked; I'd assumed this place was pretty homogeneous.

I hesitated, but couldn't stop now. If I acted afraid, these Vikings would recognize it. I needed to persuade them I was too dangerous for them to sail farther north and attack Stenford. Besides, I had my augments.

My body *would* know what to do, even if my heart was wavering. I walked toward the captive, noting that the captain still had his axe in hand.

Oh, ever-loving hell. He *was* going to betray me.

A panicked part of me knew the moment he shifted. I spun to see him winding up with the axe. Ealstan—following behind me—shouted and tried to stop it, but a Viking rushed him, shoving him aside.

I stared down that axe.

And my body, instead of fighting, cringed.

I heard shouting people from deep within my memories.

Angry voices. Flashes of light. Like explosions.

Had I fought in a war?

Shame. Utter, gut-rotting *shame* overwhelmed me, and I flinched back, laughter echoing in my mind as I raised my hands—but not as a warrior might. More as a terrified art student would. My back hit the mast, and the captain's axe expertly shifted, going for my head. I saw my death reflected in that steel.

Until the axe head completely fell off.

It *separated* from the handle—narrowly missing my cheek—and soared out over the side of the ship. The handle of the axe missed my face by an equally narrow margin as the captain—suddenly off-balance—completed his swing.

We stared at each other, dumbfounded, as a distinctive *ploop* sounded from the water outside.

He recovered first, reaching for a sword. I wasn't a warrior. I didn't have instincts! I was going to *get myself killed*!

"You dare?" I managed to sputter. "Don't you know who I am?"

"I know and believe, now!" he shouted back, smiling. "But you've stepped onto water! You shouldn't have admitted your lineage to me, prince! The Dökkálfar will pay well for your corpse! You are weakened enough to fall to mortal blades now!"

Oh, no. He did believe. A little too much.

Three Vikings had attacked Ealstan, who struggled in close quarters with them. Sefawynn's voice called over the chaos. "Master!" she said. "Flee before they bind you with boasts!"

The captain glanced at his skald, who grinned at me. I barely understood what was happening. Sefawynn's outburst had . . . persuaded them to capture me instead?

Run with that, I thought, desperate. *Buy Ealstan some time.* "They wouldn't dare!" I shouted. "My father would be *outraged* by the bounty price!"

That did it. The captain's hand hesitated on his sword hilt, and he nodded eagerly at his skald. She'd moved to the side of the ship, near two empty rowing seats. But now she composed herself, then strode forward, speaking in a loud voice.

> "Word-weaver I am   on waves wandering,
>   The dread one's daughter,   daunter of the dead!"

I needed to play the part, so I flinched.
She stepped forward again.

> "Struck-straight, strength strays,   struggles under strain.
>   A worm to the wolf   your worth will be waste!"

I sagged against the ship's mast.

> "Victorious vision   I vow through this verse!
>   Behold my bright boast,   my battle-born build!"

I hissed, then met her eyes. I acted as if I was going to obey, but then—with gritted teeth—stood back up. I stretched, as if throwing off a weight. "Is that your best, skald?" I demanded.

She backed up a step, hand going to her breast.

> "Submit to my spell-songs—"

I flipped my hand out in front of me, as if batting the words aside. "I am Runian Von-Internet of Cascadia!" I shouted over her. "Your words cannot bind me, *mortal*."

She stumbled behind the captain and muttered something. He seemed intimidated now—and his expression fell further at a groan from the side. Ealstan stumbled toward us—leaving one of his opponents slumped against the gunwale, boots scraping the wooden floor as he thrashed in his own blood. The other two had backed away warily.

The brutality made me sick. Still, I tried to regain some of my confidence as Ealstan and Sefawynn hurried to my left, placing all of us near the captive—with the captain and his soldiers gathered at the front. They didn't even look at the dying man.

"Now what, honored aelv?" Ealstan whispered. "You are strong indeed to resist such boasts, but . . . we should not have gone over water."

Damned if I knew what to do. The Vikings didn't seem eager to advance on us, but they stood between us and freedom.

My only instinct was to climb over the side of the boat and try to swim away. *Yeah,* I thought. *Outswim a group of literal Vikings. That's going to go great.* What else could I do, though? It—

A thought occurred to me.

"Sefawynn," I said, "please tell me you still have that ink."

"Yes," she said, digging out the small clay pot—for oil—in which she'd stored it. "But . . ."

"Give it to me," I said. "Ealstan, grab the captive, then jump over the side. Sefawynn, you follow. If this doesn't work, we'll need to try our best to run."

Ealstan obeyed immediately, bless the man. Sefawynn took my arm, drawing my attention from the Vikings. She'd dug out the ink, but held it away from me.

"Don't write," she hissed at me. "You will draw Woden's anger."

"Would you rather be dead?" I demanded.

"Yes!"

Huh. Hopefully the Vikings were equally superstitious. I took the ink from her and pushed her gently toward Ealstan, who had hauled the captive to his feet and cut his hands free. The two were preparing to leap off the ship.

Sefawynn scrambled after them. I turned toward the Vikings,

then smashed the ink to the deck. I knelt and began to smear it into a shape—one of the runes I'd seen on the stone at Stenford. The one that looked like an F.

I was able to get the shape right, and blessedly, it worked. The Vikings huddled away from the rune, like children who had just encountered a rabid dog.

I stood up, pleased with myself.

"You will leave," I demanded, "and you will *not* return to these lands."

At my words, thunder sounded in a sharp, demanding peal from the perfectly cloudless sky, and the rune burst aflame.

As in, the ink *started on fire*.

I was stunned. What was in that ink?

Oh, hell. Something was *very* wrong about all of this. I looked again at the handle of the captain's axe, remembering the sudden way it had fallen to pieces. Remembering the strange, vanishing offerings in the bowls. The . . .

Well, the *everything*. I'd been ignoring it, unwilling to accept it, but my ability to disbelieve was crumbling.

"We will go, álfr," the captain said. "I vow it." His expression hardened. "We will not return until we have strength enough to defeat you. The gods will stand by us, after what you have done here."

I had no response for that. I gawked at the burning rune blackening the wood in front of me. I stepped back from it as it persisted, despite the breeze.

Confused, and more than a little terrified, I ran for the side of the ship. With the help of my hand augments, I hauled myself up and over and leaped into the ocean—hoping the water wasn't too deep.

OUR FANTASTIC PACKAGES!

Here at Frugal Wizard Inc.®, we provide the highest quality experience at a fraction of the prices charged by other dimensional tourism companies.

We believe that the Interdimensional Wizard™ deserves options. Predetermined, groomed experiences are right for some, but others prefer a more rugged experience, full of unexplored lands and adventure.

As such, we offer five packages. Each comes with our triple

guarantee, except where stated! Pick the experience that is right for you!

PACKAGE ONE: DISCOUNT DIMENSIONS

For an extremely low price, you can purchase a dimensional experience that *doesn't* meet our strict filtering process. This package offers you a dimension missing *one* of the three guarantees.

PANDEMIC DIMENSIONS

These dimensions meet our other two criteria, but are experiencing (or are postulated to soon experience) a terrible pandemic on the scale of the Black Death. Perfect for physicians wishing to save the world, researchers studying infectious diseases, or others with interesting tastes. (No judgment here!)

UNINTELLIGIBLE DIMENSIONS

The population of the British Isles in these dimensions doesn't speak a language intelligible to any known Earth language speakers. Perfect for linguists or those who want an extra challenge! Visit the speedrun section of our website for current records for full dictionary creation in the various language groups.

STONE AGE DIMENSIONS

These dimensions don't provide the traditional medieval experience promised in our marketing materials. Perfect for those who *really* want to show off to the locals! Forget mesmerizing ancients with your phone; try inventing agriculture or the wheel! Note: Population numbers in these dimensions can be low, and there are often no permanent settlements.

EXTRA DISCOUNTED DIMENSIONS

For the *extremely* frugal wizard, choose a dimension that lacks two, or even all three, of our guarantees! Completely unpopulated dimensions, often including various forms of megafauna, are also available for those who want to conquer true wilderness. Or for those who really like woolly rhinoceroses.

PACKAGE TWO: WIZARD WILDCARD™ DIMENSIONS

Our most popular package is the Wizard Wildcard™. Roll the dice! Literally anything could show up in your dimension![1]

While these dimensions include our three guarantees, nothing else is disclosed ahead of time. Maybe the Irish have taken over! Or the Insular Celts may dominate. Perhaps the Norman influence is especially strong. Whatever you discover, your dimension will have history, customs, and experiences all its own. That's the true fun of being an Interdimensional Wizard™!

PACKAGE THREE: SET TIME PERIOD

Are you looking forward to a specific experience? Perhaps your heart is set on learning to joust, or you want to help the Roman legions in their push northward across Britain? This is the package for you!

You choose a specific time period—in relation to technological level and expected cultural customs—and we'll provide a dimension that meets our triple guarantee and fits the desired criteria.

---

1. Please reference "FAQ: All Right, WHY Can't I Have a Dimension Full of Talking Bananas?"—including all important legal disclaimers.

(The time periods available are Celtic, Roman, Anglo-Saxon, Early Norman, and High Middle Ages.)

PACKAGE FOUR: LUXURY EXPERIENCE

In this premium package, you choose not only your desired time period, but also one specific criterion from the following list. Warning: You might have to wait until a proper dimension is located! Please visit our website for a current list of available luxury dimensions.

Luxury Options (pick one):

- A specific historical individual from our world exists in the dimension.[2] Arm wrestle King Richard the Lionhearted! Have a rap battle with Chaucer!

- A rare time-period/cultural/technological mix. (For example, Romans with gunpowder, still-living megafauna, or a Britain with Chinese settlements.)

- A highly sought-after specific time period. (The Norman invasion is about to start, for example.) Perfect for historical war gamers! See the speedrun section on page 203 for more ideas.

- Specialist dimensions found more commonly in our band than in others, as outlined on page 113. (Includes Celtic True Matriarchy™ dimensions, dimensions with extra-high ethnic diversity on

---

2. Mythological figures, like Arthur and Robin Hood, are not available. You must choose people who are documented in the historical record.

Britain, and our Last Bastion of Civilization™ dimensions where Rome has fallen and Britain has become the center of the Roman empire.)

PACKAGE FIVE: TOTAL WIZARD™ PACKAGE

This ultimate package includes all of the benefits of the Luxury Experience and any number of *bonus* add-ons! These can include, but are not limited to:

· A small nuclear power plant and a castle to install it in.

· A full complement of modern weapons capable of outfitting a band of one hundred soldiers.[3]

· A modern helicopter, fully automated with piloting software and weapons.[3]

· Your own adventuring party! This option includes a one-year contract with an expert linguist, a historian, a bodyguard, and a dimensional guide to help you establish yourself in your new dimension.

· A fully trained complement of local servants, guaranteed to treat you as a god, and a castle to house them.

---

3. Legal Disclaimer: Controlled weapons will be delivered to the dimension by our team via a temporary gateway in international waters. This is to avoid local restrictions on arms sales. As per the Dimensional Arms Act, anyone carrying controlled weapons into a dimension must subject their in-dimension portal to government inspection. Said weapons may not be brought back through the portal into our dimension. Extra fees apply.

- Research into local diseases, a medical tent with equipment for treating wounds, and up to 2,000 vaccines prepared for distribution to your loyal followers. Also includes access to a medical team that can be called on in emergencies or for triage after a battle.

- One True Wizard™ staff with weapon functions, projection abilities, and a suite of magnetism augments to replicate telekinetic powers. Don't go wizarding without one!™

For more details on bonus add-ons, see the full list of over 30 stunning options in the next chapter! Please remember that these options may be added to *any* package! It's our way of offering our wizards the most flexibility possible.

15

I managed not to drown, though it was touch and go until Ealstan pulled me out. I sputtered on the shore.

A warning popped up in my vision.

Near-drowning detected. Nanites providing oxygen directly to the bloodstream. You have five hours left before running out of air. Would you like to contact emergency services?

I selected *No, I'm OK.*

Would you like to activate first aid mode to help others?

"How," Sefawynn asked, "did he nearly drown in a mere *five feet* of water?"

"You know how their kind are with water," Ealstan said.

I shook my head, fumbling for a bit before I cleared my vision of the message and disabled future prompts to call for help. I appreciated the thought, but at the moment I was busy coughing.

The Vikings, who were still packing up, eyed me. I didn't know if my failure to swim improved or hurt my reputation, but we made a very hasty retreat with the captive we'd saved.

Some fifteen minutes later, I stood—still damp—near the spot where we'd originally observed the Hordamen, watching their ships retreat across the blue ocean. They'd left behind their lead ship. Somehow, *despite* the fact that it had mostly sunk, the flames smoldered on.

Damn.

"You have my *utmost* thanks," the captive said to Sefawynn and Ealstan behind me. He had a deep baritone voice, and spoke with an accent that—for the first time here—I was familiar with. Middle Eastern for certain.

Ealstan had built a fire—a normal one—to warm us up. They sat beside it, treating what had happened as—if not normal—expected.

"You're from the otherlands, I assume," Sefawynn said. "I've met your kind in Maelport. Traders."

"Yes, but I am not a trader, honored skop," he explained. "I came to live among your people ten years ago—and have committed to stay here my entire life. My name is Yazad, and I am a loyal subject of the earl."

I listened with half an ear as I stared at the impossibly burning ship.

What on *Earth* just happened?

You're not on Earth, a part of me thought.

Yeah, but the rules were supposed to be the same. Gravity was still gravity. Thermodynamics were still thermodynamics. Water-based liquids did *not* spontaneously burst into flame. Unless . . . had Sefawynn swapped the ink for something else?

As the fire below *finally* went out, the black smoke dissipating, I found my confidence shaken. I mean, I would keep looking for rational answers. But for the first time since landing here, I wasn't entirely convinced I'd find them.

"Why," Ealstan asked, "would you leave your people and come live here?"

"What?" Yazad said with a laugh. "Adventure isn't enough of a reason?"

"I'd never leave my people," Ealstan said. "My lands are all I want to know."

"Well, it is wonderful that we are all different, then!" Yazad said. "Isn't creation beautiful?"

I turned toward my companions. The important thing was that we'd gotten away, and had even sent the Vikings running. Sailing. Whatever.

The downside was that I was less certain than ever of who I was. I'd *frozen* instead of fighting when it counted. I'd remembered so much— but it was all a jumbled mess. Art school. Police academy. Detective work. Those memories had returned. But there were still big holes in my most recent past. What had I done *after* the police academy? Why did I have these augments? Why did all of the pieces of my past seem like they were at war with one another?

Who was I, really?

I sighed and walked to the small fire. I settled down on the small log they'd left for me, trying to banish a chill that wasn't entirely due to damp clothing or teasing wind.

"I have thanked the others," Yazad said to me. "But not you. Not directly. Thank you, aelv. I watched your wyrd stop that axe. I have

137

not seen its like away from city protections, and certainly not on the open sea!"

I nodded to him. He was a bit plumper than others I'd seen here, and had a ready, genuine smile. He'd pulled a hat from his pocket. It had long portions down over the ears, cloth across the top, and a headband across the forehead. It reminded me of things I was sure I'd seen in Bible school.

"I thank you as well, honored aelv," Ealstan said to me. "My people are safe because of you."

"He broke Woden's covenant," Sefawynn said. "He wrote werging *words*, Little Father."

"He is an aelv," Ealstan said with a laugh. "Woden's covenant doesn't include such creatures!"

"You saw Thunor burn the ship," Sefawynn said.

"The aelv still lives, does he not?" Ealstan said. "It was a warning— to the Hordamen and us—that *we* should never try such boldness."

"Yes," Sefawynn said, her gaze making me uncomfortable. "Yes, this is true. Somehow."

"The prohibition on writing is *not* universal," Yazad told us, lacing his fingers before himself. "Though I would never insult you all by writing here, many in my lands do it freely."

"Different lands," Sefawynn said. "Different gods."

"*A* different god," Yazad said, leaning in and smiling as he turned to Ealstan. "You ask why I would come here, Little Father of Stenford? I've come to *teach*. About a god above gods. A god who *loves* his people, rather than punishing them."

Ah. This, at least, was familiar. I'd been wondering about religion in this place. Most of England had become Christians eventually, after all.

"A god who loves?" Ealstan said. "Who?"

"Ahura Mazda," Yazad said softly. "The one true god."

Wait. Who?

"Zoroaster," Sefawynn said. "I've heard of this."

Yazad raised his finger. "Zoroaster is the spiritual leader who taught us of the true god. But he was not a god himself. This is a mistake many make."

"Wait," I said. "What about Christianity? You know? Apostles, Jerusalem, all of that?"

"Ah," Yazad said. "You speak of Yeshuans? They are our cousins, you might say! Many mix us up. I'm surprised an aelv pays enough attention to mortals to know of our doings!"

"I . . . pay attention to some things," I said. "Yeshua. He was crucified by the Romans?"

"Ha!" Yazad said. "They tried. But he was rescued by Ahura Mazda. We were one people for a short time, and together we fought as a coalition of all the lands of Abraham! But this was all many centuries ago, before the Hunas destroyed Rome entirely. You know the history of our region well for a fair creature of the north!"

"I find mortals interesting," I told him.

"Excellent!" Yazad said. "Would you be willing to listen to me teach?"

I frowned. "You'd . . . try to convert an aelv?"

"I will try to convert anyone!" Yazad said. "Because all deserve to know of Ahura Mazda's love." Then he winked at me. "But an aelv would be a particular accomplishment, I think."

"You're not worried about Woden?" I asked, glancing at the other two for support. "You won't write in his lands, but you'll preach against him?"

"Woden doesn't care about worship," Ealstan said. "So long as he is obeyed. And feared. So long as we suffer . . ." He leaned forward, rubbing his chin. "How was it you were captured, Yazad? Have they been raiding along the coast? Were other villages hit?"

"Fortunately, no," he replied. "My capture was my own fault. I was sailing, you see!"

"I'm sorry," Ealstan said. "They killed the other fishermen, I assume? Preserved you because you are a holy man?"

"There were no others," Yazad said. "And I was not fishing, merely sailing. They did scuttle my poor ship. Alas."

"You were out by yourself?" Ealstan said. "These waters are dangerous! If you were not fishing, you should have returned to your home!"

"This is true, this is true," Yazad said. "Save for one thing."

"Which is?" Ealstan asked.

"I enjoy sailing!" Yazad said. "I come from a land to the northeast of Persia, where we have no waters such as these. Just hills, some desert, and a few desert hills! When I first saw the ocean, I thought, 'I must cross that. I must experience the waters as Ahura Mazda created them!' So I learned. The speed you can get, the spray of the ocean, the feeling of flying! Ah, it is divine."

The joy in his voice reminded me of the way Jen spoke about history and her studies. I remembered when we first met, I realized that I'd never felt so passionate about anything as she felt about history. I'd lived my entire life after wanting to know what it felt like to love something as much as she did.

So I'd tried. Was that why I'd gone to art school? To see if I could love something as much as she loved her studies?

"I'm confused," Ealstan said, staring into the fire.

"Confused by what, Little Father of Stenford?" Yazad said.

"You were sailing because you wanted to go *quickly*," Ealstan said. "But where were you going?"

"Nowhere in particular," Yazad said. "I enjoy the sailing itself."

I frowned. "Ealstan. Haven't you ever done something just because you like it?"

"I enjoy sitting by my hearth," he said softly. "I enjoy knowing that the larder is full, and my people will not starve at wintertime. I enjoy . . . enjoyed . . . watching my boys . . ." He stared deeper into the flames.

Yazad turned to me and sighed. "It is not so uncommon, honored aelv," he explained. "Life is harsh here, crushed between the sea and the lands of the Bear. These people think that if something is not protecting them or feeding them, it is frivolous. I try to explain that there is so much to *love* and *enjoy* about the world Ahura Mazda created. Yet perhaps that joy is difficult to feel when you live beneath the eyes of gods who mourn."

Ealstan and Sefawynn didn't respond.

"Speaking of frivolity," Ealstan said, glancing at the sun. "We should be moving. Skop, you have humored this delay long enough. Young Wyrm is still in danger."

"Our delay saved lives," she said, though you could tell the delay *had* been excruciating for her.

"They won't kill him," I assured her. "Not while they think he's useful."

"What is this?" Yazad said. "Someone is in danger?"

"My brother," Sefawynn said. "Taken during the night by strangers with odd accents and mannerisms." She glanced at me.

"Many strangers in these parts, lately," Yazad said. "We hear tales of them at the preserve."

"The preserve?" Ealstan said. He stood, then yawned, though he obviously tried to fight it off.

I was in the habit of basically ignoring sleep schedules—not uncommon in the modern day, no matter what my mother said. But Ealstan's fatigue was also manifest in Sefawynn, who yawned once he did.

"The preserve is the name of our dwelling outside Wellbury," Yazad said. "But look, you are tired! You cannot travel far in such a state. Come, stay with us tonight! It is close, not more than three hours, depending on how far north those Hordamen have brought me."

"We can't go into Wellbury in this state," Ealstan said to Sefawynn. "The riders have surely arrived before us, and the chance of surprise is lost. Sleeping somewhere safe and planning tomorrow would serve our cause best."

"You are wise, Little Father," she said to him, wilting a little. Damn, she *did* look tired.

"We accept your offer, Yazad," Ealstan said. "We'll redistribute the packhorse's burden so you can ride." He hadn't ended up sending that packhorse back to Stenford, fortunately.

"No need!" Yazad said. "I'll walk! My legs are a little jealous of the attention I've given the sea."

I was about to complain that his walking would slow us down, but then I remembered how slow our pace had been earlier. Horses were less the thundering creatures of pounding hoofbeats and unparalleled speed found in movies and more like golf carts that ran on a tank of grass and occasionally bit you.

As we stood to rejoin the horses, we found flaming letters burned into the ground.

Those had *not* been there a few minutes ago.

Sefawynn and Ealstan immediately averted their eyes. Yazad stepped up beside me, rubbing his bearded chin. "Curious, curious. Some of those letters look familiar to me. Is that Greek?"

"It's English," I said, stunned. "My language."

The burning letters read: *Nice work. You might be worth the trouble.*

Oh, hell. I couldn't keep denying it anymore, could I?

"Scrub it out," Sefawynn hissed at me.

"But the flames," I said. "What are they?"

"Logna's Fire," Ealstan muttered.

"Like what burned the ship?" I asked.

They shook their heads and hurried on, uncomfortable. Finally, I did as Sefawynn asked, and scuffed out the smoldering words with my foot.

We were soon back in the saddle and on our way. I checked to make sure the rest of the pages of my book were safe in the fold of my saddle (they were) and that none of *them* had started on fire (they hadn't).

Only then did I make the connection. The book had apparently exploded as I'd entered this place—as evidenced by the many singed portions. Was that . . . related? It seemed ludicrous that some Norse god with a few letters swapped around was watching for anyone who tried to write, and doling out fire blasts. But then again . . .

At least it would cut down on graffiti, I thought, absently reaching for my nonexistent notebook to record my review. Three stars. Very clean walls—ignore the smoldering corpses.

The Weswarans refused my further attempts at conversation, and I didn't press too hard. They were obviously exhausted, and Yazad was happy to hum to himself as he marched along with us. That left me time to think. Which was dangerous right now.

Because I was very close to believing in a group of Norse gods with the letters swapped around.

FAQ:

How Can I Be Certain My Personal Wizard Dimension™ Won't Be Corrupted by Other Visitors?

 For a deeper explanation of the dimensional travel process, please see Section Four: The Boring Science Stuff. (Specifically Chapter 4.17: Dimensional Travel in Brief.) But if that's too long for you, here's the *extra-brief* version!

As explained elsewhere, individual dimensions are too granular for our instruments to specifically target. We pick a group of generally similar dimensions, then randomly open a portal to one of them. We catalog what we find, and if it meets our Quantifiably Strict and High-Quality Standards of Dimensional Excellence™,[1] we activate a dimensional beacon and add it to our roster of dimensions for sale.

---

1. This phrase is legally defined as a Marketing Term by the Truth in Advertising Act of 2045.

FAQ:

A dimensional beacon acts as an anchor into a specific dimension, tying it to our dimension. Without one, the chances of finding the same dimension a second time would be infinitesimally small. (As in, you'd have a better chance of dropping a grain of sand onto a beach and then finding that same grain ten years later.)

Still worried that other dimensional travelers will horn in on your fun? Don't be! Your beacon features a personal quantum code of literally infinite digits, unbreakable by any known or theorized science, and is only activatable by a physical quantum key.[2] In order to visit your dimension, your beacon must be active *and* the visitor must have a physical key imprinted with your code.

For extra privacy, once you arrive in your dimension, you can imprint a new code on your key. And, if you're extra paranoid, you can *disable* your beacon!

(The dangers involved are minimal, as you are automatically anchored to our dimension from your side. Confused? Imagine the dimensions as a river with infinite branches. Choosing which branch to go down is difficult because there are so many, but there's only *one* way to go back upstream. You also can't sidestep from one branch to another; you must return to our dimension first, then "sail" down another path.)

---

2. In most nations, legal codes prevent us from giving dimensional keys to anyone who is wanted for a crime or who has an injunction against them preventing interdimensional travel pending investigation or possible trial. Similar treaties prevent us from providing dimensional keys to such people even in international waters. I know. We're sad about that too. If you need something to cheer you up, you can find a picture of a baby woolly rhinoceros on page 214.

FAQ:

In short, even if we wanted to repossess your dimension, or sell it to multiple people, we couldn't! And the likelihood of anyone else randomly finding your dimension is laughably small. It really will be all yours!

Just be certain to protect your beacon and your gateway. Both come standard with all of our packages, and will be installed at the location of your choice inside your Personal Wizard Dimension™. Both come with a lifetime guarantee and a hundred-year-minimum fusion battery. Please note: If your gateway is damaged, you might not be able to return—though considering the fantastic adventures that await you, why would you want to?[3]

---

3. Worried about being trapped in your dimension without a way home? Please invest in our Frugal Check-In option. In this add-on, a Frugal Wizard Inc.® representative will visit your dimension on a set schedule, just in case something has happened to your equipment. Note that these services require you to give us a copy of your key. You must also keep your original code and leave your beacon on. See page 332 for details. Redundant backup dimensional beacons, including smaller mobile beacons, can also be purchased and installed.

16

Yazad's "preserve" turned out to be a modest-sized hut along the edge of a vast forest. We arrived just after sundown, leading the horses up through rows of trees too neat to be natural. "Our orchard," Yazad explained, walking beside me. "We don't own this land, but were granted care of it by the Midfather of Wellbury."

That was the nearby town. Ealstan said it was much larger than Stenford—but considering Stenford had, like, a hundred people in it, that wasn't the greatest descriptor ever.

The local lord was a reeve, and though Ealstan claimed to know him, I was wary. Ulric had indicated that this guy, Wealdsig, had been supportive. We might have trouble convincing him to give Wyrm back.

Ealstan paused, looking past Yazad's home into the deep congregation of trees. "A little near the forest, don't you think?" he asked.

"We've never suffered any ill from it!" Yazad said, ambling on ahead. "The Black Bear doesn't seem intent on pushing this direction."

"Still," Ealstan said.

Sefawynn led her horse past us, saying nothing. She moved by rote, her posture slumped. I hadn't heard anything out of her in an hour, and I hoped that was just fatigue. I'd never lived without medical nanites, so I didn't *know*, but I'd read that lack of sleep zombified people.

The preserve was close to the size of Ealstan's manor, so perhaps "hut" was the wrong word. But it was difficult to avoid the association, considering the rough wooden walls and the thatched roof. Yazad ushered us up quietly, then cracked the door, startling an elderly man sitting right inside. He had a long beard that still had some streaks of brown in it, but was bald save for a few stray bits of hair sticking straight up.

"Yazad?" he asked in a quiet, intense voice. "Oh, praise Ahura Mazda!" The elderly man glanced back at the slumbering people surrounding the firepit in the center of the large open room, then slipped out to join us. He clutched Yazad's arm, tears in his eyes. "What happened?"

"I tried preaching to some Hordamen!" Yazad said with a big grin.

"Oh, Yazad," the old man said. "We *warned* you!"

"You did," Yazad said, then waved at the three of us. "But by the grace of Ahura Mazda, I was saved by this skop, the Little Father of Stenford, and that aelv with the sickly complexion!"

Sickly?

The old man gawked at me. "An . . . aelv?"

"He's harmless," Yazad said, slapping me on the shoulder. "Unless you're a boat! But come, we have exhausted guests. Sorry, Little Father—but no fine mattresses here for you. I'm afraid all we have is hay on the floor."

"It will be fine, Yazad," he said.

"Shall I wake the others?" the old man said.

"No, no, Leof!" Yazad said. "When they find me among them in the morning, I will pretend I've been here the whole time, and act annoyed that they ignored me. It will be delightful!"

Leof opened the door for us, then shuffled over to take our horses. On the way, he squinted at Sefawynn. "Skop?" he asked. "You look familiar."

She shook out of her stupor. "I often pass this way telling stories," she said, handing over her reins.

"Yes, yes," the old man said. "Well, no need for a loosing here. Our wight is quite friendly! Rarely curdles the milk, and once fixed my shoes with no offering. Hid a dead mouse in them though."

I slipped my book pages out of the saddle, then handed my horse over as well. Yazad ushered us into the hut, gesturing for us to be quiet. Yazad took hay from a box in the corner to make beds. I let him make one up for me, though I didn't plan to sleep.

The occupants of the room didn't so much as stir at the fuss. There were a good dozen of them, crowded along the floor like a giant slumber party. A couple of families, judging by the ages. I supposed if you always slept in one big room with everyone else, you got used to people making a little noise.

Sefawynn and Ealstan climbed onto their pallets with barely a word. Before long, both had fallen asleep, using their cloaks for blankets. I settled onto my pallet, which was close to the fire, and decided to get some extra reading in. I focused on the FAQ pages, as a good way to skim for quick information. My excitement flared as I discovered a section that briefly outlined how interdimensional travel worked.

The explanation didn't seem terribly familiar to me. I suspected I hadn't known much about the process before leaping into this place.

Perhaps I'd been hot on the trail of the criminals and left without any other choice.

Unfortunately, the FAQ was frustratingly vague. What did a dimensional portal *look* like? It referenced a more in-depth explanation, so I shuffled through the pages, hunting for Chapter 4.17 . . .

Which was, of course, missing. I found only a single identifiable page from the section, and the only part of the text I could make out appeared to be a joke about marmosets.

I sat back, annoyed. Then I spotted something odd—a pile of five stones sitting next to me, the largest no bigger than my thumb. They'd been arranged into a little pyramid.

That was unnerving. I moved my foot, toppling the rocks over—but then was distracted as Leof entered the room. He woke a boy and sent him out to watch over our horses and saddles, then eyed me warily before placing a few more logs on the fire.

He retreated to his stool and returned to peering through a slit in the door, when he wasn't surreptitiously glancing my way.

Well, I wanted them to think I was an elf, so . . . great? The fire burned a little hotter with the new logs—or so I assumed from the increased glow. My medical nanites regulated my temperature to my preferred specifications, so I didn't really notice temperature changes within normal thresholds. But judging from the others, it seemed like the air was chilly here at night, even in the spring.

I forced myself to dive back into the book. Frustratingly, after another hour—per my internal chronometer—I'd learned basically nothing. How could there be so many pages to this thing, but so little actual information? I'd read about the fantastic—and frugal—packages I could purchase seventeen times. But heaven help me if I needed to figure out, say, the Anglo-Saxon version of a handshake or whatever.

(One star. Barf up some alphabet soup, and you might create a more useful text.)

I absently pulled a half-burned stick from the fire and chewed on the charcoal end to get some carbon in my system to restore my nanites. Taste bud hacks made the flavor palatable—I usually picked buttered toast, though the texture mismatch was odd.

That earned me another look from the elderly watchman, so I held up the pages I was reading, which made him look away in a panic. I settled back, feeling unjustifiably smug. Why was I taunting the old man, anyway?

To avoid thinking about what happened, I realized. *It's why you've been reading about potential add-ons to packages for the last twenty minutes.*

I didn't want to accept how strange this place was. Runes burned when you wrote them. Gods left messages for me in the dirt. Why didn't the damn book say something about *that*? I paused, then timidly wrote my name on the floor with a bit of charcoal—nothing happened. Maybe I should try a rune?

Idiot, I thought. *You want to burn the hut down? Or get lightning thrown at you by a comic book character?*

I was uncomfortable with how likely I believed that was at the moment. One theme that kept coming up in the book was that these dimensions *should* have the same physics as mine. The cultures might have been tossed into an interdimensional blender, the linguistics conveniently baffling, the social structures upended . . . But the physics? That should be the same. 9.8 m/s^2, 2+2=4, object in motion. Most importantly, entropy was a thing.

Rocks shouldn't spontaneously form into piles. I felt a chill, and resisted looking. But finally, I glanced over.

The five little stones were again stacked in a perfect little pyramid. Cursing softly, I knocked them over again—then turned up my skin temperature two degrees. The chill persisted.

I closed my eyes. Maybe *I* was suffering some ill effects from a lack of sleep? Had my medical nanites or my firmware been damaged? Was I hallucinating? Or causing things to spontaneously combust?

When I reopened my eyes, the rocks were now arranged in a near-impossible stack, one atop another, on their *edges*. Perfectly balanced, like you sometimes saw in social media posts with people doing yoga on a mountain. Five stars for spectacular stacking. Creepy, yet cool. My wight had style.

Damn. I was accepting it now, wasn't I?

How could I not? It was either that, or believe I was suffering from hallucinations.

"Show-off," I couldn't help muttering, though the rocks fell with a soft series of clicks when I shifted positions. After some deliberation, I instructed my nanites to let me sleep. Maybe that would reset my system. One last, desperate attempt to find a rational explanation for my experiences here.

I fell asleep to the sight of those damn rocks once again in a pyramid shape, as if to mock me.

17

I awoke at seven in the morning, on the dot, and my nanites immediately scrubbed my mind of sleepiness. I'd chosen that hour so I could be up before everyone else. But I hadn't thought that through—the entire room was already bustling with motion. Sefawynn was entertaining some children in one corner. She'd changed dresses, and seemed to have washed her hair. Ealstan was nowhere to be seen—though the windows had been thrown open, and I heard men laughing and talking nearby.

Right. Agrarian culture. Break of dawn. Gotta milk the chickens or whatever. I stretched, sitting up and picking at some hay stuck to my neck. A ding sounded in my ear and text appeared in my vision.

Congratulations! You got a full night's rest. Your health goal is to get at least six hours of sleep every three days. So far, you have accomplished your goal 1 time this year. Keep it up!

I vaguely remembered setting that health goal after Jen had complained about my sleep habits. How did people survive without medical nanites? I seemed to remember my grandfather subsisting on coffee, but I didn't think that existed in medieval England.

Did anything seem different now that I'd gotten some shut-eye? I glanced toward the pile of rocks, which still sat in a pyramid next to my pallet. I knocked them over, then stayed close to make certain nobody snuck up and rearranged them.

I continued to pick hay out of my clothing and finally registered what Sefawynn was saying.

"And then," she said, leaning down and spreading her hands, "Runian, prince of the aelvs, spoke to the evil Hordamen:

> "'I find you faulty   and failing in fight.
> Shame is your shadow   for showing your ships.
> Run and remember   Runian the writer!'

"His boast caused them to fall back in fear, and—not being mortal or a subject of Woden—Runian used his finger to *draw a rune* on the boat's deck!"

The children gasped, then looked at me. I made a good show of wiggling my fingers and making them flash through a rainbow of colors in rapid succession.

"What happened next?" one of the older kids asked in a hushed tone.

"Thunder assaulted the open sky," Sefawynn said, "and because Runian could not be touched by Woden, Thunor's wrath struck the ship! The flames separated us from the Hordamen and allowed us to leap into the ocean. Where he, being an aelv, nearly drowned."

The other three children listened with rapt attention, but a taller girl—maybe eleven or twelve—studied me instead. "*I* don't think he looks like an aelv," she declared. "*I* think he looks like that sickly fellow who tried to steal apples last summer. He doesn't even have a beard."

"Aelvs have no beards," Sefawynn said.

"But aren't they supposed to be beautiful?" the girl asked.

Ouch. I was spared further insults as Yazad called for the children to work in the orchard. I felt a little sad to have missed his prank, though the people *did* seem happy to have him back. Each of the children gave him a hug, calling him uncle, as they rushed out the door.

I smiled toward Sefawynn, but she'd stood up and was looking out the window. She seemed melancholy.

Her brother has been kidnapped, I thought. *Of course she's melancholy.*

"You are awake, my friend!" Yazad said to me. "I have news. Strangers visited with the reeve last night and rode out early this morning, leaving one of their number behind."

"My brother," Sefawynn said. "He *is* here."

"There is more," Yazad said. "A different stranger passed this way two nights ago. Someone very odd. Come with me."

"*One* stranger?" Sefawynn said, walking up.

"Yes," Yazad said. "Come, come." He led the way out the door instead of answering our questions, frustrating man.

I climbed to my feet, then noticed the reassembled rock pile. So much for hoping it was a sleep-deprived hallucination. I kicked at the rocks in annoyance, and stubbed my toe.

What the hell? I leaned down, and found they'd been glued together by a thick amber gel.

157

"Sap," Sefawynn said. "Have you been antagonizing the wight, Runian?"

"No," I said.

She eyed me.

"They like making piles, right?" I said. "I gave it piles to make."

"For a runian," she said, "you are not very clever."

"My ways and reasonings are beyond those of mortals."

She picked a piece of hay out of my hair, eyebrow raised. Then she jumped as an older woman entered the hut, carrying a bucket of water and a scrub brush. Sefawynn quickly looked away, hiding in my shadow as we passed the woman and went outside.

"What was that about?" I asked her.

"What?"

"You hid from that woman."

"I did not," she said, chin raised, but not meeting my eyes. "I was helping your reputation as an aelv."

Right. We joined Yazad and followed him into the orchard. The orderly rows were oddly encouraging. They felt familiar in a way very little here did; even the people standing on stools and tending the trees felt normal to me.

Then we reached the edge and passed alongside the true forest. I'd seen plenty of forests before. This shouldn't have felt any different, and it didn't *look* different. But I was unnerved by those shadowed, untamed depths. It was a primal nature that didn't exist in the world I'd come from, and hadn't for centuries. Yes, I had night vision, but somehow that wasn't comforting. For a place that dark, you needed *fire*, living light.

Yazad directed us to continue along the path, saying he'd be back in a moment, then marched off. As we continued, I found Sefawynn watching me again.

"You fear the forest," she noted.

"I'm wary of it."

"Maybe you're not so stupid as I implied," she said.

"The others speak of the . . . Black Bear? Who is he?"

"A Waelish king," she said, "from before my grandfather's time."

"And he's still alive?"

"Yes," she said softly. "It is said he can only be slain by his own child, and so far, he has produced no children."

I accepted that some unseen thing was piling rocks. Was I ready to go all in, and start accepting everything she said as true? That seemed a stretch. Three stars for the creepy mythology, though.

We soon found Ealstan helping some men dig out the stump of a fallen apple tree. After only a day together, it didn't surprise me, his status as lord notwithstanding. Sefawynn and I watched as he used a hand axe on some of the roots while other men pulled hard to tip the stump back.

When they saw us, one of the men called a break and a girl brought them water in a bucket.

"Honored aelv," Ealstan said, climbing out of the hole and bowing his head to me with reverence. "Greetings and welcome."

I stifled a sigh. Honestly, you save one village from being burned and pillaged by Vikings, and look what happens.

"Yazad brought word that the reeve had visitors last night. One remained when they traveled on this morning," I told him.

"This is good news," Ealstan said. "If we plead with the midfather, I believe he will release Sefawynn's brother. But what of Ulric and Quinn? Will they be content with power over the reeve?"

"They'll *definitely* want more," I said. "They probably dropped Wyrm off because they didn't want to bother with him. I'd guess they continued on to the earl's to seize real power."

"My path is toward Maelport to warn the earl," Ealstan said. "But first, we find and rescue the youth."

Yazad soon trotted up with an older woman, who bore a basket of sticks. She moved slowly, likely because of her advanced years. She was short, and thick of body, with long white hair she kept in a bun, stuck through with wooden sticks. Her round face and cheerful eyes reminded me of someone . . .

Grandmother Dobson, I realized with fondness. We often went fishing together. Another piece of my childhood slid into place, and I couldn't help grinning widely.

"This," Yazad said, gesturing toward me, "is the—"

"I've seen an aelv before, Yazad," the woman said, tottering over to me. "Yes, this is a fine specimen!"

"Familiar with my kind, are you?" I said with a smile.

"Yes, and you won't be tricking me!" she said. "Or I'll trick you right back." She leaned in close. "I'm very dangerous, when I have a mind to be. Are you properly intimidated, aelv?"

"Yes, very," I said.

"Good, good." She selected a stick from her pile. "This is for you."

"Um . . . thanks?" I said.

"Thokk is a traveling hearth-keeper," Yazad said, gesturing to the woman. "She sells tinder."

I glanced at the woods, which were obviously full of as much tinder as you'd want. Still, Yazad was gesturing to me from behind her, as if to say, "Roll with it." So I did, nodding my thanks and tucking the stick away into my cloak pocket.

"Thokk, tell the aelv of the man you met on the road," Yazad said.

"He was an aelv too," the old lady said, a hand on her hip. "He had red hair, like a northman. He wore no beard, had an odd way of speaking, and his features were unusual."

Ealstan said, "That's the man the strangers were looking for at Stenford. Before Ulric and Quinn took the skop's brother, they were asking about a beardless man with red hair."

Something about that jogged my brain.

"Follow me," I said to the others, heading back to the preserve. There was a memory there somewhere, and I was desperate to pull on the thread.

When the others caught up to me, I'd already dug out a sheet of paper with some space at the bottom, and was trying out a few sticks from the fire that had sharper charcoal points.

Thokk slipped out a stick from the bottom of her pile. "Here. Good char on this one."

"Thanks," I said, trying it. It drew well, like the charcoal pencils I was used to. "Could you describe this man to me? Did he have a broad or narrow nose? Was his face rounder, or more angular?"

"I suppose the face would be round," she said. Though everyone else—even Ealstan and Sefawynn—kept a good distance from me as I drew, the old woman leaned in awkwardly close. "No, no. Not *that* round." She whacked me on the back of the head with a stick.

"Ow!" I snapped.

Thokk winced. "Whoops. Sorry. Thought you'd be a little more sturdy. You know, since aelvs can leap over mountains and turn themselves into steel and all."

"Those things aren't part of the stories, Grandmother Thokk," Sefawynn said.

"Could have sworn I heard it somewhere," she said, tapping my paper with a stick. "Less round, and a lower hairline."

"And the nose?" I asked.

"Narrow," she said. "Yes, like that."

I continued prodding her, my sketching accelerating in a fervor. I'd done this before, many times. After I'd dropped out of art school, I'd wanted to do something responsible with my life. Chasing a passion I didn't have had been exhausting. So I'd tried something rigid, something my parents would see as useful.

I'd joined the police academy at . . . at the urging of a friend. My art background had come in handy, and I'd trained as a forensic artist.

With the liberal use of my finger to smudge out mistakes, I created the face from Thokk's memory. As the face took shape, I felt a growing sense of familiarity. I knew someone like this—a guy who liked to dye his hair, who had encouraged me . . .

"Ha!" the old woman said. "Yes, that's him. See? I told you aelvs could summon people in flat surfaces. They're all staying quiet, aelv, because they don't want to admit how often I'm right."

I stared at the crude charcoal sketch, remembering a laughing face. Evenings at the bar together. Asking for help in my studies. Then . . . eventually . . . working together? Two cops. Friends from before the academy and . . .

His name was Ryan Chu.

He was my partner.

FAQ:

Can I Transfer Things Between Dimensions?

A: ▷ You can bring whatever you want into your Personal Wizard Dimension™! Assuming it's something you legally own, of course.[1]

However, you can't bring anything back. (We recommend you keep your original clothing for visits home.)

As explained in Section Four: The Boring Science Stuff, dimensional offshoots have less "substance" (page 285). They aren't *quite* as real as *our* dimension.

Essentially, anything (or any*one*) from your dimension would vanish in transit to our reality.

---

1. Frugal Wizard Inc.® complies with all dimensional treaties, laws, and jurisdictions. We are the only commercial dimensional travel provider who has never been convicted of a major dimensional legal code violation![3]

This is, of course, why we've never been able to verify the existence of a dimension above ours in the dimensional travel "river." Though gateways indicate that something might be there, not even electrons or photons can make the trip.

For now, such a destination remains theoretical. Regardless, if dimensional physics work the same way in all realities, the chances of someone dimensionally upstream from us locating our dimension are small. Basically nonexistent. So don't worry about it.[2]

(Note: While you *can* use your gateway to travel farther "downstream" to dimensions that branch off of yours, we highly recommend against it. These dimensions tend to be unstable.)

---

2. See FAQ: Can You Recommend a Therapist to Help Me Cope with the Existential Dread Caused by the Realization That My Reality Might Just Be an Offshoot of Another Dimension with More Substance than Ours?

3. In Canada.

18

Ryan was here.

Did he know he was being hunted? I had to find him—both to warn him, and to finally get some damn explanations.

"Where did you see him?" I asked Thokk.

"Heading into Wellbury," she said. "Two days ago."

"You know this man, honored aelv?" Ealstan said.

"Yes," I said. "He's one of my kind. A mighty soldier among us. We should try to join him."

Ealstan leaned in to study the picture. "Wellbury was already our destination," Ealstan said. "Perhaps he may aid us with the release of Wyrm, or in stopping Ulric and Quinn. We could ask the midfather about him."

I focused on the drawing, clinging to my memories in the academy with Ryan and . . . Jen? No, she hadn't been a cop. But we'd often gone out at night, the three of us. Friends. Then Jen and I had become a thing.

"Pardon, Little Father," Sefawynn said. "But I was hoping to retrieve Wyrm *without* talking to Wealdsig. The reeve is . . . not my favorite person."

"The midfather's devotion to Woden can be uncomfortable at times," Ealstan said.

"Uncomfortable?" Yazad said. "Pardon, but didn't the man once nail himself to a tree?"

Wait. What?

Ealstan looked to me, chagrined. "Woden required a sacrifice before the battle of Far Strength," he explained. "Some forty years ago now. Sacrificing directly of oneself to Woden is a . . . way to tip the scales in your favor."

"Woden forgets himself and thirsts for increasing devotion," Thokk said softly. "Like a drunkard calling for more wine."

"You should not say such things, hearth-tender," Sefawynn said.

"I'll say what I want," Thokk snapped. "It's true."

Yazad grinned widely.

"Don't give me that," Thokk said to him. "I'm not converting to your feely-lovey god with his pillows and smiles. He wouldn't want me anyway."

"Ahura Mazda wants everyone, no matter how lowly or incapable," Yazad said. "I am proof of that!"

"Can we talk about the nailing to a tree?" I said. "That part sounds important."

"Wealdsig needed strength for the battle," Ealstan said. "He considered sacrificing one of his warriors, but felt that would give *them* the honor. In one of the old tales, Woden nailed himself to the world tree. So, to draw upon that strength, Wealdsig . . . emulated him. His right hand isn't of much use now, but people respect him."

"Fools respect him," Yazad said.

"You can't fault his heart," Ealstan said. "That's one part of him that remains unbroken."

"Unlike his brain . . ." Thokk said.

Great. I settled onto the floor beside the hearth.

Ryan had come through this region two days ago—and yesterday, Ulric and Quinn had followed. They'd left this morning, probably toward the earl's seat. They'd told Ealstan they represented the earl, and if I knew Ulric, he'd make his base impressive and well fortified. If he had a portal out of here, he'd keep it there—at the center of his power.

Maybe Ryan was tracking their activities in this dimension? Maybe I was making too many assumptions. I barely knew my own name; it seemed a stretch to try to guess at other people's motives.

"If you trust Wealdsig," I said to Ealstan, "it seems like it would make sense to talk to him."

"But Ulric said Wealdsig was working for them," Sefawynn said.

"Wealdsig is not the type to give outlanders his devotion," Ealstan said. "He's not that . . . dependable, honestly. He'll do what he finds amusing at the moment. For now, that might be listening to Ulric— but it also might mean listening to me when I talk to him."

I wasn't certain if I liked that idea or not. "We *should* try to see what Wealdsig knows."

"We are decided then," Ealstan said. "We ride in and announce ourselves, then plead our case."

"No," Sefawynn said quickly. "We should sneak into the city. Even if we're going to talk to him, we should be certain not to be seen entering. In case the enemy left someone at the gates to watch. They might recognize . . . an aelv."

I narrowed my eyes at her. There was something familiar in her eyes, her posture.

She glanced away, arms folded.

"Oh!" Yazad said, clapping his hands together with a joyous *crack*. "I can help with this! I often bring fruit from the orchard and our storerooms to distribute to the townspeople! The hearthmen rarely take much note of those I bring with me. You shall accompany me with sacks of fruit, and nobody will think to look at you. It is a way I can repay you for your service to me!"

I supposed it was a good idea, and Ealstan obviously thought so as well, because the two of them went to see how many sacks of apples were ready for transport. Thokk tended the fire, as Leof was still dozing in the corner.

I looked at my sketch. Ryan would be annoyed at me if he knew I was here. The thought confused me. We were partners; didn't we get into problems together?

No . . . I thought. *Something happened between us . . .*

I flexed my hand. It was something to do with these augments. They weren't standard police equipment. Where *had* I gotten them? And why had I frozen when that Hordaman attacked me?

Flashes of light. Shouts of anger.

I started to wonder again. About myself, my heart, who I'd been . . . and what I'd done. For the first time, I wasn't sure I *wanted* to remember. I knew, deep down, that I'd latched on too tightly to the memory of being a cop. It didn't explain everything I could do, my instincts for lying and hiding.

No. I was a hero. I *had* to be a hero. I'd always wanted to . . .

To be like Ryan. But things hadn't turned out like I'd wanted, had they?

Hell. I spent a few minutes digging through my submenus, and again could not enable the inactive platings. I was baffled. Why did I have them, if not to use them? I poked and prodded, until—oddly—a new message came up.

Platings forcibly disabled by external command, it read. *You aren't getting them back, Johnny. Stop trying.*

Oh, hell. Someone had *done* this to me. Intentionally. I exited out of my menus, and felt a distinct impression to *hide.* I wanted to stop digging into my past, stop looking for answers beyond what floated at the surface. I wasn't going to like what I found.

Shame almost overwhelmed me.

I knew that emotion well. But why had I seen it in *Sefawynn* a few minutes ago?

Both Sefawynn and Thokk had left the room while I was distracted. So I stood up, brushed myself off, and poked my head out of the hut. Several women were working on the thatching of the roof, while others worked in the orchard. One fellow was replacing the stones in the pathway. Life didn't leave people with a lot of leisure time around here.

I did notice several bowls of berries out front, with various requests in front of them. Worn-out shoes, a pile of reeds for weaving a mat, some milk? I couldn't decide if that was an offering, or if they wanted it turned into butter. Guess even mysterious invisible forces had to work for a living.

Feeling a little foolish, I said, "You want to give one of those a try while I look for Sefawynn?"

No reply, of course.

I eventually found Sefawynn sitting on a stump, staring into the dark forest. I strolled up, hands in my pockets, wind tugging at my cloak. Handy piece of clothing, that. I didn't need the warmth, but I sure felt more dramatic wearing it. (Four stars. The weird kids might be onto something.)

"Hey," I said to her.

She nodded.

"Leof thought he recognized you," I continued. "Now you're worried the guards at the city gate might too. And you've been acting strange ever since we got here. Like you're . . . ashamed of something."

She sighed, elbows on knees, resting her head in her hands. I leaned back against a nearby tree.

"Our boasts don't do anything," she whispered. "The skops all know it. I think they used to work. I mean, the Hordamen skalds make theirs work, so it's possible ours used to as well, isn't it?"

"I don't know," I said softly. "I don't know much about any of this."

"You baffle me, Runian," she said, finally looking at me. "I've figured out the voice trick—I met a skop once who could make it sound like objects around him were talking, even though he didn't move his lips. It's something like that, isn't it? That's how you run that grift?"

"I'm not a grifter," I said, with too much force. That was a raw nerve. "But it is a similar ability."

"I have no room to chide you," Sefawynn said. "We skops should admit that we *can't* loose wights, or bind them, or intimidate them. But . . . it helps people to believe we can." She grimaced. "That's a justification. Truth is, if we were honest with everyone, they'd throw us out and we'd starve. So we keep acting like we know what we're doing . . ."

"And Wellbury?"

"I came through here a few years back," Sefawynn said, "after the Bear took my parents. He was pushing this direction, so the midfather asked for bindings on a nearby settlement. Extra protections, because the runestones . . . well, you know.

"I performed my best boasts, though I knew they wouldn't do anything. Wyrm and I got paid, then moved on."

"And that settlement?" I asked.

She nodded out into the forest. "Used to be right there."

I followed her gaze into the dense forest, past stone-column trees that had to be a hundred years old. There couldn't have been a settlement out *there*.

Though, what did I know? I'd started talking to the air and believing in ghosts or whatever. So I looked closer. As I studied the forest, I saw shadows that *might* have been old stone walls, or foundations.

"People are starting to figure it out," Sefawynn said. "When I loose a bog, it returns the next night. The protections I promise don't materialize. People die, and their kin wonder why they fed that skop. Why they listened and believed . . . There aren't many places these days where I won't be recognized—I keep forgetting where I've been."

No wonder she thought I was a grifter; she was living that very life. She was the medieval version of a psychic. In my time, those people were mostly harmless. But here, where some of it was real? Maybe the psychic comparison was a bad one. She was more like a scam artist, selling bad augments that didn't protect you.

None of my business either way; I had mob bosses to deal with. I just wished that tone in her voice didn't feel so uncomfortably familiar. The look in her eyes made her seem hollow, like a cheap plastic toy. The kind painted to look like metal, but you knew the difference the moment you held it.

"I'm so tired of lying," Sefawynn whispered. "Of always being worried . . ."

"Of never staying in one place too long," I said, "because you're afraid it will catch up to you. Of being worried that each person you pass is someone you stole from. Of never sleeping except when you have to, because even your friends are . . . the kinds of people you don't sleep easily around."

She glanced at me. For a moment, I worried her show of vulnerability had been an act to get me to admit to something. Then she nodded.

I tried to summon a rousing speech. Tell her something properly honorable, like the honest detective I'd once trained to be. *Turn your life around, kid,* or *Get an honest job. Go volunteer at a shelter for diabetic kittens.*

"Life is awful sometimes," I said instead. "So you cope."

"Others cope without grifting," she said. "Ealstan does it by helping people survive."

"And those Hordamen do it by ripping people apart," I said. "Burning down villages. On that scale, you're not doing so bad."

She stretched, then stood, brushing off her dress. "Thanks," she said. "For not judging."

"You think I'm a grifter too. Why would I judge?"

"That's the first thing you've said that makes me doubt," she said. "Because every grifter *I've* known is a judgmental aers."

There it was again. They called people ears as an insult? (Two stars. Better than calling someone a nose. I think.)

"The midfather might recognize me," she said as we walked toward the preserve. "He might not. But it might be best if I'm not there when Ealstan chats with him."

"That's fine," I said. "It might be best if *I* approached him."

"You're going to try to convince Wealdsig that you're a lizard, aren't you?"

"*Wizard,*" I said. "And yes. I am. It's supposed to work quite well. My book says so. And I impressed those Hordamen."

"Your eyes should have burned out reading all that writing," she noted. "You have a strange wyrd to you."

"All of your words are strange, really."

"*Wyrd*," she said. "Fate or luck or . . . It's not really either, but . . . how do you not know any of this? Where *are* you from?"

"Seattle." I glanced at her. "We don't have many Anglo-Saxons there. Good coffee, though. And great bookstores. I'm telling you the truth, Sefawynn. I've only been in your country for a few days."

"And yet, you speak our language."

"*You* speak *my* language."

She rolled her eyes.

"Stop that," I said.

"I was checking the time of day."

"The sun is *literally* behind us."

"Which one knows by looking at the sky."

"There are plenty of shadows. They're long enough to tell the time by."

She stopped in place and squinted at me.

"What?" I asked.

"I'm seeing if the shadows are dark enough."

"For what?"

"To obscure your face. Nope. I can still make it out. It's not *nearly* dark enough for my taste."

I caught a smile on her lips. An unspoken honesty grew between us. We both had uncomfortable bits to our pasts. I didn't want to confront mine, but they were there, just beneath the surface. But we kept moving forward. Now that we'd admitted a few things, her lack of powers in particular, the air seemed clearer. She walked a little closer to me.

I froze in place.

"Wait," I said. "Was that flirting? Were we *flirting*?"

She rolled her eyes again and kept walking.

Nice, John, I thought. *That's a pro move.* I appeared to be terrible with women. Good to know.

I hurried to catch up. People gathered around the front. What was wrong?

Oh. They were staring at a stack of some *twenty* woven mats. And a mound of butter the size of a small child.

The shoes, though, had been unraveled into their component pieces. Even the *laces* had been stripped down to bits of fiber. It was like the wight was saying, "I did what you asked—but to show you I'm not a pushover, I ruined the shoes. So there."

Leof reverently picked up one of the mats. "What manner of wight could do this . . . ?"

Sefawynn looked at me, then pulled me away.

"What?" I whispered when we were out of earshot.

"Did you do that?" she demanded.

"I don't know how to weave mats. I can barely make ramen."

"Their wight is nice," she said. "But weak. I talked to the kids this morning—it can only manage one small task at a time, and does it over many days. Did you ask your wight to do that?"

"Look, it's not a big deal. Maybe the one following me has a better work ethic."

"How have you bound such a powerful wight?" she demanded. "And not to a place, but to a *person*. You make no sense!"

"I know!" I said. "Try being me! Zero stars! Worse than diet soda with sugar dumped in it!"

Wait.

How in the hell did I know what *that* tasted like?

There really *were* some things in my past it would be best to forget.

Sefawynn frowned. "What is zero?"

"Seriously," I said. "That's the part of my statement that confused you?"

"It's the confusing part that I almost followed," she said. She glanced back at the preserve. "Come on; let's talk to Yazad about specifics. I want to see my brother."

19

Wellbury wasn't the giant fortress the others had made it out to be. It was larger than Stenford, sure, and had a wooden wall surrounding the entire place. But the only stone structures I saw on approach were the two towers beside the gate.

I was beginning to think I wouldn't see *any* castles. Still, if I were an invading Hordaman, maybe that thick log palisade would be daunting. Certainly, the moat would be annoying to cross, assuming the archers up on the wall were filling you with splinters.

The town wasn't far enough inward from the coast to make me comfortable, though. Ealstan had been telling me of invasions of dozens, or even *hundreds*, of Hordamen ships.

I tried to picture that as I walked up along the road, surrounded by Yazad's faithful, lugging a basket of apples tied to my back. A hundred ships, flooding this approach with burly men and their manicured beards. I tried imagining the people of the preserve, who didn't have a fighter among them, running for their lives.

These poor people; crowded on one side by the forest, the ocean on the other. It would be prime real estate to my people—but here, both were dangerous. Their enemies were mobile, but they were tied down, locked in by their homes, farms, and families. In the face of that, the wall seemed toothpick-flimsy, the moat barely a puddle.

We'd come in the evening, hoping the shadows would help obscure our activities. Yazad set down his baskets of apples—carried with a pole across his back—and chatted up the guards at the gate, lightly trying to convert them with talk of Ahura Mazda's greatness. The guards took it with a laugh, accepting the apples Yazad offered.

I examined them closely. But if Ulric had left someone to catch Ryan, they'd be watching from somewhere more secretive.

None of the guards gave us a second look. The town was busy, despite the fading light. Men locked animals into several large round pens inside the walls, as others visited the blacksmith, carted firewood, or headed to their homes.

A lifetime of video games had taught me to watch for a tavern or an inn, but I didn't spot one. I got the impression that if you were here, you either knew someone, or you were of a trustworthy traveling profession—like Sefawynn or Thokk—and people were glad to have you in their home in exchange for your services.

Huddles of single-story, thatched homes, like too many baby birds sharing a nest, squeezed the streets narrow. The only exception was right next to the wall—where ladders were placed for men to access the heights to watch and guard the approach.

The stench was a surprise.

I'd expected the people to stink, but my companions seemed no worse than my hippie friends who elected not to wear deodorant. Sefawynn usually smelled nice.

But this place . . . Farm smells were pervasive here—but only as counterparts to the worse human smells. I took a few whiffs, then elected to breathe through my mouth.

I could vaguely remember studying about ancient times, wondering why someone would live out in the boonies instead of a comfortable town. Cities were superior. A source of convenience and culture. They had things like bakers and butchers and . . . uh . . . candlestick makers?

Culture seemed a stretch here, though. No symphonies were being performed, unless you counted the sound of buzzing flies against that of boots ripping free of mud. This place must be *rife* with disease, and the noises were distracting. It might be better defended, but I soon found myself missing the peaceful air of the preserve.

That said, I was surprised by how many different kinds of people I saw in here. While there were far more pale people with the two-layered dresses or trouser-and-tunic getups that I associated with the Anglo-Saxon people of this dimension, there were a number of people with tan skin, dark skin, and a variety of clothing styles—from hats like Yazad wore, to clothing with colorful patterns. I even spotted an Asian family. I'd always thought people would stay where they were in medieval times, being without steam engines or airplanes.

We entered a less crowded area of the town. Small fields, or vegetable gardens, stretched between homes. Yazad ushered us into a storehouse populated by sacks of grain and prowling cats. One rubbed against my leg, then nipped at me when I tried to pet it. Cats. The same in every dimension.

"All right, my friends," Yazad said quietly as we put down our baskets of apples. "By Ahura Mazda's grace, we have delivered you into the town. Reeve Wealdsig will be at his manor, preparing for his nightly feast and boasts. If it's possible, please don't get my people into trouble with whatever you do here."

"We'll leave the robes with you," Sefawynn said, shucking hers—we'd all worn them over our clothing—"and won't mention you, Yazad."

"Take care, friend," Ealstan said, handing over his own robe. "And if it's true that your god cares for men as you say . . . perhaps give him an offering on our behalf."

"Ahura Mazda accepts only good words, good deeds, and good thoughts," Yazad said. "But I will send him prayers on your behalf. After you rescue the lad and find the evil men you hunt, return to me. I'll prove to you how much better life can be without fear of the heavens."

"I think I should fear them *more*, if I listened to you," Ealstan said. "Your god is far, Yazad, and your lands distant."

"He is only as far as your heart," Yazad said, slipping the pole from the baskets he'd been carrying. "Your staff, Runian."

"Thank you," I said, taking it. It was of apple wood, smooth beneath my fingers. I'd mentioned wanting one, and Yazad had offered this one, as it was "reminiscent of that of the magi."

"We will make our way back home," Yazad told us. "Delm doesn't count numbers at the gates, unless they are the number of apples I've yet to give him!"

He gave us each a hug in turn. Then, Ealstan nodded to Sefawynn and me, and we raised the hoods of our cloaks. Together, the three of us made our way to the side door of the storehouse—followed by a fourth, smaller figure.

"What?" Thokk said as we turned toward her.

"Perhaps it would be best if you stayed with the others, Grandmother Thokk," Ealstan said.

"I'm my own woman," Thokk said.

"Our mission is dangerous," Sefawynn said.

"I know," the old lady said. "And you'll end up dead without my help. Besides, the apple farm is boring and you're interesting. The decision is made: I'm with you."

I expected the others to forbid her outright. This wasn't a place for someone who had to be pushing eighty, but Sefawynn and Ealstan shared a look and said nothing more.

I didn't say anything either. Thokk knew how to care for herself better than I did in this world. Hopefully, I could make up for my shortcomings with my particular advantages—it was time to prove that I was a wizard.

FAQ:

Why Does Everyone in Britain Speak Modern English in My Pre-Norman-Conquest Dimension? Shouldn't That Require an Incredible Alignment of Social and Linguistic Factors That Would Never in a Million Years Align in Such a Convenient Way?

A: Apparently not.

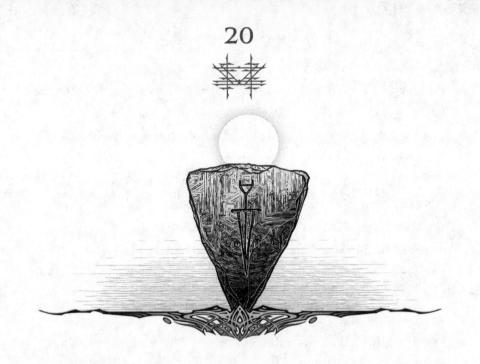

20

We started toward the manor. The crux of our plan again depended on me. Hopefully, it would go better this time. I didn't want to resort to flaming words again; I did *not* trust them.

With Ealstan's guidance, we kept to a less-traveled pathway. Perhaps someone would have noticed we didn't belong in the full light of day, but at night, Ealstan's bearing prevented anyone from questioning us. He looked like an official man on official business.

Again, I was struck by how small the town was. It was one of the largest settlements in the region—surpassed only by Maelport, the earl's seat. Yet we reached the manor in less than a minute; this entire compound couldn't be much larger than a football field.

The manor was similar to the one in Stenford—longer than it was tall, made entirely out of wood, but with open glassless windows showing a hearth's glow from inside. A woman puttered around in front, setting out offerings. The runestone rested in a large, flat courtyard before the building. It was black and jagged across the top, and bigger than the one in Stenford, maybe four feet across and three times that tall.

This time, I couldn't deny it. The symbols etched on the black stone were glowing a soft blue.

The three of us loitered in the shadows while the woman finished her work. "Hey," I whispered. "Is the runestone here more powerful than the one in Stenford?"

"Yes," Sefawynn said. "It was created to protect a larger area. It expels bogs and helps soothe helpful wights. Any residing in the region should help defend the city during an attack."

"And my wight?" I said. "Will this affect it?"

"It might weaken it," Sefawynn said. "The stone wants it to either settle down and protect the region, or to leave. Your wight is resisting both, staying bound to you. Whatever has attached to you—nicor, draca, or some variety we haven't defined—it's strong. Frighteningly so."

"Wait," I said. "How can you tell? How can you even see that I have a wight?"

"It's a thing of skops," Thokk said. "How could they know if a wight was bound or loosed if they couldn't see the signs?"

How indeed. I glanced at Sefawynn, whose face was hidden in the shadows of her hood.

"So . . ." Thokk whispered. "Why are we sneaking about again?"

"Again, elder," Ealstan said. "This is dangerous. Perhaps you should—"

"Why should I care if it's dangerous?" Thokk said. "Do you know how old I am? I probably only have a few months left. Not much to risk here! So what are we doing?"

"Runian is going to persuade the reeve to tell us what he knows about Sefawynn's brother," Ealstan said. "Once we know his location, Sefawynn and I will free him while Runian distracts the reeve."

It was the compromise we'd come to. I'd decided to chat him up and learn what I could about Ulric and Quinn's plans while the other two pulled off the rescue.

"So we're going to simply walk on in?" Thokk asked.

"No," Sefawynn said. "Runian wishes to, as he put it, 'make an entrance.'"

If the book was to be believed, I needed to wow the reeve from the start. I doubted this was the standard policeman's way of getting things done, but more and more, I wasn't certain I was the type who cared.

"We should move," Ealstan said. The woman who had been preparing the offerings had stepped into the manor. There would be hearthmen—soldiers—inside, but this wasn't a people who seemed to worry about assassins. Their eyes were outward, toward the ocean and the forest. The back of the building wasn't likely to be watched.

We hurried across the dirt path to the side of the building, where we found an alleyway between it and the city wall. The alley was empty of people, and perfect for our purposes. An open window ahead painted the area with a rosy orange light.

"Wait here with me at the corner, elder," Ealstan told Thokk. "If you please."

"Not a chance," she said. "This will be entertaining."

She followed Sefawynn and me as we snuck through the alleyway. I was impressed with her ability to move quietly. Not that it took a ton of skill to sneak through the dark along the back of a building.

That said, I'd gotten a board to the face the last time I'd done this, so . . .

A glance inside the window showed me a similar setup to basically all the other homes I'd seen so far. A large chamber with a firepit at the center. A set of massive tables with thick log legs framed the room. There were several guards around the space, but only one table—just inside to our left—was occupied. There sat a tall woman with dark hair and a thin, scraggly-haired older man. He had one eye and was drinking a large mug of something frothy.

"Reminds me of my brother," Thokk whispered.

To the right, I spotted the door Ealstan suggested I use—the way out to "do one's business," I'd been told. We were on the east side of the building, and that doorway out was on the north edge of the room. It would be locked.

"You sure you can do this, Runian?" Sefawynn whispered.

"Nope," I said. "Just be ready. And pray this plan works . . ."

"Pray?" Thokk said. "I doubt you want Woden watching this."

I took a deep breath, then started on my way. Thokk, blessedly, remained behind with Sefawynn. I rounded the north side of the building—passing a long trough that smelled even worse than the rest of this place—and approached the door. Farther along the wall, I could see the back gate. It was guarded, but the soldiers probably thought I was visiting the latrine.

I examined the door. I'd bummed a thin knife and a piece of wire off of Yazad. It shouldn't be too hard to outsmart a thousand-year-old lock.

Where was the lock?

The wooden door had a handle and a hole. I tried it to be certain—and yeah, it was shut tight. They'd made it sound like the lock was something simple, but hell if I could figure it out. I hadn't even seen a bar on the other side.

Fortunately, I'd come prepared. I leaned my staff against the wall, then fished in my cloak pocket for a berry, which I sat on the ground. "Could you open this, please?" I asked softly, then turned my back on the door and counted to a hundred.

The berry was still there. Oh, right. I took a small white cloth from my pocket and sat it down, then put the berry on top of that.

"How about now?" I asked, repeating the process. The berry was gone. I wouldn't want to eat off the ground here either.

The door was now loose. I grabbed my staff, took a deep breath, then burst into the chamber. I slammed the butt of my staff against the ground.

"I am Runian," I declared. "I am here to tell you of your future!"

Wealdsig gaped at me, a mug halfway to his lips.

I rapped my staff on the floor again, using my vocal augments to make a sound like thunder. The book had extolled the virtues of their patented True Wizard™ staff, which did things like this on its own, but I figured my augments could do a good imitation.

I waited. Ealstan had warned me this man might be unpredictable, and—

Wealdsig laughed loudly and slammed his hand on the table several times. "Delightful!" he said. "Woman, fetch my best drink. Stranger, what other tricks can you do?"

"Uh . . ." I said. I'd been expecting objections, maybe anger, not immediate buy-in. The woman at his side rushed out of the room on his errand, but I kept my attention on the reeve. "I can foretell the future! But first, I must prove to you that—"

"Tricks!" he snapped, pointing at me. "Now!"

"Right!" I said. "Have one of your hearthmen hold up a cloak, so I cannot see your table."

189

Wealdsig slapped his hand on the table again—by the way the fingers curled and didn't move, I guessed that was the one he'd nailed to a tree. A soldier hopped over and, as Wealdsig waved impatiently, took off his cloak and held it up to obscure the table.

As I waited, I noticed some pieces of wood on the floor by the door. A lock, perhaps? And my wight had disassembled it.

"Now what, stranger?" Wealdsig said, ale froth sticking to his scraggly grey beard.

"Now," I said, "select an object from the table and point to it behind the cloak. I will use my powers to read your mind and see your choice!"

The book suggested I use a drone with its optics attached to my visual inputs, but I had a more . . . analog solution. As Wealdsig fiddled behind the cloak, I turned up my hearing augments. The crackling of the fire became a roar in my ears, but I spliced that out with a few commands. A few moments later, I was able to pick out Sefawynn's voice as she whispered from beside the window.

"It's his knife," she said, "slipped from the sheath at his side. I think it has a wolf's head on the pommel."

I closed my eyes and held up my hands. With my sleeves rolled to my elbows, I made a flame effect dance on the skin. I was proud of that; I'd spent several hours earlier inputting the commands.

"Yes . . ." I said, adjusting my hearing to normal levels. "I see! Midfather, you have chosen your own knife! Marked with the sign of the wolf!"

"Ha!" Wealdsig said. He tossed up the knife, caught it, then slammed it into the table. "Again!"

"I first wish to—"

"*AGAIN!*"

Okay . . . I made a show of closing my eyes and holding up my hands, readjusting my hearing as he made another selection.

"Oh my," Sefawynn whispered. "He's . . . ah . . . pointing at his crotch, Runian. He thinks himself clever, judging by the grin."

I thought I heard Thokk snickering.

"I see . . ." I said. "A mighty member. A source of great creation. Midfather, you have chosen your source of heirs and heritage."

He threw back his chair, letting it slam to the floor. I winced at the sound, having forgotten to dampen my hearing. But he hit the table again, grinning wildly. "Ha ha! You're far more fun than the other outlanders, spindly one."

Spindly?

"Midfather," I said. "I must—"

"More tricks!" he said.

The sound of thunder boomed from my mouth. I hoped it sounded more intimidating than silly. When I'd practiced, Thokk had . . . Well, never mind. It worked on Wealdsig, who quieted.

"I must give you a terrible warning about your future," I said, pointing at him, flames flickering on the surface of my skin. "But first—the other outlanders who passed through this city. What can you tell me of them?"

"Ulric Lordslayer?" he said.

"Yes!" I said. "What did he tell you before he left?"

"He had to get to Maelport," the reeve said. "He's expecting visitors from another world in three days."

Visitors? In three days? "Did he leave a youth with you?"

"Yes," Wealdsig said. "I threw him in the pit near the compost heap. Why? What does this have to do with my future?"

"He is a changeling," I said, and I heard whispered thanks from

Sefawynn. Now I had to keep Wealdsig distracted long enough for her and Ealstan to rescue the boy.

One of my plans—finally—was working the way I'd intended. I turned down my hearing and prepared to launch into my next trick. I walked over to the fire, where I'd planned to pick up coals and not be burned, thanks to my platings.

As I prepared, I noticed someone standing in the doorway into the hall from the front chambers. The woman who'd been sitting with Wealdsig earlier had returned.

Quinn, Ulric's right-hand man, was with her. "Johnny?" he exclaimed. "What the hell are *you* doing here?"

O h, hell.

That was Quinn, all right, shovel-faced as ever.

Wealdsig laughed, dropping down into a different seat and throwing his empty mug at the soldier who—awkwardly—was still holding up the cloak. "You said he'd have red hair," Wealdsig told Quinn. "Can he change his appearance?"

"This isn't the one we're watching for," Quinn said, stalking across the room. He was wearing tactical camo instead of period clothing. The woman hovered near the doorway. She'd been sent to get him when I arrived. They'd been expecting me.

No, not me. This had been a trap for Ryan. And I'd fallen into it.

I raised my hands and dropped my staff, backing away. "Oh, hey Quinn. Uh . . . how's Tacy?"

"Cut the pleasantries," he said. "You realize the boss wants your balls, don't you? What were you *thinking*? Stealing from Ulric him-self?" He paused, then laughed. "Wait. *This* is the code you copied?

You tried to hide in *this* dimension? Johnny boy, you've made *terrible* decisions in your life, but this one is *precious*!"

Oh, hell.

"Not even bright enough to destroy the original key," Quinn said. "Not that it would have mattered, with the backups. But tell me honestly, Johnny. Did you have *any* idea what you were doing when you leaped in here?"

"I'm . . . not one of you," I said. "I'm a cop."

"A cop? You're barely a *door guard*, Johnny. We've purchased *real* cops in the force; why would we need a dropout?"

Dropout.

Damn. It was true.

I sank down to the floor, against the table beside the wall. Another big chunk of my life slid into place.

I wasn't a detective. I'd washed out after six months. I'd left the academy, disgraced. Just like I had with art school. Just like I had in everything I'd ever tried . . .

I'd tried to make ends meet, but failed, so I turned to petty thievery and grifting. I'd spent years on a downward spiral, until I'd ended up sleeping—literally—in a gutter.

Then, ten years ago, Ulric had invited me in.

This dimension was supposed to be my escape, I thought, mind dull. *I wanted to get away. Go someplace where I wasn't a failure a dozen times over . . .*

After Jen's death . . . I ran away. Stole a code.

Came here.

Jen always wanted to visit one of these dimensions. And Ulric had hundreds stashed away in case he needed somewhere to hide. I'd thought he surely wouldn't miss one, or even notice . . .

Quinn was still chuckling as he turned away from me, helping himself to a mug of ale on Wealdsig's table. He pulled something from his pocket—a phone? How on Earth had they gotten those to work here?

"Should we be worried?" Wealdsig said, gesturing to me. "He has powers, like your kind."

"What, Johnny?" Quinn said, looking up from his phone. "You're kidding, right? Does he *look* dangerous?"

"You all look weak to me," Wealdsig said.

"Johnny wasn't even dangerous when he was *supposed* to be."

Quinn held up his phone to me. "I'm going to tell the boss you're here, Johnny. You could go beg to him, if you want. He might not toss you off a cliff. Then again, he's been in a terrible mood lately . . ."

"You set a trap," I said, trying to keep him talking. "But not for me?"

"Your old roommate is here," Quinn said. "We got the dimension locked off after he entered, but with his augments . . . Well, the boss isn't taking risks. He's been hunting us for what, ten years now? Struck at us a week ago, disabled some of our equipment. That man is a real pain.

"So, we've been trying to nab him. We're kidnapping kids and spreading rumors. You know how Chu gets about kidnappings. And you know how the boss gets about *him*. Chu getting some backup made him . . ." Quinn trailed off, then grinned. "Hell! That wasn't backup that the tracker spotted warping in up north. That was *you*, wasn't it?"

"I guess . . ." I blinked. "I don't really remember how I got here."

"It hit you hard," Quinn said. "You've got the look. This dimensional stuff can wipe your entire brain." He thought a moment, then sat his phone on the table, taking a long slurp of his ale. "Boss might be willing to forgive you if you agree to be bait. You're the only person Chu might want dead more than he wants the boss."

I was barely listening. It was a lot to sort through. Memories, still fragmentary, but fitting together. I'd joined Ulric's cartel . . . but the next few years were still blank. Something had happened, and I'd . . .

I'd become Ulric's *door guard*. A glorified bouncer. The butt of jokes. Whenever anyone wanted a laugh, there was Johnny to poke. It made me *livid*. I could have strangled them all.

Except I'd run away. Like I always did. And I'd picked the exact *wrong* place to go. I slumped down—hating the way Quinn snickered at me—while remembering hundreds of similar moments.

Only one major piece of my life was missing. Art school was clear, the academy mostly so. The grifting and the gutter were coming into focus . . . but what came after that?

Wait. If Quinn and Ulric had laid a trap for Ryan using kidnapped children, Ealstan and Sefawynn were going to fall right into it. I needed to . . .

Do what? I'd frozen in the fight against the Hordamen. I was barely a door guard. I was a coward.

You can't let anything happen to her, I told myself, panic welling up inside of me. *This time, you* can *do something. So do it.*

I was a coward, but I was also a very, *very* good liar. Could I get rid of Quinn? He was by far the most dangerous thing in this city.

"You . . . you *really* think Ulric will give me a second chance?" I said, turning back toward him.

"Depends on what you can do for him, Johnny. Like always."

I stood and shuffled from one foot to the other. I bit my lip. Then, "I saw Ryan," I blurted.

Quinn perked up.

I hurried over to him, then palmed a berry from my pocket and sat it next to the phone. "Please," I whispered.

"Please what?" Quinn asked.

"Please help me," I said. "I promise, I saw Ryan right after I dropped in here. He held a knife to my throat, quite near gutted me. But he let me go. Old history and all."

"Surprised about that," Quinn said, reaching for his phone.

"Don't tell Ulric!" I said, grabbing Quinn's arm. "Not until we come up with a plan. Maybe we could package Ryan for him? Only . . . Quinn, Ryan is hunting the boss. Heading to some place called Maelport?"

"That's where our base is," Quinn said. "Idiot. Chu must know about the rescue party, so he's going to try to stop the boss before it arrives . . ."

Wealdsig watched us with a wild grin. There was something seriously wrong with that fellow. He seemed erratic, like he didn't care about anyone or anything. The wight couldn't work if people were watching, so when Wealdsig tipped his head back to drink from a new mug, I turned Quinn away from the table, my arm around his shoulder.

"Quinn," I said softly, "Ryan's gone rogue. He wants to kill the boss here, beyond the reach of the law. You know their history."

Quinn nodded gravely.

"Let *me* tell the boss," I said.

Quinn legitimately considered it, which surprised me. He was loyal to a fault—considered himself old-school mafia.

"Can't do it, Johnny," he said, turning to the table. "Boss needs to know now, and he needs to hear it straight, no spin." He picked up the phone.

Which fell apart in his fingers.

"Ha!" Wealdsig laughed, pointing with his good hand. "The wights don't like you, outlander. I warned you."

"Hell," Quinn said, trying to get the pieces together. It was a lost cause—the phone crumbled in his fingers. Screws, the plastic shell, even the motherboard seemed to have been divided into their base components.

"I hate those things," Quinn muttered, then looked at me. "I need to get to Maelport. Follow if you want, but I'm taking my bike. Run, Johnny. I doubt the boss will find you on the continent, if you can make it there."

"Thanks," I said. "I . . . didn't expect that much."

"I owe you," he said. "For the thing with Tacy. You know."

Nope. I didn't. I nodded anyway.

Quinn was off a moment later. I took a deep breath. He'd probably taken the only gun in the city with him. So, well, I'd done *that* to help. Maybe I could lie my way into tricking Wealdsig again to help Sefawynn?

I picked up my staff and turned toward him. The reeve was leaning back in his chair now, his feet up on the table. "More tricks?" he asked.

"Can you take me to the changeling prisoner?" I asked. "The one Ulric left here?"

"Nah," he said. He tried to take a drink, but the mug was empty, so he sighed and tossed it away. (Three stars for the durable mugs. One star for the ambience. Floor excessively sticky.) He seemed moderately drunk at this point. "Sorry, harmless one. Your friends can tear holes in men's chests by pointing at them—so I'm not inclined to . . ."

He trailed off, frowning. Then he clambered to his feet, waving to his two hearthmen, who had watched all of this with mute concern. *They probably watched Ulric and Quinn annihilate a few of their friends when they first came through,* I thought. Which may have happened a lot earlier than I'd assumed. They'd been here for a while, if they already had allies and plans in motion.

What had drawn Wealdsig's attention? With a curse, I realized I might have turned my hearing down a little *too* low. I raised it enough to hear shouting outside; one of the voices belonged to Ealstan.

They'd been discovered.

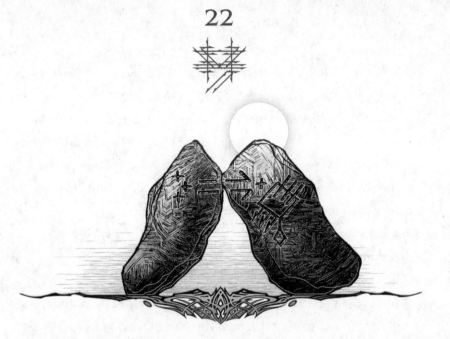

22

I pushed out the front door of the manor, accompanied by a tipsy Wealdsig and his hearthmen. The courtyard was lit brightly by torches. People ran around, crying about an attack.

"There, Midfather," one hearthman said, pointing to the wooden wall nearby—where a small huddle of soldiers surrounded a beleaguered Ealstan. Behind him, Sefawynn clutched her brother, her back to the wall. Ealstan waved his axe about in broad arcs, trying to get the soldiers to stay away. Nearby, several archers set up in the courtyard. There was no sign of Thokk.

"Please, Midfather!" I said to Wealdsig. "Call off your soldiers. Those people are friends of mine."

"Are they?" he said. "Let's see how they fight, coward!"

A moment later, the soldiers parted and an archer took aim.

The arrow lodged in Ealstan's gut, perhaps hitting his spine. He gasped, stumbling, blood spilling out of the wound, staining his fine tunic.

The sight provoked something visceral in me, like an arrow through my own guts. Sefawynn's scream echoed in the air.

Ealstan had *believed* in me. He was the only person in *any* dimension who thought of me as anything other than a con man and a joke.

The person he knows is a lie, I reminded myself. Looking back, I saw the signs of my delusional thinking easily. The effort I'd made to convince myself I'd been anything *but* the obvious.

I knew the truth now.

But damn it, Ealstan *saw* me. Met my eyes. And smiled.

Then two more arrows hit him.

I dropped my staff and started running. I barreled toward the crowd of soldiers, sounding thunder from my mouth. In a fantastically bad tactical decision, I tackled one of them to the ground.

I managed to get to my knees above him and raised a fist to punch.

I froze as I heard the phantom shouting again. Saw the flashes. Felt the terror. The shrinking of my soul as I . . .

As I threw a match?

The last piece clicked into place.

The augments, paid for by Ulric so I could fight in the Enhanced Fighting League. Years spent rising through the ranks. Then a title match against Quinn.

I remembered a crowd shouting with anger as I fell to the mat, my ribs crushed. Bets lost.

A hero, failed.

Flashing lights. Cameras.

Quinn standing above me, fists bloodied.

And I remembered kneeling there, letting him kick me so hard, it broke me. Literally.

THE FRUGAL WIZARD'S HANDBOOK

Ulric had ordered my chest and skull augments compromised, so my fall would be worse. Better for the margins, you see. I'd spent years trying to bring them back online after he laughed when I asked him to do it.

He liked me being weak, bearing the scars of my fall. The dive he'd *ordered* me to take, then mocked me for.

I *hated* him. I *hated* it all.

A shadow of motion. I blocked the axe from an oncoming soldier with my forearm, which turned steel grey. Then I threw myself to my feet and *slugged* the guy in the chest with full augments, hurling him back some ten feet and into the dirt.

I was tired—

Of being called—

A *coward*.

I was tired of *believing* it.

My training took over. I'd spent six years in the ring, fighting in the bloodiest version of the mixed boxing sport—where they allowed specialized bladed weapons, then patched you up afterward. And none of these medieval idiots had blades that could cut through plating, while I had a *whole* lot of pent-up anger.

I caught a sword on my arm, then smashed the blade with my other fist. It wasn't enough to shatter the sword, but I might have broken some bones in the soldier's hand as the blade whipped out of it. Another man came at me from the side, and I gave him a flying lesson, sending him tumbling end over end. As I broke a third guy's arm, the others got a clue and dashed away, shouting that I was one of *them*.

Damn right, I was.

But then there were those archers across the courtyard. They hesitated—perhaps worried about drawing the attention of the guy who had just punched two of their friends into next week. But if they released, I was as good as dead. Archers lined the wall now. Even if I managed to block a few arrows with my arms or back, more shots would follow.

"Put down your weapons!" I shouted, enhancing my voice with thunder. "And I will spare you!"

A few of them glanced toward the reeve. He was laughing wildly; he was *enjoying* all of this. "You were supposed to be a coward, outsider!" he called to me.

"That's what Ulric thinks," I called back. "Join with me, Wealdsig. Together, we can bring him down and steal his weapons!"

He squinted at me with his one eye. He seemed to be considering it, but I didn't have time to wait. Ealstan was groaning softly, as Sefawynn and her brother tried to staunch the blood flow. Dared I turn my attention away from the archers to help?

If only I could get my other platings online. I called up the password screen.

Why did I think I could guess it now, with my brain still full of holes? I'd spent the last *three years* trying to figure out this password, Ulric laughing at me the entire time.

I was again confronted with what I was. *Who* I was. My tense battle readiness faded.

Other soldiers, urged on by Wealdsig, approached. The reeve joined them, his axe out, crowding us. He'd seen me crush two soldiers, but still he came up on me. He wasn't a coward. I'd give him that. This was a people accustomed to fighting against terrible odds.

"Sorry," Wealdsig said, axe at the ready. "If you had the powers they had—and could kill at a distance—you wouldn't look so frightened!"

Ealstan was gasping, staring heavenward, blood leaking from his mouth.

I really was useless. I couldn't stop this.

I lowered my arms from the guard position and slumped to the ground.

"Take me," I whispered. "I have knowledge that can help you. Let my friends go."

"He's dead," Wealdsig said, gesturing to Ealstan. "Poor fellow. I liked him."

I winced. But then, I *distinctly* heard an unfamiliar voice in my ear.

"This is the best you can do?" it asked. "And I thought you were worth the trouble I was putting into this."

Was this the best I could do? I looked at Ealstan's wounds, and realized that while *I* was useless, my medical nanites were *not*. I pushed aside a distraught Sefawynn, then yanked out the arrows. Her brother sat back, hands bloody, horrified.

I brought up my medical nanite menu and instigated first aid mode. Then I deactivated the plating on my palm. With Ealstan's own knife, I cut a slice in my skin, then pressed it to his wound.

Institute emergency person-to-person medical nanite transfer? popped up in my vision. With a click, I sent them crawling from my bloodstream into his. As I pressed my hand against the wound, medical data scrolled by on my vision.

Microsutures complete. Bleeding staunched.

30% of nanites transferred.

Bacteria scrubbing begun.

70% of nanites transferred.

Tissue reconstruction initiated.

90% of nanites transferred. Please disconnect and contact emer-

gency services. Be aware that your personal nanite levels will remain low for approximately 48 hours as your supply is reconstructed. Seek an infusion and take extra care. Consume additional carbon as soon as possible.
Process complete.

I relaxed as Ealstan's flesh regenerated. He groaned—with an emergency rescue like this, the nanites wouldn't numb the nerve endings. They'd break down one another to form tissue and blood cells out of their organic structure, and they couldn't afford to waste time or energy on pain.

I knew how that felt. In the Enhanced Fighting League, you'd often end up in emergency resuscitation—cut literally to pieces—after a bout. Then again, it was better than dying a slow, painful death via gut wound.

Ealstan's groaning stopped and he sat up, poking at his wounds, which were already scabbed over by a restoration poultice made from deactivated nanites. We were still surrounded by enemies, so it wasn't much of a rescue, but Ealstan looked at me in awe, and Sefawynn and her brother both stared at me agog.

I raised my fists again, but my heart wasn't in it. I knew how it would end. I'd get in a few hits, but then one would stab me in the vitals, or those archers would loose. With my nanites so low, that would be it. We'd all be dead.

Except . . . Wealdsig was staring at me, slack-jawed.

"You can *heal*?" he asked softly.

I glanced at Ealstan, who had pulled up his shirt, more fully revealing where the three arrow holes had been.

"I can," I lied, meeting Wealdsig's eyes. "I lack the ability the others have to kill from a distance. But I can restore the dying to life."

"Can you . . ." Wealdsig said, "bring back the dead?"

"No," I said. "But here. Cut your palm."

He did so eagerly, the bizarre little miscreant. I put my own still-bloodied wound to his and initiated the process again, ignoring the low-nanite warning that flashed over my vision. This was a small wound, and easy to heal. I was left with around five percent of my nanites. My system wouldn't let me go below that threshold, even with an override.

It worked, though. Wealdsig held up his newly repaired hand. Mine would take longer, as my remaining nanites worked overtime to replicate themselves and—hopefully—keep me from getting the bubonic plague or whatever strange diseases they had in this reality.

Wealdsig laughed, still staring at his hand, wiggling one finger, then another. Oh, hell. That had been his wounded one. The nanites were slowly repairing the old damage as well as the new.

"With this . . ." Wealdsig said. "We could go to battle and not worry that our sons and brothers would die . . . We could stand against the Hordamen. We could thrive . . ."

The others murmured and nodded. Ulric had been wielding guns to awe them, blowing apart people who angered him. But these people were *used* to bullies. They already knew what it was like to be afraid of a foreign invader.

They weren't impressed by the ability to kill. Cowed by it, yes. But impressed? No.

They were impressed by the ability to live.

I reassessed the wild look in Wealdsig's eyes. The frantic way he'd acted. Maybe he wasn't erratic or uncaring. Maybe it was the opposite.

"How many?" I asked him. "How many sons have you lost to battle?"

"Seven," he whispered. "All seven of my boys." He looked to

Ealstan, who had carefully climbed to his feet. "Guess I'm glad you're not dead. How are you feeling?"

"Shockingly fit," he said. "You?"

"Lonely," Wealdsig said, examining his fully functional hand. "Very lonely."

"I know that feeling," Ealstan said softly.

"I tried to curry Woden's favor," Wealdsig said. "It didn't work."

"Woden is mad with anguish and loss."

Wealdsig grunted. "I tried that too. Helps a little."

I glanced over and smiled at Sefawynn. "All this time," she whispered, stunned. "I . . . I called you a charlatan. I didn't want to see, or accept what you could do, because it didn't fit with the world as I saw it. I didn't want to admit to things I didn't understand."

Then she *bowed* to me, touching her forehead to the ground. "Forgive me, Great One, please."

This was the exact reaction I was supposed to provoke, according to the book. And I didn't mind it from Ealstan. But from Sefawynn? It made me nauseous.

"Sefawynn," I said to her, "I'm not . . ."

Hell. I really was terrible with women—

Wait. I had most of my memories back now, and I *knew* I was *great* with women. I had all the best pickup lines, and knew how to order women around to show I was dominant, and . . . and I had high standards, which is why I often left the bar alone. Well, *always* left the bar alone . . .

Nothing like a therapeutic bout of amnesia to force you to look really hard at your life, eh?

For now, I sighed, restored the platings on my hand, and faced

Wealdsig. "You've seen my power," I said. "You can't kill us. I'll just heal everyone." I purposefully didn't show off my own hand, which—now that the adrenaline was fading—throbbed with pain.

He glanced at his soldiers. Nobody responded.

"If I let you go," Wealdsig finally said, "those other two will kill me."

"No," I said. "You let me go, and I'll go kill them. Then you'll have *me* as an ally. The man who can preserve your people, not just kill your enemies."

"Ulric can call down thunder and lightning," Ealstan said, "but that hasn't saved us in the past. We should trust Runian. It's the best choice, Wealdsig."

"Fine," he said. "But you're going to have to punch me."

I frowned. "Excuse me?"

"Punch me," he said. "Then leave. If Ulric and Quinn come back, I'll show them my wounds, tell them you fought your way out, and hope they believe we did all we could to stop you."

He braced himself, closing his eyes.

So, with a shrug, I punched him. Don't judge. I'd been wanting to do it all night. I took care to punch him hard enough to leave a solid bruise but not break much. You got good at that sort of delicacy when you were a mob fighter trained to carefully win or throw matches.

Wealdsig groaned from the ground. "Kill them," he said. "Once you do, remember I let you go, and that all we really want is to live."

I nodded, picked up my staff, then ushered my companions toward the front gates.

"They said you were harmless," Wealdsig said from behind. "Do they know what you're *actually* capable of doing?"

"No."

"The fools! They won't know what is coming for them."

I kept walking, head up, back straight. Another lie. But at least I finally knew why I was so good at those. When you lived a life like mine, you got plenty of practice trying them out on yourself.

THE END OF PART TWO

PART THREE

Bagsworth Ruins Everything (Again)

HOW TO BE A WIZARD

The following is an excerpt from *The Truth About Truth: A Call to Adventure* by Cecil G. Bagsworth III, *The First Interdimensional Wizard™*. (Frugal Wizard™ Press, 2098, $39.99. Signed editions available to Frugal Fans™ subscription club members.)

It was during my tenure as royal advisor to King Henry the Second, the great Plantagenet king, that I realized the incredible ramifications of my wizardry for our entire dimension.

Up until this point, dimensional travel had been restricted to the great explorers—like myself. Once we determined a place was safe, we'd allow the historians in for carefully guarded investigations.

Many thought all alternate dimensions should remain forever relegated to the dusty bins of scholars and specialists.

And yet, the power of wizards has been incredible in our own world. Now, you might claim that wizardry is a myth—and *magic* is, indeed, whimsical nonsense. Fortunately, the wizard is more than magic. A wizard is the mind behind the throne, the king's advisor.

Makbul Ibrahim Pasha's wisdom and diplomatic sense steered the Ottoman Empire under Suleiman. Thomas Cromwell fundamentally changed the relationship between church and state in the Western world. Chanakya literally wrote the book on statecraft. It could be argued that Rasputin, for all his charlatanry, was the root cause of the fall of the Russian monarchy.

These people changed the world, and the simple, incredible truth was awe-inspiring to me: Anyone could take this mantle upon themselves, if given the opportunity.

In the early 1960s, science fiction writer Arthur C. Clarke formalized what would become his most famous truism: Any sufficiently advanced technology is indistinguishable from magic. This can be further extrapolated to Bagsworth's Law™: Any sufficiently trained modern person can become a god to those from previous eras.

You may be mediocre by today's standards. But in grade school you were taught a fundamental understanding of science, nature, and medicine—power that can establish dynasties, save millions of lives, and fundamentally change the world.

And there are enough dimensions that each and every one of us can have our own.

I strongly encourage you to purchase this book's companion volume, *Science for Wizards*™, where we explain vital skills like crafting gunpowder, administering vaccines, and establishing fusion cultures. But heed this important warning: In most ancient mythologies, even gods can die.

Basic medical nanites can work wonders for preventing your demise. They can absorb oxygen from water, or even scrub the CO_2. They can staunch wounds. They can let you eat almost anything. But if a bunch of knights chop you to pieces, you *will* die.

Even if you can afford augments and platings, you are *not* immortal. If the local villagers chain you to a wall, you will eventually run out of carbon, your nanites will be unable to self-replicate, and you *will* die.

You must wow the people of your dimension so thoroughly that no one will ever dare turn against you. And you must never, *never* let them know that they—with sufficient training—could do what you do.

The past is a brutal place, my friend. You can change that. But first, you must tame it.

bout an hour later, we knocked at the door of the preserve. Yazad threw open the door, spilling light across us, then raised his hands in praise toward the heavens. "Ah! My friends! We prayed all evening for you, and look, you have survived!" He squinted at us. "Where is Thokk?"

"I don't think anything happened to her," Sefawynn said quickly. "She ran off in the city, laughing."

"She is like that," Yazad said.

They all shared another of those looks I *felt* I should understand.

"Regardless," Yazad said, "is this young Wyrm?"

"That's me," Wyrm said softly, grinning. Sefawynn had barely let go of him the entire walk, hugging him at least six separate times. "They said you have food here?"

"What are your thoughts on stewed apples?" Yazad asked.

"Yes, please!" Wyrm replied.

Yazad stepped aside, welcoming us to his hearth. Inside, I got a good look at Wyrm. It had only been two days, so it was probably my mind playing tricks on me, but he looked *thinner*. And he'd smelled so bad at first that we'd made him jump in the river.

Now he sat down to warm himself by the hearth as Yazad's disciples cheered him—and us—as if we were heroes returning from the underworld itself. As Ealstan spun a tale of his miraculous survival, the air turned electric with excitement.

Yazad served bowls of stewed apples. Wyrm took his bowl eagerly, and Ealstan took his with a bowed head of thanks. I felt off, and hung back near the wall. Sefawynn hesitantly approached me, then bowed deeply.

"Thank you," she murmured. "A hundred times, Great Prince. Thank you."

"Sefawynn, please," I said. "I'm just me. You don't need to act like this."

She bowed lower.

"Maybe an eye roll?" I asked her. "For old times?"

"Please," she whispered, "don't remind me of how I treated you. I'm so sorry."

She hastened toward the fire. I reached for her, but then let my arm fall back down.

Dammit. I'd spent our entire time together trying to persuade her I wasn't a scoundrel. Now I'd give almost anything to go back to that. It had felt so *comfortable* in those brief hours when we'd understood one another. Now she accepted I had powers, and it ruined everything.

I sighed and settled down on a stool. I was still trying to decompress from everything that had happened—including having my memories back. The recovery of my time as a boxer was the last chunk. I mean, I couldn't remember what I'd eaten for breakfast last week—but who did? I knew who I was, where I'd come from, what I'd accomplished—or not.

I remembered my time with Jen, which had been . . . uneven. Passionate at times, but full of as much (or more) arguing and shouting. I remembered Ryan, and how he'd grown more and more disappointed in me as we'd entered our late twenties, then thirties. I remembered fighting for Ulric, getting heavily into his debt, and then . . .

Losing that title bout to Quinn. Becoming a bumbling door guard. Damn, there really *wasn't* much worthwhile to remember. I did have some fond memories of my parents and sister, who all lived in Atlanta—but I hadn't seen them in years. It was hard to look my parents in the eyes.

When my mind had been blank, I'd imagined I was Ryan's partner, a heroic detective. Now I knew the truth: I was the proud owner of a zero-out-of-five life. I had a dead girlfriend I'd driven away, an alienated best friend, and a family that didn't call or mention me on social media.

I was tired. And hungry. Strange sensations for all that they were innately human. Without my nanites, was I worth anything?

Yazad walked over with a bowl for me. "Do you eat?" he asked.

"Today I do," I said, taking the bowl. It was warm through the wood, and smelled of some of the same spices Sefawynn liked to wear. I glanced at her again, then looked away. She was enjoying Ealstan's tale, though she was the better storyteller.

"So," Yazad said, settling down on a stool next to mine. "What are you?"

"What do you think I am?"

"In my homeland," he said, "we don't have wights. Our spirits of

219

the air are far more dangerous, and only prayers keep them away. Once in a while, you find a less dangerous one. We think, perhaps, they are the remnants of the gods that ruled the deserts before we received the light of Ahura Mazda."

I stirred my apple stew, nodding. If wights were real, why not creatures of Middle Eastern folklore?

"At first," Yazad said, "I was convinced you were something like that. A god from a foreign land. Because—and forgive me—I do not believe that aelvs are real. In all my travels, I've found only spirits that cannot be seen!"

"I'm not an aelv," I said. "I guess the easiest way to explain is to say I'm from the future."

"Ah!" Yazad smacked his forehead with the heel of his hand. "Of course."

"What?" I said. "You *believe* me?"

"It makes so much sense!" he said. "You have incredible powers, but seem so ignorant. In your time, people have discovered things we have not?"

"Many," I said.

"It is taught that Ahura Mazda will continue to grace us with light and knowledge," he explained. "In my grandfather's time, there were no windmills. But now they are common in my lands. I have tried to build one here, but even *explaining* the idea confuses people.

"'How can you harness the wind?' they ask. 'Is the wind a wight?' 'What offerings does it take?' 'Will it not be angry with your device?'" He heaved a sigh. "It is hard to understand something you have not seen. And during your time, you have many such things?"

"Incredible things," I said, holding my staff across my lap. "Honestly, Yazad, in my time, I'm less than special. I'm worthless as a person."

"That is why Ahura Mazda sent you to us," Yazad said, eyes twinkling. "Here, you are far more than you could have been—and we are blessed for it!"

"I feel like a charlatan," I said, looking down.

He tapped my arm, then pointed to Sefawynn. She was smiling in a genuine, open way, for maybe the first time since I'd met her. She kept reaching out and putting her arm around her brother, as if to reassure herself that he was really there. Ealstan, normally so stern, seemed electric by the firelight, talking almost like a skop himself, to the glee of the children. Wyrm took it all in with a goofy grin, finishing his third bowl of stewed apples.

"Are those the faces of people taken in by a charlatan?" Yazad said. "Or the faces of people who are grateful for your help?"

"I've only managed to help three people," I said. "And now they think I'm something to be worshipped."

"Only three people?" Yazad leaned in. "Runian, my friend. Ahura Mazda's love manifests inside our hearts. When you feel it, you are feeling infinity itself. There is no *only* when it comes to goodness and joy. The smallest amount is as large as the universe, and one boy saved from a pit is a precious work beyond that of any king's treasury."

He tapped the staff with the end of his finger, knocking his fingernail on its wood. "You *are* something special. Here. Now. That is what matters. So what if your knowledge is common among your kind? It is rare here. Perhaps every magus sent by Ahura Mazda to teach, instruct, and protect is like you. Simply someone who knows a little more—a little better—than everyone else."

He patted me on the arm, then wandered off to collect bowls and refill them for guests and members of his flock.

It was time to make a decision. We'd rescued Sefawynn's brother. I had my memory back, and I knew I hadn't come here to stop Ulric.

So . . . what now?

Quinn had suggested I run to the continent. With my medical nanites, my augments, and a little practice under my belt, I could find a tribe somewhere and become their king. Sure, there'd be no pay-per-view sports to watch, but it could be a good life.

Did I really think Ulric would leave me alone? He was planning something for this world. It had *literal* magic. I was a confirmed coward, but I was a smart one. Smart men never bet against Ulric. Word would get around. I'd never be able to rest, knowing I was playing king in his Personal Wizard Dimension™.

I needed to go to Maelport and find a way to get out. Escape back to the real world, then save up to buy a regular, boring dimension to hide in—one where I could smash the beacons and portals and be truly safe.

And alone.

"Hey," I said softly. "Thanks for the nudge in Wellbury."

No response.

"I *heard* you talk," I said. "So there's no use pretending."

"I do not take orders," the voice said in my ear—making me jump. "I accept bargains. Tonight, I want none, John of Seattle."

It . . . knew my name? And it knew of Seattle?

Damn.

"—and that is the story of how I died!" Ealstan said, poking his fingers through a bloodstained hole in his shirt. "And how I am back from the dead! Now . . ." He hesitated. "Now I don't know what comes next."

Both he and Sefawynn glanced at me. The room fell quiet.

I took a deep breath. "Next," I said, "you're going to go home to your wife and your people, Ealstan."

"And what are *you* going to do?" he asked.

"I'll travel onward to the earl's seat in Maelport," I admitted.

"You're going to stop Ulric and save the earl!" Ealstan said.

"I . . . I'm going to try to escape," I said. "Ulric has the only way for me to get out of your world and return to mine."

"You cannot fool me, Great One," Ealstan said, giving me a seated bow. "You fear for my safety, so you wish to send me away. I will not allow this. The highfather is in danger. I will accompany you, if you will have one so weak as I."

I sighed.

"This Ulric is planning something," Sefawynn said. "What did Wealdsig say? Ulric has to meet with visitors in three days?"

A rescue party, Quinn had said. Were they trapped? That would explain why the place wasn't completely under their thumb. If Ulric was isolated . . .

He'd be low on resources and reinforcements. For two days at least. Sefawynn looked to Ealstan and nodded. Hell. She was going to insist on coming along on my quest to stop Ulric.

A quest that didn't exist. I only wanted out of here. Right? I stared through my mostly full bowl of apples as I took a long, hard look at myself. I didn't like what I saw. It had been fifteen years or more since I'd looked in a mirror without feeling disgusted.

I'd washed out of everything I'd ever tried. Was that why the way Sefawynn and Ealstan treated me made me nervous? Because I knew that I'd ultimately fail them?

What if, this time, I didn't?

What if I tried to stop Ulric? Yes, I knew how stupid that idea was.

But running in to help Ealstan had been stupid, and I'd done that—and succeeded. Maybe it was time to *try*.

Why not? I hated my life outside of here. Why would I go back?

"Yes," I said. "I'm going to stop him."

He'd probably kill us. But at least I'd go to my grave knowing I'd finally stood up to Ulric Stromfin.

24

I had to bathe the next morning, since my remaining nanites had their little hands full maintaining my immunities. I found the experience novel, particularly since I had to use a cold river.

I wished Jen was around; she could have told me how long it would take society to develop indoor plumbing and heated water spigots. When I complained to Yazad, he laughed and said they had those things in Persia. But the northerners, he said, preferred to freeze their bits off.

An hour later, I helped the others pack our things onto our horses. Yazad bid us farewell with characteristic boisterousness, promising to pray for us in our travels. As I'd expected, Sefawynn told her brother to stay behind—and though most youths from my time would have complained about being left out of some grand adventure, most of them hadn't spent two days in a pit. Wyrm gave his sister a hug, listened to her instructions for a third time, then waved goodbye as we mounted up and took off.

After only two hours of riding, I started to feel sore. Horseback riding was not as pleasant without microrobots reconstructing your muscles to alleviate things like repetitive motions. Random parts of my body started itching without warning, and my teeth felt slimy and *gross*. Then my nose started running from allergies. How did people *live* like this?

Zero stars. I'd like to go back to being a demigod, please.

To pass the time, I moved up beside Sefawynn. "So . . ." I said to her.

"Yes, honored aelv?"

"Can we maybe just go back to how we were?" I asked. "I'm not mad at you."

"It wouldn't be appropriate," she said. "You know me for what I am. And I know you for what you are."

"You don't, truly," I said to her.

She rode in silence.

I sighed. "All right. If you really respect me now, please explain how you knew a wight was following me. You say"—I eyed Ealstan, riding proudly in front of us, and chose my words carefully—"that you question your skills. Yet, in my experience, you've got some incredible ones."

"I . . . was born with the Night Marks."

"Which are what?"

"Three deep blue spots," she said. "Birthmarks, on your back. It means you are chosen by Woden."

"Or cursed by him," Ealstan noted. "The two are often interchangeable, honored aelv."

"And these marks mean you can see the wights?" I asked.

"Nobody can see wights," she said. "If it were to happen, either

226

you—or the wight—would die. Some imagine little people with red hats, others imagine forest spirits with fog for bodies. But we don't know."

"So how . . ."

"I see shadows, honored aelv," she said, her voice small. "At the corner of my vision. The size of the shadow indicates the power of the wight. They're almost always there. I often worry that one day I'll turn too quickly, and I'll see one in full. And that will be the end."

"That . . ." I said. "Sefawynn, that sounds horrible. I didn't know."

"Blessing," Ealstan said, "and curse."

I shivered, trying not to think too hard about what it must be like. To always have those shadows at the corners of your vision. Then again, there was a certain horror to knowing they were always there while I *couldn't* see them.

"Sefawynn," I said, voice softer, "that means . . . what you can do, it's a *real* power. You're not . . ."

"A charlatan?" she replied. "The fact that I was chosen makes it more embarrassing. Woden expects much of me. And I fail him."

I felt like an utter heel. I tried thinking of something to say to fix things, but every option felt stupid. I'd tasted my own foot too many times already this trip, and even after a bath, it wasn't a flavor I relished.

Instead, I guided my horse up beside Ealstan. I was getting the hang of this horse stuff, wasn't I? Like riding a self-driving motorcycle. That farted.

"What I don't get," I said to him, "is why you worship Woden if he sends you all these curses."

"We must be patient!" Sefawynn said from behind. "Suffer long enough, and we'll return to his favor."

"To one extent, she's right." Ealstan held the reins lightly as he swayed in rhythm with the beats of the hooves. "This is our punishment. For the war, and for the loss of Friag, though our failures began long before that. When Logna brought us writing, stolen from Woden, we accepted it. In that moment, humankind took a step toward joining her worship, instead of *his*."

"And how does that Black Bear fit into all of this?" I said. "Sefawynn told me he still lives?"

"In his dark forest kingdom," Ealstan said, nodding. "Logna's children, the monsters, live there too. My grandfather was in the war, when Friag fell. He thought it was the end. The death of the gods, and of the world itself."

"The Black Bear," Sefawynn said, "slayer of gods, binder of monsters, king of men. When he turned Fenris the Wolf against Friag at the battle of Badon, he took upon himself the curse of the land, binding it to his soul. Now his hounds haunt the forests, and he looks ever outward . . . Immortal, yet fearing his own spawn more than anything."

Damn. These people had some messed-up mythology. History. Both. Either.

"Woden is our only hope and defense," Sefawynn said. "If it weren't for the gods, the Black Bear would slay us all."

"Woden is afraid," Ealstan said. "The gods don't fight because they fear the monsters, and the end. They know it should have been Tiw who died."

"We shouldn't have had writing anyway," Sefawynn said. "It was Friag's heritage!"

"Who can argue with a skop about the histories?" Ealstan said. "Not me. Not today."

So . . . they worshipped a god who was afraid of being killed, who blamed humanity for the death of his wife—and basically wanted *them* dead. Seemed about right.

"Where did Woden come from?" I asked.

"The womb of his mother, obviously," Sefawynn said.

"Gods are born," I said. "And they can obviously die. So what makes them gods?"

"Thunder," she said. "Burning words. Striking people dead for questioning them. Have you not been paying attention?"

I glanced back at her, encouraged by the tone—but she immediately looked down, embarrassed.

"So where did the *first* god come from?" I asked Ealstan.

"Licked from a rock by a cow," Ealstan said with a perfectly straight face.

"Uh . . ."

"It was a very special cow."

This particular line of questioning wasn't going anywhere useful. I sat back, trying to enjoy the ride. These were probably the last moments of peace I'd know. We were riding to stop *Ulric the Butcher*, after all.

That knowledge kept me stewing. Yes, there was a pastoral beauty to this land—heightened when we'd pass a break in the trees and see out over the churning ocean. And yet, that only reminded me of the Hordamen. These poor people, crushed between forest and ocean, with a god that didn't like them and an evil mobster from the future looking to dominate them. It was like the rock and the hard place had been joined by a bulldozer and a jackhammer.

We were riding straight toward the worst of it. What was I doing? I should be riding the *other* way, to . . .

Wait. What was that? There was a person hiding beside a large rock near the road up ahead. Ealstan tensed too, but then relaxed, shaking his head at me. So . . . not dangerous?

We rode past, and the small figure moved out from behind the rock and joined us. It was Thokk.

Sefawynn jumped, spotting the old woman for the first time. She looked around—as if wondering where the woman had come from—but didn't say anything.

"Ealstan," I said, "why is nobody bothered by her?"

"Hmm?" he asked, then made a show of being surprised. "Oh! The hearth-keeper has joined us. Welcome, elder." He didn't offer her his horse, as someone from my time might have. But then again, we weren't moving particularly quickly, and Thokk was spry for her age.

"I think I'll travel with you for a while," Thokk said to him. "Safer that way. There are bandits on this path."

"As you wish," Ealstan said with a nod.

I frowned at him, then at Sefawynn. This was getting ridiculous. I struggled to stop my horse. Thokk, perhaps sensing my frustration, fell back with me until we were several lengths behind the others, who made a show of being unconcerned as they pulled up together.

I leaned down. "All right," I said to Thokk, speaking softly. "What the *hell* is going on with you?"

"Just thought I'd go out for a walk," she said.

"I *saw* you behind that rock," I said. "You were waiting for us. Then you popped out when you thought we weren't looking, so you'd appear mysteriously."

"I have no idea what you're talking about."

"The others always glance at each other meaningfully whenever you are mentioned," I said.

"And what kind of glance would that be?"

"You know," I said. "Like this." I gave her an intense look, leaning down beside my horse, then nodded knowingly.

"Ah, that," she said. "Just means they're constipated."

"Thokk . . ." I said. "Please. Life has been particularly frustrating for me lately. Can you just give me this one?"

The old lady grinned, walking along with her fire implements tied in a sack on her back. "You don't know many stories, do you, outlander?"

"Stories?" I asked. "About what?"

"Tales that are passed down, family to family. Not the great legends of epic deeds or heroes. Simple stories, about people living their lives—and finding rewards, or not, depending on their actions."

"Oh," I said. "Like fairy tales."

"I don't know that term," she said. "But it has the right air. If you've heard any such stories, tell me: What kinds of roles do old women play in them?"

"Well," I said, "they're usually witches. Or witches in disguise. Or sometimes beautiful women cursed to look like witches . . ." I frowned. "Not a lot of nonwitches in those stories."

"We'd use the word 'wicce,'" she said. "But ours are very much the same! When I was younger, I needed someone with me to travel. Young women don't travel on their own, except maybe skops—even bandits need their help. But the rest of us? Never!

"But as I got older, something happened. People started acting strange around me. Oddly respectful, even frightened. And the older I got, the more it happened, until . . ."

I smiled. "They think you're a witch."

"Or a forest spirit," she said, "or a god in disguise—you have to watch out for those. Ha! *Nobody* believes I'm a regular old woman, walking the roads. Too suspicious."

"So you play it up."

"It's great," she said, with a surprisingly toothy grin. "I don't have to be afraid. First time in my life I can have some fun, travel the world, see what trouble I can get into. Why let the young folk have all the dumb ideas? Not fair, I say. And if I get caught, well, no respectable old matron would do this, so they go back to being frightened, and let me go."

"Clever," I said. "And it works?"

"Sure," she said. "Unless I'm in a group. Then I turn back into a regular old woman. I hope you all appreciate what I'm giving up by joining you."

"We . . . didn't ask you to."

"Tough," she said. "Just don't expect me to get you out of the trap the bandits have set for you."

"Bandits?" I asked, straightening in alarm. "What bandits?"

As soon as I asked, I spotted motion in the trees nearby. Figures, moving to surround us.

"Those ones, there," Thokk replied. "I *did* warn you. Twice!"

Wait. Did I Just Do a Colonialism?

We here at Frugal Wizard Inc.® are dedicated to doing our part by listening to and advancing the causes of marginalized people. We support real change in our communities through corporate awareness and authentic and honest discussion regarding the difficult topics facing BAIIHPOC people today.

Through our Give Back Initiative, we support social programs that inspire a better tomorrow and a future where all voices are heard. In conjunction with the Leave It Alone Movement of Northern America, we have donated over one thousand dimensions to be preserved and left untouched—each featuring culturally significant issues regarding historically oppressed minorities.

We strongly encourage our customers to avoid traveling to the Americas or Africa in their dimension. If you want to join with us in helping marginalized peoples throughout all dimensions, please purchase our I Refuse to Use™ wristbands—all proceeds go to the fight for equality.

For those wanting an extra-personal fight against oppression, might we suggest one of our exclusive ~~White~~ Unstated Ethnicity Savior Packages,[1] where you can help the people of the British Isles repel the Roman invaders. Be a liberator and fight for the underdogs!

---

1. This package has been vetted by ten independent sensitivity professionals to ensure it is "absolutely not problematic in any way."[2]

2. This phrase is legally defined as a Marketing Term by the Truth in Advertising Act of 2045.

25

The newcomers surrounded us. They didn't *look* like bandits. They were better dressed than I'd have expected—their cloaks, tunics, and trousers were well kept, and a few were brightly colored.

They didn't have bows, which was good. I didn't have a great track record with those. Still, a part of me was disappointed. You think of bandits living in the woods of England, and you expect bows.

I nudged my horse, but the stupid animal had locked up. I climbed out of the saddle, my worry increasing. We couldn't afford for Ealstan to take another mortal wound for at least—I checked my chronometer—thirty-three hours.

I slid my staff out of its place on my saddle and prepared for some wizarding.

"Be careful. These are desperate men," Thokk said softly. "They have nothing to lose. They have rejected their fathers, their hearths, and their gods. You can't scare them. They're already terrified."

I hesitated, staff in hand. "So . . . what are you saying?" I whispered to her.

"Keep quiet for now," Thokk whispered back.

She was the one who traveled these paths regularly. I turned off my vocal augments. Thokk and I stepped toward Ealstan and Sefawynn, and my stupid horse finally decided to join us, huddling so close to the others that she nearly squished me.

Ealstan's hand was at his axe, but he didn't draw it. Twelve bandits—he probably didn't like those odds, even with an aelv on his side. I'd warned him in private that I could only heal someone once every few days, so hopefully he wouldn't do anything stupid.

One of the bandits strolled around us in a circle. His cloak was a deep red and his belt buckle was silver, as was his cloak clasp. He seemed . . . more refined than the others. His beard was trimmed, almost to a point, and his long dark hair was full and perfectly styled. What was it with these thugs who looked like they spent half their time in a salon?

(What products did one use in Anglo-Saxon England? Beaver snot? A grudging four stars.)

He stopped beside a particularly large tree and tapped it with his knuckles. "This is a very fine tree," he said to us. "Would you not say so?"

Ealstan glanced at the rest of us, befuddled. I shook my head. What was this guy on about?

Sefawynn, however, released a breath. "Very nice indeed," she said loudly. "It seems important."

"It was grown from a seed of the world tree," the man said. "Mighty and tall, it is. Worthy of being seen and appreciated."

"Indeed," Sefawynn said. "One might expect a toll to be paid for visiting said tree."

The man spread his hands, looking toward the other ruffians. "See? Some of them do get it."

"Which village are you from?" Ealstan asked the bandit, hand still on his axe. "What's your lineage, fallen little father?"

"Li—" I began, but Thokk elbowed me. Apparently, she'd meant what she'd said about me staying quiet.

"Yes, he's a lord," Thokk told me in a hushed tone. "You thought bandits were rogue commoners? Weapons are expensive, outlander."

Huh. I guess it made sense. I'd spent almost half my life working for a crime boss in Seattle—and this was basically the same thing. Even their methods seemed familiar.

"A fine tree indeed," the head bandit said, gesturing with gloved hands. "And this is our road. Do you see any other armed forces nearby, guarding it?"

"You take advantage of our crumbling society," Ealstan said. "The highfather cannot defend these lanes any longer—so you become wolves. You should be better than this."

The lead bandit sighed, then thumbed toward Ealstan. "He pays a double toll. Once for himself. Once for his ego."

"I—" Ealstan began, but Sefawynn cut him off.

"Ealstan," she said softly, "they know. Anything you'd tell them, any condemnations of their character . . . *They know.* Trust me."

He fell silent.

The lead bandit eyed her, then nodded. "You're a smart woman."

"I'm a skop," Sefawynn said, meeting his eyes.

Several bandits backed up immediately, muttering.

"You may pass without a toll," the lead bandit said. "Our road is your road, story bearer."

She nodded to him. She *was* proud of her heritage—of her profession. If she hadn't been, maybe it wouldn't hurt her so much to fail.

"I see three tolls to be paid, then," the lead bandit said. "High tolls for the rich, which his lordship here has proven you are. I'll take the horses. You have four, so you can keep one—for the skop."

"There was a time," Ealstan said, "when all men in this land fought together against outsiders. What happened to those days?"

"Ask the skop," the bandit said, waving for Ealstan to climb down.

It took the thegn a moment of consideration, but he obeyed.

I was tempted to go on a punching spree and see how many of these guys I could get stuck into trees. But that was bravado talking. Without my chest platings . . . I furtively pulled up the lock on those platings and tried *JohnnyIsACoward* as the password. No luck.

Thokk was probably right. We didn't *need* the horses. Maelport was only a day's walk away. It was still hard for me to grasp just how small things were in this place. Tiny cities, tiny towns, and tiny earldoms.

These bandits did the shakedown the way I'd been taught. Leave just enough to keep your prey capable of continuing on, so you might be able to rob them again in the future. I worried they'd kill us to remove witnesses, but if nobody was protecting this roadway—if things really were bad enough that no army would follow at our complaint of being robbed—then there was no need.

If travelers vanished too often on the road, people would hire guards—or not come this way. But if the banditry took the form of a toll, and you were free to pass after paying . . . you could factor that into the trip's cost.

They let us move our things—other than the saddles—to the packhorse, which is the one we decided to keep. As we worked, the lead bandit eyed Thokk. "You a skop too?" he asked her.

"She—" Ealstan said.

"Let her answer for herself," the bandit said.

"What need have I for stories?" Thokk said. "I'm basically dead already."

The bandit grunted, then turned to me.

"He's my nephew," Thokk said. "Slow of wits. Good luck getting anything useful out of him."

Was that really called for? I didn't complain, though. I wanted to keep moving. Once we got our things loaded, the bandits let us go. Interesting. Two thousand years of progress, and the mafia used the same tricks. Some people pretended that thievery was about anarchy, or sticking it to people in power. But most thievery was run by people with a different sort of power.

"Strangely," I said as we walked away, "that's the first time an experience here has made perfect sense to me."

Thokk immediately sighed.

"What?" I asked.

At that moment, something slammed into me from behind.

Everything went dark.

26

I found myself in darkness as my nanite system rebooted, and I immediately knew what had happened.

Someone had hit me with a damn blackout grenade!

Blackout grenades use a jolt of energy to send a forced command through your nanite system. Each of the little machines emits a small shock, knocking you unconscious. The nanites then go through a reboot sequence. As my system was sitting around twelve percent efficiency, it had been enough to lay me out.

Blackout grenades were single use and expensive. We'd employed them once in a while on jobs, when we didn't want to kill a person we were grabbing. But they weren't terribly practical for most occasions—after all, any weapon powerful enough to fry your augments could also rip a hole in you.

Right, then. I had no idea how I'd gotten here, or where *here* was. But by now, I was an expert at ignorance. All I had to do was avoid any boards to the face. Also, maybe I should avoid getting pulled into any more personally revealing quests to stop interdimensional mobsters.

I waited until my optical augments came back online. Once they did, I saw I was in a small room, some kind of tool shack. I slipped off the mat where I'd been placed. If I'd been hit by a blackout grenade, that pointed to Ulric . . .

Those bandits! They'd hit me from behind the moment they'd heard me speak. They'd been watching for *accents*. Holy hell. Were my friends all right? I felt a brief moment of panic, breathing quickly and sharply.

They took me captive instead of killing me, I thought. Maybe they'd done the same for my friends. Plus, there was a small chance these bandits didn't know I had augments. They'd left me alone in here and let me reboot. Maybe they'd stolen the grenade, and were watching for people with accents from my world to ransom back to Ulric?

I didn't know enough to make such guesses. But I also didn't want to stumble out of here into a potentially dangerous situation. I turned up my auditory augments, and could pick out a crackling fire and laughter. Wind blew through the trees right outside and rattled the door. Were we in the deep forest? Wasn't that supposed to be bad? Some-thing about hounds, dark forces, and that guy who had a wolf kill Woden's wife?

I turned my ears down to normal levels and moved to the back of the room. One nice thing about being a coward: You learn all sorts of ways to run away. With a little work, I found a loose board and was able to pry it off, thanks to my wrist augments.

I slipped out to find that my little shack directly abutted the forest. A seemingly infinite field of quiet monoliths. Though their endless, ancient nature was daunting, seeing them with my augments on dispelled some of the mystery. I'd seen plenty of trees before. Granted, those had mostly been cultivated, solitary trees, carefully planted along streets. Trees, it occurred to me, were like teenagers. They loomed in aggregation.

Out of curiosity, I flipped off my augments. Immediately, the shadows returned. An impenetrable wall of darkness. And yet, things *did* move in there. Skulking. Shifting.

Hell. I flipped my augments back on, but now I felt unnerved— whatever was moving out there turned invisible when I used night vision.

"That," I muttered, "is cheating."

A part of me *still* wanted to run off into those woods, be done with all this. Find someplace to hide. During my amnesia, I'd constructed an entire life from the glimpses I'd remembered. But those hadn't given me a full picture. That time I'd remembered being on patrol with my partner? That had been Ryan picking me up for lunch, and we'd talked about a case he was working. The times I'd remembered saving or helping people? Role-plays from my training.

Truth was, I'd run from my failures like I ran from everything. Like I should run now.

I shoved down those feelings. While I wasn't the hero I'd imagined, I didn't have to be the wretch Ulric and his goons saw. I inched along the perimeter of the forest, toward the bonfire pushing back the gloom. All twelve bandits sat there, laughing and chatting in the night. They had Ealstan; I recognized him sitting with too-straight posture beside the fire, on a log. He stared forward with a quiet intensity. Probably contemplating all the terrible things that happened to, say, birds.

At least he was alive. A dozen enemies, with a hostage? I knew enough to recognize what a cop would do: call for backup, and *don't* engage. But there was no backup for me to call. My wizard trick wasn't going to work here either—not if they knew enough to recognize my accent and hit me with something that would disable my nanites. So . . .

Hell, I didn't know. I was new to this not being useless thing. I did spot someone standing by the fire, their back to me, wearing an ornate hat with a plume. They seemed leader-ish. Maybe if I grabbed the leader I could make the others give me back my friends?

That didn't seem particularly heroic, but you know. Baby steps. Before I could talk myself out of it, I took a deep breath and dashed toward the fire. Only then did the irregularities start to pop out at me.

Ealstan was eating a bowl of soup. Sefawynn was sitting nearby, just out of sight from where I'd been standing, chatting amiably with another woman.

Most importantly, the guy I was running toward turned at the sound of my approach.

It was Ryan Chu.

FAQ:

What If I'm Still Worried About the Ethics of Essentially Colonizing the British Isles, Influencing the Course of History for an Entire People?

First, let us reiterate that you needn't worry. The Dimensional Law Act, the Ethical Consortium Decision on Interdimensional Rights, and the consensus of over a thousand noted philosophy professionals all agree that our world's ethics and laws cannot be transposed to alternate dimensions, where the very laws of physics might (but likely won't[1]) be different.

Many misinterpret these resolutions and decisions to say we shouldn't

---

1. See FAQ: All Right, WHY Can't I Have a Dimension Full of Talking Bananas?

interfere with alternate dimensions. However, a better interpretation is that we shouldn't use *our* laws, practices, and ideas as a basis for dealing with people of other realities. By definition, *even these resolutions* have no bearing upon alternate dimensions—because anything we decide in our dimension cannot be binding for other realities.

Though you will find ethical discussions and arguments along a variety of philosophical lines, the ultimate decision is yours. There are infinite realities. There are, reasonably, an infinite number of approaches you could take toward interactions in your dimension. We're not going to tell you which one to pick. Once you step through that portal, you leave our dimension and enter one where only *your* conscience matters.

If you're still concerned about the ethics involved in your impending purchase of one of our perfect (for you) dimensions, perhaps you'd enjoy looking at what other wizards have done! We recommend *Case Studies in Hope: Ten People Who Changed the World in Their Personal Wizard Dimensions™*, by the Frugal Wizard™ editorial team. (Frugal Wizard™ Press, 2099, $39.99. Limited illustrated edition available to Frugal Fans™ subscription club members.)

In this book, you can read about Apinya Pan, who set up a "free city" in her dimension. Nobody was conquered or forced to join her. She simply built a city with comprehensive health care, modern food supplies, and other advancements—then invited people to move in. She brought security and peace of mind to millions as she turned her city into a modern metropolis—an oasis of reason in a time of darkness!

You can do the same, or you can find your own way. Anything you decide will be right in *your* dimension—don't let anyone judge you. Just as you can't bring things back from your dimension to ours due to their fundamentally incompatible nature, you shouldn't carry the baggage of our societal expectations when you leave.

The new world you enter might find *them* fundamentally incompatible.[2]

---

2. For those seeking a different perspective, we suggest the book *Case Studies in Awesome: Ten People Who Ruled the World in Their Personal Wizard Dimensions*™, by the Frugal Wizard™ editorial team. (Frugal Wizard™ Press, 2099, $39.99. Limited illustrated edition available to Frugal Fans™ subscription club members.)

27

I pulled to an abrupt stop. It isn't every day you find one of your best friends standing in the center of an Anglo-Saxon forest, wearing a Robin Hood outfit.

Ryan Chu, detective extraordinaire, star of the Seattle PD Anti-Cartel and Illegal Augments Division. Tall, friendly, and confident. He succeeded at everything he tried—he even had impeccable fashion sense.

Worst part was, you couldn't hate the guy, because he was so damned nice. He'd been chatting with Thokk—who I could see now that he'd shifted. She was laughing at whatever he'd told her.

Ryan was innately likable. No wonder I'd imagined myself as someone like him when I'd started to recover my memories. He'd never been my partner, but it's what I'd always dreamed about.

I'd *wanted* to be successful like him. More, I'd wanted to know where I belonged. Ryan had chosen the academy from an early age, shot for it, and hit dead center in the target. Jen had picked history in high school, and had excelled from the get-go. Why was it so hard for me to figure out what *I* should be doing?

Quinn and the others thought Ryan hated me. I'd encouraged that idea, worried they'd manipulate him through me if they'd known the truth. Ryan didn't hate me. He was *disappointed* in me. And maybe a little bitter about how things had gone with Jen.

Tonight, he turned from Thokk and lowered his cup from his lips. "Oh," he said. "Hey, Johnny."

"Uh, hey. So, it seems I've been out for a while?"

"My fault," said the pointed-beard guy, raising his hand. "Used the aelv stunning device on you. Wasn't supposed to knock you out that long, though."

"They told me you saved this man's life yesterday," Ryan said, gesturing to Ealstan. "Your nanites must have taken forever to reboot. Good to see you up."

"I keep thinking I'm starting to understand your aelv stuff," the beard guy said. "Then you say something like that, and I'm lost again."

The others of the band laughed nervously. I caught Sefawynn's eyes. Though she seemed uncomfortable—her arms were pulled in tight and she held her bowl of soup in a clawlike grip—she nodded at me. *We're all right,* that nod said.

"Johnny," Ryan said, nodding to the side. "Want to chat in private?"

I felt a surreal disconnect as we walked away from the fire. Ryan was a part of my other life, even more so than Ulric and the others.

"So," Ryan said, "didn't expect to find you here."

"I . . ." Well, the truth would have to be enough, this time. "You know when we had lunch last month? And you talked about how

250

you were working on an investigation involving dimensional travel? It reminded me that Ulric had a bunch of spare dimensions. I thought maybe I'd borrow one, you know? He'd never miss it. And if he did, so what? I'd be tucked away where nobody could reach me. That's how it was supposed to work, anyway . . ."

"You picked *this* dimension," Ryan said flatly. "Randomly, out of the list."

"Yeah."

"The only dimension in history that's *ever* been discovered to have something resembling magic. The one dimension where Ulric was building a criminal enterprise."

"In my defense," I said, "Ulric keeps the list in one big file. There's no way to tell if any of them are important."

"Oh, Johnny," Ryan said, rubbing his forehead.

"What?"

"That's the *point*. If someone breaks into his system and pulls his list of dimensions, they won't know which one is the important one and which of the other thousand are decoys."

"Huh," I said. "That's smart."

"Assuming one doesn't run into Johnny West and his own brand of dumb luck."

"More dumb than lucky," I said. That had been Ryan's line back when I'd been successful in the high school boxing league. Before my luck had run thin, but my dumb had proven to be a renewable re-source.

Ryan eyed me, his face lit by the distant bonfire. He didn't quite trust me; he thought I was lying. That maybe I'd been sent here by Ulric to find him. I couldn't blame him.

Truth was, there'd been a wedge between us for some time now. There'd been a nice few years when he'd thought I was in the Enhanced Fighting League on my own merits. But he *was* a detective, and his job *was* to track the cartels.

He'd pushed me for info on Ulric. Ulric had pushed me to lay down false trails for Ryan. In the end, they'd both realized I was useless, so life had continued—though things had never been the same between me and Ryan. It was like a sitcom. The cop, his best friend the thief, and the woman they both loved.

Except I'd always felt like the bit character who lived next door. The one with the bad hair and the worse catchphrase.

"I wanted to get away," I whispered. "That's why I'm here, Ryan. I woke up one day, and realized I hated it."

"It?"

"Everything. My life. My job. My world. And then, Jen . . ."

Ryan looked away. Jen was a sore spot. The only time I'd beaten Ryan at anything was when she'd chosen me, two years ago.

I knew he resented me for what had happened. If my relationship with Jen hadn't gone south in such a spectacularly awful way, she wouldn't have run off to Europe. No Europe, no accident.

I looked down at my feet.

"Did you really save the thegn's life?" Ryan asked. "Run in, fight off his foes, use your nanites to heal him?"

"Not hard to fight a bunch of medieval soldiers when you're the only guy around with platings."

"You still only plated on your arms?"

I shrugged. "Haven't ever found the password."

"And that skop says you're all off to stop Ulric and save the earl."

I looked back up at him, then smiled. "Yeah. I might have let their better natures nudge me a little."

"A little? You were going to tackle me. You didn't know who I was, did you? You really thought you'd been taken by bandits?"

"Yeah," I admitted.

He stared at me. Hard. Then he smiled. "Johnny."

"Don't give me that look," I said.

"What look?"

"The 'I knew there was someone better inside of you' look. You're not my grandma."

"Well, your grandma did always say she preferred me."

"Because you pretended to like opera," I said. "If she knew what you thought of her goulash . . ."

Ryan grinned. I grinned back. For the first time in forever, there wasn't an edge to either smile—it felt like we'd rewound ten years. All it took was getting stuck in an alternate dimension.

"So," Ryan said, "they think you're an elf?"

"Sure do," I said. "You?"

"Yeah. I figured it was because nobody here knew what to make of a Chinese dude. I guess it's more the superpowers, eh?"

"And, in my case, generally acting strange. I basically forgot everything about myself at first."

"You didn't take the pill?"

"What pill?"

"The dimensional stabilizer?" He rubbed his forehead like he was my *dad* or something. "Oh, Johnny."

"It's not *all* my fault," I said. "I bought one of those stupid books about getting around in these places. Only it *exploded* when I brought it through. Plus, I ended up in the middle of nowhere. I've spent the last four days trying to catch up."

"Wait," Ryan said. "Four days? You came in that recently?"

"Yeah. Why?"

"I sabotaged Ulric's equipment a week ago," he said, "including his beacon. You shouldn't have been able to get here at all. No beacon, no dimensional travel—at least not *accurate* dimensional travel." He began pacing, punching his hand into his fist. Same posture he'd used when figuring out how to talk a professor into giving him better grades. Then he stopped and looked at me. "He must have another beacon! That explains so much!"

"I'm . . . not following," I said.

"Did you really learn that little about what you were doing before you jumped in?"

"That part of my book exploded! I thought I could pick it up along the way."

"To get to a specific dimension, you need something called a beacon," Ryan explained. "Which is set up *in* the dimension. It sends a signal back to our Earth. Without one of those, turned on and sending information back, someone from Earth won't *ever* be able to find their way here."

Okay. I did know that part.

"A week back," Ryan continued, "I blew up Ulric's beacon and his portal, trapping him here."

"And . . . trapping you here too?" I asked.

"No," he said. "I have my own beacon—a small, portable one. It was supposed to allow reinforcements to join me, or at least let someone through with a portal to collect me. But they didn't come. I don't know why."

"And you can't ask them?" I said. "Flip the beacon on and off to make Morse code or something?"

"It doesn't work that way," he said. "The equipment back on our Earth can't distinguish a beacon turning on or off. The signal is either there, or it's not. And it takes time to lock on to an active beacon. Something to do with information getting distorted as it travels upstream. The important part is, I was supposed to get help, but none showed up. I thought something was wrong with my beacon, that I was trapped. But now . . . it makes sense."

I looked at him, and tried *not* to look stupid.

Ryan sighed. "Johnny, there can only be one signal per dimension—and the stronger beacon overrides the weaker one. He must have an extra, larger device overriding mine. That's why my backup hasn't arrived."

"But . . . how did *I* get sent all the way up north?"

"No idea," Ryan admitted. "Maybe I damaged his equipment in such a way that when people enter, their landing is no longer accurate? Sorry. When I busted up his equipment, I didn't realize my childhood best friend was going to pop in for tapas."

I shrugged. "It's probably better I didn't land somewhere near him. Still, he did notice that someone had entered the dimension—he thought it had to do with you. He came *in person* to look into it. He's afraid of you, Ryan. Really afraid."

"Good."

"Not good," I said. "Really *not* good, Ryan. Ulric is—"

"I've spent ten years hunting him, Johnny. I've got an idea of what he can do."

I supposed he did. "I know, but . . . I had a run-in with Quinn yesterday. They think you're gunning for Ulric. And they've got help on the way. Quinn said they've got a rescue team arriving tomorrow."

"Wait. A rescue team?" Ryan cursed softly. "He definitely has a working beacon. Destroying the portal is only half the equation. I'd hoped Ulric would be too paranoid to give someone else authority to visit, though check-in teams are a common precaution in dimensional travel."

"Nah," I said. "He's too paranoid *not* to have backup." I'd read about this in the book—you could arrange for people to check on you periodically. Ulric wouldn't trust a company to do it, but he'd most certainly set up his own team.

"We need to get that beacon," Ryan said. "Use it to get backup—and keep him trapped. We need to move."

"We?" I said.

Ryan gestured to the group of bandits sitting around the fire. "My merry men. I had to use what I had."

I raised an eyebrow, then glanced at Ryan's fancy hat. Maybe I needed to revise my opinion of his fashion sense.

(Two stars. And his men weren't all that merry.)

"I'm leading a bandit troop in the forests of central England," he said, noticing my scrutiny. "I *had* to act the part. Maybe all those legends about Robin Hood are about me, and things got muddled over the years."

"We're not in our dimension, where those legends exist," I said.

"Okay," he said, "so maybe an alternate-reality version of *me* came to our world fifteen hundred years ago, and did *this* to a different alternate-dimension version of Ulric. Who knows, right?"

"And the magic?" I asked softly, taking Ryan by the arm. "What about that?"

"I think it's a strange quantum fluctuation involving collapsing probability fields," Ryan said.

"Ryan!" I said. "That sounds positively scientific. You hated it when your parents talked like that."

"Yeah, well, I became a cop—but I couldn't escape it entirely. I think probability physics is somehow influenced by *public perception* here. They *think* there are invisible beings helping them, and this dimension changes the laws of probability. Unlikely things occur to fulfill people's expectations."

Now he sounded like his father explaining why free will didn't exist. The Chus were . . . fine folks, really. That said, they didn't pay attention to anything but physics. I suppose that's natural when you each have one-sixteenth of a Nobel Prize. Or, perhaps you're more likely to end up with an eighth of a Nobel Prize in the family when that sort of conversation happens regularly.

"Ryan," I said, "you're overlooking the obvious answer. What if there *are* invisible beings? Maybe the same things used to live in our world. That would explain all the stories."

"The stories don't need explanations other than human imagination," Ryan said. "You don't *actually* think fairies are real here, do you?"

"Have you seen how writing can burn? My book *literally* exploded!"

He shook his head. "You always did like the easy answers, Johnny. There's far more to this than invisible monsters—something Ulric is trying very hard to exploit."

"What's he up to, anyway?"

"You don't know?" Ryan said. "You were on your way to stop him, and you don't even know what he's doing?"

I blushed. "Extorting people. Making money. I assume."

"I thought you were in his gang."

"You don't tell the *door guard* about your interdimensional domination plans, Ryan. But why does he care? He can't take anything out. So even if there is magic here, he can't use it in our world."

"He doesn't need to take it out to use it, Johnny."

I frowned.

"This place plays strangely with luck and fortune. Ulric brought a bunch of blank lottery sheets in here, and something about this place—the wyrd, they call it—let him pick which numbers to play to win. In *our* world."

"What, *really?*"

"Really."

Damn.

That was bad.

People make all kinds of wrong assumptions about people like Ulric. I blame the elaborate supervillain "take over the world" type movies with their Doomsday lasers and pocket nukes. I'd never met a cartel boss who wanted anything to do with world domination. If people thought you were building a nuke, you went from dealing with cops like Ryan to having the president order drone strikes on your yacht. Ulric was *not* stupid.

So what did a smart mafia man want? Money. Money bought politicians. Money opened doors. Money, these days, bought universes. Ulric got most of his money from lucrative black market augment sales, but it was dangerous. *Clean(ish)* money was better. Money from fixed fights was relatively clean—and hard to pin down in court. And if you did get convicted, punishments were light, easy to wiggle out of. But the opportunities were fewer.

So Ulric ran other operations. Most notably, black market augments. Lots of money in that, but it was far more dangerous. If he could influence probability instead . . . He'd never run out of working cash. He could pay his men with lottery tickets guaranteed to win small pots. Hell, he could bring down rival bookies and casinos.

Worse, he could determine which stocks would rise, which insurgents would prevail in taking over small countries, which politicians to back . . .

With enough money in his pocket, Ulric's potential for evil—as proven by current dimensional understanding—would be *literally* infinite.

"This is dangerous," I whispered. "This entire dimension is too dangerous for anyone to control."

"We'll let the feds decide that," Ryan said. "For now, I'm going to have to move up my timetable. We need to take down Ulric while he's vulnerable." He looked to me. "Is there enough cop in you to help, Johnny?"

I paused only briefly before nodding. It was what Sefawynn, Ealstan, and I had been planning to try anyway. With Ryan and his "merry men" on board, our chances of stopping Ulric skyrocketed.

But for some reason, I was a little disappointed.

Yes, I'd been marching into an unknown situation with no realistic chance of success. But . . . this had been *my* fight. My way to prove that Ulric didn't own me.

Now someone *capable* was involved, so it wasn't really my fight anymore. That's how it had to be when Ryan was around. He was everything Sefawynn and Ealstan *thought* I was. He was . . .

Wait.

Could I use that?

A plan started to form in my mind. Not for dealing with Ulric, or figuring out what was up with the wights. No, this was a plan to fix something more vital to me: my relationship with the quiet woman sitting by the fire, light reflecting off her tight blond curls.

If I wanted to repair our relationship, I simply had to ruin things! A goal that, for once, played directly into my personal talents.

28

I followed Ryan back toward the fire. Now that I was paying attention, I noticed a few modern conveniences. Solar panels set up in one of the trees, barely visible against the night sky. A closed laptop sitting on a stump near a tent. A multitool shovel-axe hybrid, like they used in the military, leaning against a tree.

Ryan was prepared for life in the Middle Ages, and he always did like working with locals. He acted less like an invader into urban spaces and more like a resource to train people to rid themselves of diseases like cartels. It was completely believable that he'd recruited an entire team of local bandits.

People liked Ryan. He was more than the perfect cop—he was a perfect human being. Trustworthy, reliable, honest to a fault.

Which was something a guy like me could exploit.

"Hey Sefawynn, Thokk, Ealstan," I said to the three of them. "I've got good news. Ryan here is willing to help us against Ulric."

"The timeframe is tight," Ryan said, pulling a black commando duffel from the shadows near his tent. "We need to leave early in the morning in order to reach Maelport tomorrow. I would appreciate any help I could get."

"Ryan and I were partners back in our world," I said, thumbing toward him. "I was the little father, and he was my hearthman."

Ryan smiled, the chagrined one he used when putting up with me. "That's not strictly true."

"Okay, maybe we were more like equals."

"He was a student," he said to the others. "I took him with me *one* day, when I knew it would be peaceful."

"You were impressed by how well I was doing in school," I said. "And what a great cop—um, warrior—I was going to make."

Ryan continued grinning in that same way, shaking his head, like he didn't want to contradict me outright—but it was painful for a guy like him to let something so blatantly untrue hang in the air.

He was getting better, judging by how he kept it in. He really *was* a good man. However, right now, I needed a little more of the old him. So I poked a little harder.

"I talked him into becoming a warrior," I said to Ealstan. "He'd never have gone to training without my help."

"All right, Johnny," Ryan said. "You know I can't let that slide."

I looked at him innocently.

"Johnny is a thief," Ryan said to the others. "Now, the rest of my team are bandits—"

"Recovering," one of them called out. "That's what you told us to say, right?"

"Right," Ryan said. "I obviously have nothing against working with people who have been pushed into rougher professions. But I've known Johnny since we were kids. He didn't get *pushed* into a rough profession—he let himself slide in. You should all know that he used to work with Ulric."

I shrugged, looking away, as if I didn't care. Those by the fire were silent for a moment. Then blessedly, she spoke.

"What kind of person was he?" Sefawynn asked.

"He . . ." Ryan hesitated.

"He was good enough for Jen to choose," I snapped. I cringed to use her like that. But she was dead, so she wouldn't care. Plus, this was the only thing that got under Ryan's skin.

Ryan sighed. "Johnny is a chronic underachiever. He's failed out of everything he's ever tried. He wasn't a great warrior. He was a scam artist. The one time I thought he was going to do something good with his life, I found out he was a cheat.

"Among our people, people pay good money to watch men fight one another—and they'll wager on the outcome. Johnny betrayed their trust. He lost fights on purpose so his friends could bet against him and win. Eventually, he lost so often that nobody wanted to watch him anymore. He didn't even get rich off all his scheming— Ulric took it all!"

His words stung, but that's what I'd wanted him to say. I'd pushed him to—

"Johnny is a drain on everyone he knows," Ryan continued. "He's asked me for money *every time* I've talked to him. His relationships wither. His parents eventually moved away. His sister won't talk to him, because of how much he owes her. He's exhausting to be around."

Okay. *That* was uncalled for. Maybe I should stop mentioning Jen to—

"In addition," Ryan said, raising his hands in the air, "everything I do, he's right there, shadowing me. I think about going to

263

art school? Well, Johnny enrolls first. I graduate from the police academy? He's there the next week. I mention I like a girl? He asks her out that night. I walk into a damn *alternate dimension*, and there he is!"

I blinked at the onslaught.

Ryan breathed deeply.

Was that how he really felt?

Was that how he'd *always* felt? I was a drain? A person whose failures . . . pulled him down too?

I mean, I wasn't *surprised*. Deep down, I'd known these things. Being a *nobody* without memories had somehow been *more fulfilling* than being myself.

But hearing someone say it . . .

Hearing *Ryan* say it . . .

I left. Out into the darkness, where nobody could see me. I didn't go far. I simply didn't want to face them, or subject them to my presence, I guess.

Or maybe I was just a coward.

I settled down near a rock, my back to the stone. Ryan probably felt terrible. Damn him. I'd ruined his day by making him ruin mine.

I thumped my head back against the stone, breathing out, long and slow. Finally, I turned off my night vision and opened my eyes. That let me look out through the shadowed trees, and see the night. That strange darkness—alive, untamed, of a genus I'd never encountered before coming here.

The forest itself was awake with groaning branches and chittering leaves. Things in the underbrush and the canopy alike gave the world a good scratching, unseen. The wind blew through, chill but crisp. And the scents . . . Soil and leaves, water stagnant and musty.

Nearby, the shadows seemed to move and quiver. Was I imagining that? Or was it something more? I could almost make out shapes.

"Can I join you?" I whispered to them. "I'd like to be unseen. It's why I came here."

They darted in close. From outside, these unnatural shadows had terrified me. In here, I didn't care so much. They didn't seem dangerous so much as . . . curious. They lingered near me, then one at a time, fled into the deeper dark of logs and thickets.

"Your presence hurts them," a voice said in my ear. A voice of dried leaves dead on branches, shivering in the late fall as they finally dropped free.

"Them too, eh?" I said.

"It's not only you," the wight explained. "It's everyone from the other world. You carry an aura that hurts us, slowly kills us. Your world bleeds into ours, and it poisons the wights."

"But not you?" I asked.

"Me also," it whispered. "I'm merely strong enough to live through a little poison."

People from my world . . . hurt the wights? What had the book said? "We have substance," I said. "Our world can overwhelm yours."

"Not substance. Poison. An opposite to us. Deadly."

"So what happens if Ulric sets up a permanent base here?" I asked.

"Death to wights," it whispered. "To wyrd. To *gods*."

"Damn. He *can't* control probability, can he? He'll end up destroying the thing he's trying to dominate."

"Yes."

The little flitting shadows danced around me, dodging in, then shying away. Like feral puppies, curious, but also nervous. I watched them, and listened to the forest chattering to itself.

If Ulric had his way, this would all wither.

I had to stop him. Or try, at least.

I could actually *do* something. *Mean* something.

Leaves crunched behind me, and I jumped, spinning and looking back across my rock. Sefawynn stood halfway between the boundary of the forest and my position, holding a frail candle—the flame cupped by her hand.

Her eyes wide, she whispered at me. "Runian? Is that you?"

"Yeah," I said, causing the shadows to dart backward.

"Please come back to the fire," she pled. "It's not safe in here."

"And it's safe in the clearing?"

"Yes," she said softly. "It has to do with that other aelv, the one you call Ryan." She glanced to the side as some of the shadows drew close to her. "The wights and dark things are frightened of him."

"They stay away from me too," I said. "People from my world bring them pain."

"That's not true. One is attached to you."

"It's the one who told me about the pain," I said.

She stepped forward, her candle flame flickering. "It *spoke* to you?"

"Yeah."

She stepped closer. "What did it sound like?"

"Like . . . something natural," I said. "I can't really explain it."

At my urging, she joined me. She set her flickering candle—in its bronze stand—upon the rock beside her. I faced her across the candle's light. We sat in silence for a while, the shadows forming a perimeter around us, some ten feet back.

"Ryan the aelv," she finally said. "You two have quite the history."

"He knows me better than anyone. Maybe better than my parents do."

"Aelvs have parents? I suppose it makes sense. Gods have parents. I've never been able to figure out if wights do or not."

"Ryan and I aren't what you think, Sefawynn," I said.

"The things you can do . . ."

"Do you think you're better than anyone else because you can see wights?"

"No," she said. "But that's different." She studied me. "I'm sorry he said those things," she continued. "I saw how it hurt you."

"I provoked it," I said. "I wanted you to understand. What I am."

"They were true, then?"

"Yeah."

"You cheated those people who bet on you?"

"I did, though I wasn't ever the one making decisions."

"You were a pawn of this man, Ulric?"

"He used me up," I said, "then made me guard his door. Mostly so he could make fun of me."

"You're among the lowest of the aelvs . . ."

"Yup."

"Practically a mortal."

I smiled. She smiled back.

"You told me you weren't a grifter . . . which is true," she said. "But it's also a lie."

"I exist as both at once," I agreed. "A quantum probability state."

"I have no idea what that means."

"Trust me, it was profound."

"Oh, look," she said, rolling her eyes. "The stars are out."

"You can't see them through the trees," I said.

"I know they're there." She stood up, then hesitantly held out a hand to me. "The stories all say to avoid aelvs, *particularly* the handsome ones."

I grinned, taking her hand and standing up.

"So," she said, "*you're* probably safe."

"I'll have you know that I'm considered *incredibly* handsome among my people."

"Is that so?"

"Yes. I have it on good authority from my mother."

Her smile widened, but then she paused. "Did your parents really leave you?"

"They retired to Atlanta," I said. "So yes and no." I squeezed her hand. "The things Ryan said *are* true, Sefawynn—but I left that person behind. In your world, even a terrible aelv can help."

Together, we walked back to the fire. She held tight to my hand—perhaps because of the shadows in the forest, but I didn't mind. I was holding on tight for a different reason. It was the first time in years I felt happy to be *me*. Somehow, being a screw-up had *fixed* one of my relationships.

Maybe, this whole time, all I'd needed was someone who saw herself as a little bit of a screw-up as well.

(NEW!)
BETTER THAN TRUE LIFE™
EXPERIENCES

I n this new revised edition of the handbook, we'd like to introduce our most incredible innovation ever: the Dimensional Versus Sport Challenge™![1,2] (Our standard Better than True Life Experiences™ are still available,[3] and can be found in the next section.)

---

1. D.V.S.C.s can be added to any package—though they aren't recommended for beginners.

2. D.V.S.C.s are available at a fifteen percent discount to repeat customers. Travel and save!

Inspired by our popular reality show, *Wizard vs. Wizard: Conquest of Britain,* D.V.S.C.s are intended to be used by two or more wizards at once.

With each D.V.S.C. dimension, we'll assign a neutral referee to your group for a period of one year. (Extensions available.) This referee will inspect your dimension and determine the criteria for your challenge, individualized to the terrain, cultures, and political setup of your world. (Standard rulesets apply: You can't hurt opposing wizard(s). You can't bring in weapons or resources beyond your initial starting gear. You can't leave the play area to recruit in other nations. Specific details available on request.)

We offer four D.V.S.C. games.

CLASSIC CONQUEST

Both players/teams are assigned a fixed number of resources and a starting region of control. The objective is to gain political control of your city, build up an army, then conquer your opponent's lands before they do the same to you!

CAPTURE THE CASTLE

A real-life variation on a capture the flag game, where players/teams compete to hold several strategic points. Usually involves hiring local mercenaries, rather than building up an entire army.

---

3. Except for our popular Nanite Mutagen Zombie War™ experience, which has been delayed due to the regrettable closure of MutaTech. We hope to provide this experience again as soon as we can find a new source of zombie nanites (or as soon as the members of MutaTech finish their prison sentences)!

GAME OF HOMES

Two players only. Each player is assigned a region to conquer and is dropped in with no resources. Players race to be the first to hold complete political sway over their assigned area—defined as all locals accepting you as their monarch. (No declaring war on the other group, though certain other interferences are allowed. See current official rules on our website.)

AUGMENTED INSANITY

The ultimate, insane war game! Players/teams each get a random—and different—assortment of modern advantages, such as modern weapons or short-term nanite injections. Give them to the locals, and see which can employ them best on the battlefield!

Be certain not to miss season four of *Wizard vs. Wizard: Britain on Fire*—where we will provide in-depth access and coverage of three exciting teams as they attempt to become the ultimate rulers of Britain! This time in a Stone Age dimension, with actual living mammoths!

29

B ack at the bandit camp, everyone was starting to turn in. They had bedrolls clumped together, and Ealstan was making a place over by them—though Thokk suggested that Sefawynn join her in the little shack where they'd put me to sleep off the effects of the blackout grenade.

I found myself awkwardly standing next to the fire. My nanites were coming online again, and my systems said I wouldn't need sleep tonight. But staying up meant facing Ryan, who sat quietly beside his tent, tapping on his laptop. He looked up as I regarded him.

"Hey," I said.

"So, um," Ryan said. "Shall we focus on how we're going to take down Ulric?"

Complete and total avoidance of uncomfortable emotions? He was speaking my language. I settled down on the ground as he turned the laptop around to show me the screen.

"Here's what I have on Maelport," he said, revealing a detailed map of a small city.

"Oh, is that all?" I said. "Just a full map of the entire place?"

"I also have 3D renderings of the earl's mansion and associated buildings," he said, tapping a key. "The earl is being kept in a pit over here—these people have no concept of proper incarceration techniques. I've outlined guard routes here, in green."

I took a screenshot of the map with my eyes. Ryan had highlighted a large meeting hall beside the mansion.

"What's this?" I asked.

"Ulric's saferoom and tech depot," Ryan said. "That's where he had his portal set up. It's the only building with modern security—so I suspect it's where he'll have the beacon, assuming it's not a portable one on his person."

I nodded slowly.

"He has a security field with micromotion-detection alarms," Ryan said. "I've outlined my best guess at the field's perimeter in blue. It follows the inside wall of the city, and alerts him if anyone with nanites or augments crosses the threshold. It's what gave me away last time."

"Your competence is a tad nauseating sometimes," I said.

"You wouldn't say that if you knew how ill-prepared I am," Ryan said. "I was only supposed to scout out the area, so I brought minimal gear and a handful of weapons. We used the last blackout grenade on you. I'm down to two guns, a laptop and solar panels, a radiophone, and my flak vest. Embarrassing, I know."

"I came in with a cloak, a mostly empty ballpoint pen, and a handbook that turned out to be ninety percent marketing material."

"Right," Ryan said. "Gotta love that Johnny West spontaneity!"

"You mean that Johnny West *incompetence*, Ryan. Just say it. You weren't worried about doing so earlier."

Avoiding uncomfortable emotions, totally my language. Saying something awkward at an inappropriate moment? That was *expert-level* John West.

"Johnny," he said. "I didn't mean those things."

"Yes, you did. We both know it."

"The emotion was real," Ryan said, "but I went further than I intended. I guess I had some pent-up issues. You know?"

Yeah. Whatever. "Can we cut his power source?" I asked, pointing at the screen. "Bring down the alarms?"

"Not easily," Ryan said. "He's got a fusion reactor inside that meeting hall. Takes in hydrogen, spits out gold."

Can you believe people used to *pay* for that stuff?

"We need to neutralize his beacon before the prearranged team comes to check on him," he said. "On Wodensday."

". . . Wodensday?"

"Sorry," he said. "Local vernacular. That's where we get the word 'Wednesday,' though, you know? From Woden's name?"

"Sure. Of course." I hadn't known. "You sure the check-in team will arrive at his beacon? I landed pretty far north."

"The people coming to check on Ulric know what they're doing."

That one was totally fair.

"So what do *we* do?" I asked.

"We leave early tomorrow morning through the forest," Ryan said, zooming out his map to view a scan of the entire region. "If we push hard, we'll arrive late tomorrow. Then, in the morning on Wodensday, we'll launch a two-pronged attack.

"I'll alert my inside contact via radiophone. They can't disable the perimeter alarm, but they should be able to let me in through the back. Then you'll—"

"Wait. You've got someone *inside* Ulric's organization? Who?"

"Can't reveal that, Johnny. Sorry."

"It can't be Quinn."

"It's not Quinn," he said.

I'd only seen Quinn and Ulric himself so far, but it made sense he'd have a few more people here. He was shockingly independent for how powerful he was, but he also understood the value of meat shields.

"So, you go in the back," I said. "What do the rest of us do?"

"Distract him," he said. "Take my men and go in the front door. The alarm will put the focus on you."

"Wait, so I trigger the trap?" I said. "While you go in the direction where nobody shoots at you. Can't *I* do that part?"

"Can you identify a beacon?" Ryan asked. "Can you turn it off without destroying it? Use these readouts to infiltrate Ulric's hideout?"

No. I couldn't. I mean, I was only a mediocre thief. A mediocre artist. And a slightly-above-average brawler. And Ryan had augments like mine, was even better with them, and had some police-specialty ones, like full video recording and IR scanning.

Beyond that . . . Ryan knew better than to entrust me with the part of the job that required reliability. I could see it in his posture, the way he stared at the screen and wouldn't meet my eyes.

I can't afford to have you screw this up, that posture said.

Ryan pulled something from his pocket. A black, diamond-shaped metal device, vaguely reminiscent of a very pointy grenade.

"This is a dimensional beacon," Ryan said. "If something happens to me, you need to be able to spot one. His will be bigger. The moment we destroy it, we can activate this one and my team should be able to join us."

Ryan waved toward the sleeping lumps nearby. "They're good men," he said softly. "They're outcasts because they didn't like seeing the earl buddy up to strangers. They're willing to fight to protect their homeland. I respect that. But if they meet up with *modern* soldiers? They'll be cut to pieces.

"I'll feel infinitely better if they have someone properly augmented among them. Once the beacon is disabled, we can retreat. We don't need to fight him. We just need to isolate him. We'll bring in our own backup, and we'll win. This is important, Johnny. Your part is important. For once, I'm begging you to *follow through*."

I nodded. I doubted any plan I'd have come up with would have been half as well thought out or rational.

"I suppose," I said. "I just hate being bait. Three stars—a pretty good score, under the tight deadline."

"Still judging everyone and everything, eh?" He shook his head at me. "Johnny, if you're going to make some changes in your life, you could throw away that notebook and stop taking notes on everyone. Nothing is ever good enough for you."

"I lost the notebook. And I don't judge everyone."

"You assigned my plan a rating."

"Yes, but—"

"And I'd bet money you gave my Robin Hood costume a score the moment you saw it."

I glanced toward the dark forest. I'd left my night vision off, and I could see the wights wiggling out there. "Is that how it looks to you? Like I'm . . . judging everyone?"

"Johnny," Ryan said, "you try something, decide it's not as good as you imagined, and give up. You try something else, and wash out of that too. Because you have these crazy standards you apply to everyone and everything but yourself."

"I just have trouble with decisions," I said, blushing as I glanced downward. "When I lost my memories I kept wondering why I scored things. Was I an art critic? A foodie? And then . . ."

"And then you remembered you're weird?"

"Then I remembered that my life is a mess," I said. "Everyone else seems to innately know what they love. When things were going poorly for me in the academy, I started keeping a list of things I liked and didn't like. I thought if I rated things, it would give me the proper context to compare. I hoped . . . it would lead me to who I am. What I like."

Ryan just shook his head, bemused. "Johnny, how can you not know what you like?"

He didn't get it, but, typically, I hadn't explained it well. It *was* why I'd started keeping that list, though. To see if there were trends I wasn't noticing. About myself, the world.

It hadn't really helped. But I'd *liked* it. It didn't have to mean anything, not really. I'd started doing it with a purpose in mind. Then I'd kept on because it felt fun. It felt interesting. I *enjoyed* it.

Five stars. This is me. Who I am. And I didn't have to explain that to Ryan Chu.

The fire was burning low, so Ryan walked over and put some more logs on it. As the flames brightened, I noticed that a few of the men had set out offerings, along with some work to be done. A shoe needing repair. A knife to be sharpened.

"Do they usually do that out here?" I asked softly.

"No. That woman claimed your group had a wight, so . . ." He shook his head. "I've tried talking to them about their superstitions."

"The work gets done, Ryan. You'll see in the morning. How do you explain that?"

"I told you, it's some kind of quantum probability manipulation," he said.

"Shoes getting repaired is *quantum probability*."

"We don't see many outlandishly unlikely things happen in our dimension," he said, "but a great deal is *possible* that never happens for its *implausibility*. For example, all the oxygen molecules in a room *could* bounce to one side at once, causing a person on the other side to suffocate. The odds are just so infinitesimally small that it's a practical impossibility in our universe. Here, those kinds of things happen far more often."

"Spontaneously repaired shoes don't seem like something that could randomly happen, no matter how unlikely."

"Maybe," Ryan said. "But there's got to be some kind of explanation. We *know* probability is odd in this dimension. That's why Ulric is here."

"There is an explanation. People make deals with the wights."

Ryan shrugged, but he let the matter drop. Instead, he dug in his pack for a moment, setting aside a nasty handgun that could cut through platings. Then he tossed me something white and puffy.

A bag of marshmallows?

"I knew I'd be camping," he said. "I was saving them, but if we've only got one day left . . ."

"These guys don't want any?" I asked, gesturing to the sleeping men.

"Have you tried feeding them modern sweets?" Ryan asked.

I shook my head.

"Let's just say they don't appreciate sugar the way we do," he replied, tossing me a stick.

We held the sticks over the flames, the way we used to when camping with his father. It was nice. The crackling fire, the scent of burning marshmallow as I inevitably ruined mine. Ryan handed me a perfectly browned one as a replacement, just like always.

I watched the devilish glow of the deep coals, which seemed to breathe as they blackened and flared in the wind. "When did it go so wrong, Ryan?"

"Probably about the time you signed up with criminals."

I shook my head. "I was in the gutter, Ryan. I signed up *because* I was desperate, because everything was ruined *already*."

"Maybe you should have stuck with school, then."

Such a Ryan thing to say. "They kicked me out of the academy," I said softly. "I didn't quit."

Ryan turned to me.

"Said I didn't have the right attitude," I continued. "Said I had a . . . failing mindset. I did try, Ryan. I *kept trying*. Doing what everyone said. Trying to do what you'd done. If I tried hard enough, I'd succeed, right? But nothing ever seemed to turn out my way."

"You're avoiding responsibility," Ryan said. "Life isn't just about luck."

"Oh?" I whispered. "And when I failed the OM3 test because of the forced nanite update that turned out to be faulty? Remember that? It set my clock back by an hour and I missed class."

"One incident, Johnny."

"You had Venessa in your class, and she invited you to her father's party," I said. "Then you ended up in his department."

"Good networking."

"Lucky networking," I said. "Ryan, if it's possible for all the atoms in a room to bounce to one side, isn't it possible that a guy like me could have things break against him, time and time again? I'm not trying to say everything that happened with me was luck. But it played a part."

"A little part."

"A little pebble starts an avalanche," I said. "Life isn't like the craps table, where the next roll has the same chance of winning as the last one. In real life, you lose a little—and that makes you wonder if you *deserve* to lose. You get nervous, make mistakes, overcompensate. That makes you lose more, then it compounds. Eventually, you're so far gone . . ."

I heaved out a sigh. What was I doing? Trying to justify it all? Heap my bad decisions upon other sources?

No, I thought. *You've never had a problem taking responsibility. You've always thought you were worthless.*

No one thing had ruined me. It had just . . . piled on.

"I suppose you have a point," Ryan said, pulling off another perfect marshmallow.

"I do?" I said. "I mean, you agree?"

"When you say it like that," Ryan said, "it forces me to wonder. How much of my confidence is because things *did* go my way? When I look at a loser—no offense—I guess I want to assume he deserves it. Because it helps me believe that it could never have happened to me."

I nodded.

"Still," Ryan said, "responsibility is important, Johnny. The way we respond to bad turns is the only thing we have control over."

"Do we have control over it?"

"We have to. Otherwise there's no choice."

"Maybe it's complicated," I said. "Maybe it's simply a complicated, soggy, broken mess."

We fell silent for a time, listening to the chatter of the fire feasting on logs.

Finally, I spoke, even softer. "It wasn't until Jen left that I realized I was poisoning everyone around me. But my terrible life, it just perpetuated itself. Like a virus. I couldn't be anyone else, not as long as I was there. I had to leave."

"So you bought one book and jumped through a dimensional portal?"

"I wasn't thinking clearly," I whispered. "I killed her, Ryan."

"No. You *didn't*. Don't talk like that."

"I drove her away." I closed my eyes. "She'd have been better off with you all along. We both know it."

"Maybe," he said. "But Johnny . . . I don't blame you."

"Talking about her gets under your skin. It always has."

"For other reasons," he said. "It's not what you think."

I looked at him, questioning.

"You're a lot of things," Ryan said. "But you're not responsible for Jen's choices. I've never, *never* blamed you. Loving Jen was one of the most relatable things you ever did, Johnny."

I met his eyes. Hell, he seemed to mean it.

"You came here for a new life," Ryan said. "Well, I think you'll have your chance. We'll bring Ulric down together—and you'll forever be the man who did that. You'll have accomplished something truly special."

"Which is?"

"You'll have gotten out from under that avalanche, Johnny. You'll have *escaped*."

282

30

"Drawing people isn't as hard as you think," I said from horse-back.

"Craeft is not as hard as I think," Sefawynn said, walking alongside. "Right."

"It's not cráeft," I said.

"Just like turning aside steel weapons with your skin is 'not craeft.'"

"That's a different kind of not craeft," I said, smiling. "Look, if you went back in time to talk to some cavemen, they'd probably think your ability to control fire is magical."

"Sure," she said. "What is a 'caveman'?"

"Uh . . ." I guessed that comment didn't make much sense without a background in modern archeology and anthropology. Her lack of experience made the conversation more difficult than the one I'd had with Yazad.

I thought about it as I rode my old, placid horse. Most of the beasts had been needed to carry equipment, but everyone insisted that the "aelvs" take one, while Thokk appropriated the third.

On one hand, Ryan and I didn't need horses. Our nanites did wonders for our endurance. On the other hand, the others were accustomed to walking long distances. Even with my enhancements, I suspected I'd be slower on foot. To keep a good pace on our ride to Maelport, I'd agreed.

We rode straight through the forest itself, which wasn't as gloomy during the day. Fortunately, the enormous trees kept the scrub minimal in this region. I tried to keep my mind off the final confrontation with Ulric, but it wasn't working. Was I ready? I was the same person who had let Ulric mock him. The coward who *told* himself that *next* time he'd stand up for himself.

Time and time again.

No, I thought, then began rummaging in my saddlebags. I pulled out a pad of paper Ryan had given me, along with a pencil. A glorious pencil! The things you miss when you can't have them. What was a pencil even made of? Wood, yes. And graphite? What *was* graphite? I tried to look it up, but of course, my system had no link to the net.

"Look," I said to Sefawynn, turning the pad toward her. "Drawing is about two fundamental things," I explained, my hand stabilizers compensating for the motion of the horse. "Use of shapes and use of shadows." I did a quick sketch of her head, using broad, firm pencil strokes for the parts of the face. Some shading, a little more work on the eyes, and it started to pop. I'd always been good at faces; just don't ask me to do hands.

"I've seen art before," she said, curious. "But how do you make it seem so real?"

"One of the tricks is something we call perspective," I explained. "Some things are farther away, right? And some things closer? That goes for parts of a person too. On a face, some parts are close to you, other parts are farther away. The trick is to make it seem that way in a drawing.

"You can't draw it like it's flat. If I use shadows—and put the eyes on a curved line like this—and use just a touch of foreshortening . . ."

There's a moment in drawing, at least for me, when a face transforms from shapes and lines into a *person*. The eyes were a big part, and the dots of light reflecting in them, but the lips were important too. There.

"Craeft," Sefawynn breathed.

"If so," I said, "it's craeft you could learn." I offered her the pencil and pad.

She took them, intrigued. At my urging, she tried out the pencil—drawing some common shapes as she walked. "The parchment is so smooth," she said. "And this quill . . . It never runs out. But the lines are dry . . ."

She'd seen me alter the color of my skin, create thunder sounds with my voice, and block weapons with my arms. But to her, this was the most marvelous of my modern wonders. She drew swirls, tried a face at my prompting, and practiced shading by holding the pencil lightly.

Then she hesitated, stopping and making me pull my horse to a halt. She held out the pad, fingers quivering. "Take it back," she said softly. "Before I do something foolish."

"Like write?" I asked.

She nodded. She knew the runes, obviously. She was a bearer of lore and stories.

"Woden forbids it," she said.

"Woden laughs at us," Ealstan said, walking up. "Woden wants us weak. It amuses him."

"He tests us," Sefawynn said.

"Why does he not test the Hordamen?" Ealstan asked. "He blesses them and curses us."

"They show more faith."

"They're simply stronger," Ealstan said, "and he rewards strength. Why would he listen to our prayers instead of theirs? Why would he support us instead?"

"We sacrifice more," Sefawynn said. "And he loves sacrifice."

Ealstan fell quiet at this, then nodded, walking on past. Thokk rode by after him—but slowed to shake her head at Sefawynn. "Fool," she muttered pointedly before riding on.

Sefawynn looked down. Feeling her shame, I got off the horse and led it for a while. I was tired of towering over Sefawynn. "Hey," I said. "I don't know much about your world, but I'm pretty sure you aren't a fool."

"She's right about me though," Sefawynn said. Then she wrapped her arm around mine. "I talk like a skop, but I've never truly been one. When I say things like that to Ealstan, I'm not being myself. I'm pretending to be a person with the moral authority to reprimand someone speaking the truth. That's foolish."

"Or hopeful," I said, pulling her a little closer, so she leaned against me as we walked. "I like that hope."

We continued in silence for a time, just . . . being together. I wasn't completely sure what to make of this thing sparking between us. I knew I *liked* it, but it also seemed abrupt. I held on anyway, keeping her almost awkwardly close as we walked. Perhaps both of us sensed we were marching toward something inevitable and terrifying. And I'd rank our—or at least my—abilities below the eighty-year-old woman who spent her time being amused by other people's mistakes.

Up ahead, I spotted Ryan waiting beside a tree. Ealstan had stopped with him, ever vigilant in case something went wrong.

We'd fallen too far behind, and Ryan wanted to check on us. How was it he managed to look so regal up there? He held the reins lightly in one hand, a rifle strapped to his back, his cloak falling dramatically around him. He should have been just as out of place here as I was. Instead, he looked like some damn hero out of a movie.

"We need to keep up the pace," he said to us.

I nodded, but didn't let go of Sefawynn or climb back on the horse. I did try to walk a little faster.

"That weapon on your back, Lord Ryan," Ealstan said. "It can kill others of your kind?"

"Yes," Ryan said, nudging his horse into motion. "But it's keyed to my nanite signature—nobody else can use it. Not even Johnny, I'm afraid."

"Like those wielded by the man Ulric and his hearthmen," Ealstan said.

"I know stories of such weapons," Sefawynn said. "The Black Bear's sword cannot be wielded by any other man either."

"Johnny," Ryan said, "this would be faster if you'd get back on the horse."

"I can keep up," I promised.

Ryan eyed the way I walked close to Sefawynn.

"Just trying to make the best of the time I have," I said to him. "You know. Carp—"

He groaned. "Please don't say your stupid carp joke."

"What? It's a classic."

"Johnny, it's *literally* the worst joke I've ever heard. It requires people to know a specific Latin phrase—"

"—Carpe diem," I said, glancing toward the others. "'Seize the day.' Everyone knows that."

"Nobody knows that, Johnny," Ryan said. "Besides. It doesn't even *work*. If you replace 'carpe' with 'carp,' it means 'fish the day.' If you said something like 'carpe dime'—'seize the money'—that would make sense. 'Carp diem' means nothing. It's stupid."

I thought it was funny. But when he broke it apart like that, I guess he was right.

Sefawynn squeezed my arm. "You two say such strange things. Runian, your world . . . what is it like?"

"Why do you call him that?" Ryan asked.

"It is the name he asked me to call him."

"It's silly," Ryan said. "His name is Johnny. Everyone calls him Johnny."

"Runian," she prodded again, "what is your world like?"

Ryan sighed, but kicked his horse forward to catch up to the others. Ealstan stayed with us.

"He is a regal man in bearing," he said to me. "But are you certain he is your friend?"

"Better than I deserve," I said.

Ealstan grunted. "Well, I too would like to know what your world is like. Can you tell us? To help pass the hours as we walk, honored . . . Runian?"

A name was a simple thing. But Ealstan deliberately saying it like that, and Sefawynn doing the same, made me a little emotional. Ryan had known me all my life. But he'd never noticed I didn't call myself Johnny. My name was John. It was how I'd always introduced myself.

Sefawynn and Ealstan listened to what I wanted. If they cared enough to call me what I'd asked them to . . . maybe they actually *cared* about *me*.

"My world is a strange place," I said. "We harness lightning, make it work for us. We force it to glow inside glass globes when we want, flipping a switch to illuminate a room."

"What's a switch?" Ealstan asked.

"A tiny lever," I said. "Instead of horses, we—do you guys have carriages?"

They shook their heads.

"Chariots?"

No.

"You have boats," I said. "Imagine a boat, only it has wheels and moves on land. It's also powered by lightning, and you can sit in it and go places."

"Why not just let the wind blow in the sails?" Sefawynn asked.

"There are no sails," I said, scratching my head with the pencil. "Here, let me show you."

Over the next hour or so, I drew. That was harder on foot, so I reluctantly let go of Sefawynn and did most of the work from the saddle. First I drew a room with light glowing from the lightbulbs and a fridge holding food, a microwave to warm it up. Then I drew a skyscraper, and pointed to that room among the many windows. From there, I drew Seattle's skyline—the postcard version, with the Space Needle and everything. In this, my skyscraper became one of many giant shadows along the bay.

Sefawynn's eyes widened as the implications sank in.

"So," Ealstan said, pointing at the skyline, "each of you lives in one of these enormous structures? A monument to your grandeur?"

"No," Sefawynn whispered. "Each of those windows is a room, with one of his kind living in it. Hundreds upon hundreds in each structure. And there are dozens of these structures . . ."

"And thousands of smaller ones," I said. "One city in my world probably covers more land than we've traveled since leaving Stenford." At least, if you included the suburbs, the nuances of which I didn't want to explain at the moment.

"Gods . . ." Sefawynn said. "It's so . . ."

"Crowded?" I asked.

"Peaceful."

Peaceful? I hadn't been expecting *that*.

"So many people living together," she said, "but not fighting. You only learned to fight as a contest, for others to watch. There might be people among you who . . . who have never seen someone die . . ."

"Most don't even know how to fight," I said. "You'd think us all weak, Ealstan."

"You misunderstand, Runian," he said. "Killing is desperation, not strength. To live without killing . . . that is a strong society. If the reverse were true, my lands would not be withering away, like crops long without water . . ."

Damn, that guy could be profound. And depressing. Five stars. Should be narrating documentaries about disasters like Chernobyl. Or my love life.

Ealstan was right, though. Their wights, runes, and wyrd were magical, special, and beautiful. But honestly, there wasn't a ton else about their world that one might envy. The book I'd bought talked about the "pastoral simplicity" of the medieval era. The "natural connection" of the people to the land and the "primitive wisdom of agrarian societies," whatever that meant.

The book lied. This place wasn't simple or pastoral. It was brutal. Terrible. Soul-crushing. Minus the murderous Vikings, the people had been wonderful. Inspiring. Cleaner, friendlier, and cleverer than I'd ever imagined. But the general feel of the time?

It sucked. These people lived such hard lives, even if you discounted the constant threat of invasion. Without modern medicine, what would happen to my friends here? Would Sefawynn die in child-birth? Would Ealstan survive countless battles, only to die of an infection from cutting his finger on a nail or something?

I wanted to protect them, help them. Bring them technology—on this point, I agreed with the book. Its goals, if not its motives. Yet, did I dare? What if doing so destroyed the magic that made their world so unique?

Is there a way to do both? I wondered. *Lead them to things like vaccines and antibiotics without destroying the wights?* That would require a professor or engineer, not a failed boxer turned mafia punch-ing bag. Something else bothered me, thinking along these lines. Something—

A touch on my leg distracted me.

"You left all of this," Sefawynn said, still holding my sketches, "to come help us against these evil men."

"Don't you dare get reverent about me again, Sefawynn," I said. "Or I'll do something *extreme* this time to make you realize what a fool I am."

"You almost make me want to, just to see what you come up with."

"I'll insult the gods."

"You already did that," she noted.

"Fine then. I'll tell Ealstan how great bows are," I said, "and how axes are mundane and lack finesse."

"Here, now," he said from the other side of my horse. "Don't involve *me* in this. Heresy is one thing, but insulting Rowena is something else."

"Wait," Sefawynn said. "You *named* your *axe*?"

"Um, yes," Ealstan said, looking away.

Sefawynn giggled.

"That's not a thing?" I said. "Not something you normally do, I mean?"

"I've never heard of it before," she said.

"Isn't Rowena your *wife's* name?" I asked.

"Yes," Ealstan said, sounding solemn. "I like my wife. It makes perfect sense to use her name for something else I like."

"If you're a weirdo," I said.

"Wyrdo," Sefawynn said. "A wyrd. A wyrd-o. Someone strange, yes? With a strange wyrd? I like it." She looked at me. "I get a chance to use *so* many interesting words around you, Runian."

"Handsome," I said. "Brilliant. Inspiring."

"Questionably handsome. Brilliantly strange. Inspiring to other rodents who wonder if they can ever pass as human . . ." She grinned at me. Whatever I'd expected from people in Anglo-Saxon England, it hadn't been *wordplay*. She was illiterate and still talked circles around me.

The other thing I hadn't expected was . . . well, *this*. The way she touched my leg, the comfortable, natural way we chatted together. The joy I felt.

It was never like that with Jen. It was always tense. We'd argued so much. I'd thought that was just a part of passion. Yet here was something so different, so wonderful.

I was so wrong for you, Jen, I thought. *I'm sorry.*

"Honored Runian," Ealstan said. "I don't mean to pry, but you *are* a warrior, of sorts. You have seen death?"

"Unfortunately," I said. "But most of my fighting was done in the ring."

"Like sparring," Ealstan said, nodding. "We have such things, but not as . . . formalized as it appears to be in your world."

"At my height," I said, "I drew crowds in the tens of thousands."

"Of *people*?" he said. "That many . . . It boggles the mind."

"But your job was to fail?" Ealstan continued, hesitant. "And to . . . cheat?"

"Yes," I admitted softly. "Though I only threw a single match. At the end, on Ulric's orders."

"Why did you do it?" Ealstan asked.

"He owned me, Ealstan," I said. "He paid the money to give me my powers. Even still . . . he took many of them away before that last fight. So I'd get beaten up good and bloody. It's why I can stop an axe with my arms, but can be knocked out by a good blow to the face."

Still felt like a sucker for that. I didn't have a glass jaw. Of course, two-by-fours weren't allowed in the ring, so I didn't have a lot of experience taking them to the face.

"Why did Ulric take away your powers, if you were commanded to fall anyway?" Sefawynn asked.

"He wanted it to be more dramatic," I said.

"I think he wanted to leave you with no choice," she said. "In that context, you did not lose to cheat those people—he set it up so you couldn't win."

It was a poor rationalization—I'd gone into that fight knowing I'd lose, and played along. At the same time, I *hadn't* had a choice. Not really.

Unfortunately, my ruminations were interrupted as I saw Ryan, impatiently waiting for us. We'd fallen behind again.

"We'll speed up," I called to him. "I—"

My brain shorted out for a moment as Sefawynn hauled herself into the saddle in front of me. She took the reins and started the animal forward at a faster clip. "He doesn't know how to ride properly," she said to Ryan. "I will make sure we match your pace."

There wasn't enough room for both of us in the saddle unless we pressed ourselves extremely close together. In other words, it was great.

"You should hold on, Runian," she said. "Just in case."

I wrapped my arms around her waist.

"Tighter?" she asked softly.

I was happy to comply.

Ryan shook his head. "You two should focus on the mission, not on foolishness best left to teenagers." He turned his horse and hurried to catch up to the others.

I blushed, but didn't let go. How on Earth did she manage to smell so good while basically spending her entire life camping?

Ealstan kept pace with us as we caught up with the others. As we reached them, he spoke. "Do not be ashamed of your joy," he told us, his voice intense. "Regardless of what aelv Ryan says. This is not a thing of shame. It is why I fight. It is why my sons bled. *Never* be ashamed of joy."

Spoken only as he could. For all the place's faults, I don't think I'd ever been so purely happy as I was in that moment. Holding Sefawynn. Feeling Ealstan's approval. Moving toward something I believed in, rather than away from what I feared.

And yet.

The worry from earlier returned. The truth I had to acknowledge. The knife that was at my kidneys, point sinking through the skin.

I couldn't be with her. I couldn't stay here. My presence was ruining her world.

This beautiful thing I'd finally found, after years of restless searching, was the one thing I couldn't keep—not without destroying it.

THE END OF PART THREE

PART FOUR

No Refunds

FAQ:

What If I Don't Like My Dimension?
Are Refunds Available?

 Many people fear their dimension won't live up to expectations. Don't worry! We are extremely proud of our dimensions and think you'll love the one you pick! If not, your purchase is backed by our 100 Percent Super Wizard Guarantee™!¹

---

1. We guarantee 100 percent that you will be released from your contractual obligation to post on social media about how wonderful your dimension is. Instead, you will be forbidden from talking about it. You may not disparage Frugal Wizard Inc.® in any way, as per section 2003 of your contract. All sales are final.²

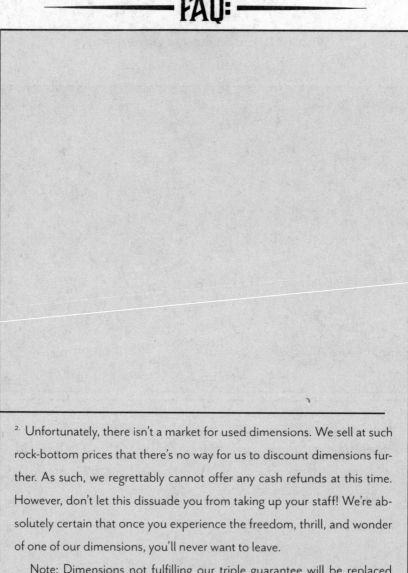

[2.] Unfortunately, there isn't a market for used dimensions. We sell at such rock-bottom prices that there's no way for us to discount dimensions further. As such, we regrettably cannot offer any cash refunds at this time. However, don't let this dissuade you from taking up your staff! We're absolutely certain that once you experience the freedom, thrill, and wonder of one of our dimensions, you'll never want to leave.

Note: Dimensions not fulfilling our triple guarantee will be replaced following the execution of item 131 of your contract. You promise to accept arbitration rather than litigation in the event of dissatisfaction, to be arbitrated in the dimension of our choosing. This contract is binding in all countries that have signed the Dimensional Law Act. Do not taunt Frugal Wizard Inc.®

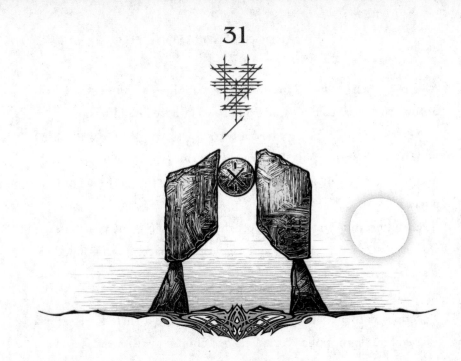

31

We took a short break that night for everyone to sleep for three or four hours while Ryan and I finished our plans. Then we roused everyone and hiked the last mile.

My nanites were starting to resume full function again, and I had some emergency services back. They would be able to keep me alive through some fairly serious punishment, which gave me an incredible amount of relief. I'd felt almost naked with them down so low.

We approached Maelport as the sun was rising. The woods began to thin near the outskirts, but we were able to find a sheltered area with a decent vantage to let us study our target. Ryan climbed a tree, where he could use his optical augments to better survey distances. I walked in a crouch up to the edge of the forest, along with Ealstan, Thokk, and Sefawynn.

By the scale of modern American cities, Maelport was tiny as hell. I suspected that it would have been dwarfed by even contemporary cities in this dimension, like Rome. But considering these people's resources,

Maelport was a vast and impressive metropolis—with full stone walls around the *entire* thing—and around two hundred buildings.

Yes, those buildings were basically cottages. And yes, the wall wasn't more than eight feet tall. But with those docks just beyond the wall, and the major roadways of packed earth leading into it, Maelport was a true city.

Early-morning fog rolled in off the ocean, but it broke right near the city, so it didn't obscure our view of the place. Ryan pointed toward the road that led northward. Dozens of people were trailing toward Maelport. I zoomed in with my optics.

People with hunched shoulders, dragging exhausted feet. They carried bundles or pulled carts, and had children with them. Refugees.

"What's going on?" I asked, pointing to them. "Those people . . ."

"Victims of Hordamen attacks," Thokk said. "They've been striking at hearths all up and down the coast."

I shared a look with Ealstan, who knelt nearby. "So," he said, "the ones we met were not isolated ships. As I feared. The Hordamen increase their raids."

"What good is all this, then?" Sefawynn said. "Even if we stop Ulric, we'll fall to *them*."

I squeezed her shoulder. I wanted to tell myself that the runestones might start working again if the people from my world left. But the decline of this people had been happening for far, far longer than our arrival could explain.

Ryan dropped down nearby with a thump. "We're in luck," he said, turning toward his followers. "Another village was hit by those Vikings. You can hide among the stream of refugees. Leave the equipment we don't need and the horses, save one, with Hend. If you get split up, meet back at this point."

They nodded. Hend was the youngest of the band, still in his teens. The guy with the pointy beard—Godric—unwrapped a bundle of sticks from the back of one of the pack animals. The men took them and began bending them and using strings to . . .

They were short bows! Nice. They hid these under a cloth on the back of one of the horses, along with . . . What was the right word? Magazines of arrows? Then they tucked axes beneath their cloaks.

"Perhaps you could stay with Hend and make certain he doesn't run into trouble," Ryan said to Thokk.

"You're not very bright, are you?" she said.

"Grandmother," Ryan said, "these men are terrible killers. My people say most would leave you alone—I guess it relates to honor? Ulric and his band will have no such hindrances. They *will* kill you."

"They can try!" she said. "The fact that they might succeed is part of the fun!"

"But—"

"I'm *going*," she said. "Don't make me curse you, young man. You seem mostly good-hearted, even if you're a bit of an aers."

That word again. Aers. Ears? Why . . .

Oh.

Arse. It meant *arse*. That made *way* more sense. I was starting to figure this place out!

Ryan sighed, then turned to me, Sefawynn, and Ealstan. "You still willing to do this?"

"We are," I said as the others nodded.

"Thank you," he said, then spoke to everyone together. "Don't take risks beyond what the mission requires. If it goes poorly, retreat. When Ulric or Quinn shows up, let Johnny face them. Remember,

303

this is about the beacon. Once we disable that, he'll be trapped in here without backup, and that will make him *infinitely* less dangerous."

I had worried I'd feel resentful taking orders from Ryan. I was beginning to feel possessive about this place—but that emotion was *exactly* what made me *want* someone as capable as Ryan in charge. Besides, there was a part of me that had been waiting for this day, the chance to be his partner.

Before we broke, Ryan stepped up to me. "Your internal chronometer still accurate?"

"It says 6:03," I said.

"Good. Mine too. I need you to start the distraction *exactly* at 7:15."

"Will do."

He stepped in close. "You promise, Johnny? *Please* tell me I can rely on you."

"This is important to me, Ryan," I said. "More important than you can know. Don't worry about my part. You just find that beacon and shut it down."

He nodded, then slipped his P-330, with antiplating rounds, from a holster on his leg. He handed the pistol to me grip first. I hesitated, then accepted it. I wasn't the best shot on the block, but I'd done some time on the range.

"Code 1929193," he said to the gun. "Reassign control to current nanite signature."

"Reassigned," a voice barked from the gun. "Nanite signature registered. Weapon active."

"Thanks," I said.

"Ulric's bound to have a thug or two besides Quinn. I swear I saw Janice when I broke in the first time."

I nodded. "I doubt he has a full crew, though. He'd have this entire region on complete lockdown if he did. So we have a chance."

"Agreed," Ryan said. "A chance." He offered his hand. I gave him a hug instead, thumping him on the back.

With that, we parted. Ryan would approach by what he called the sally port and make contact with his inside man. The rest of us hiked back for a bit less than half an hour, then ducked out into place. From there, we walked slowly, backs bowed, hoods up.

I felt horribly exposed. But before I could panic, I reminded myself that being spotted was our entire plan.

Create a distraction while Ryan did the important work. I could do that, couldn't I? Hell, Sefawynn and Thokk didn't seem frightened, and they weren't even armed. Still, as we drew closer, I took Sefawynn by the hand.

"You don't need to do this," I told her. "You're not a warrior. If something happens to you, what will become of Wyrm?"

"Yazad will care for him," Sefawynn replied. She turned her head, smiling at me beneath the hood of her cloak. "I am accustomed to danger, Runian. I live in a world without magical healing, without cities full of people who have never known what it is like to kill. I want to do this. I might not be a warrior, but I am a skop. I will not be useless to you."

I doubted Ulric's people would think twice about her being a skop, but I didn't push harder.

I did my best to adjust our speed so we arrived near to 7:00. I felt as if all the nearby refugees were watching us. That the guards would pick us out immediately once we arrived. What was the best escape route? Should I run down the road, or go cross-country to get back to the woods faster?

Follow through, I reminded myself. For once in my life, I needed to stick to something long enough to see it to the end. Once we could see the walls, I faked a coughing fit to give us an excuse to wait another few minutes. Then I looked to the others and nodded.

At exactly 7:15, we strode into Maelport.

My last fight had begun.

32

A bell—triggered by the perimeter detecting my nanites—rang in the center of town. At the sound, Ryan's soldiers yanked the bows off the horse while Sefawynn and Thokk ran to the side, their heads down. They'd pretend to be actual refugees, but stay ready to back us up. Ealstan looked up, searching for foes to fight— and his attention focused on the enemy soldiers gathering on the wall.

Soldiers with bows. Ealstan muttered a soft series of curses, then immediately followed Sefawynn and Thokk. What was he up to?

I didn't have time to think about it. Instead, I yanked out the pistol and positioned myself near Ryan's men. I probably should have shot at the enemy archers, but dammit, that would be unfair. Instead, I scanned the area.

There, I thought, picking out someone running up through the crowd. Janice Vault. She stopped when she saw me, then raised her gun.

I fired first. She dropped in a spray of blood.

Damn. I'd been in firefights before, but I'd never killed anyone I'd *known*. I didn't feel *specifically* bad about killing her, as I knew full well some of the things she'd done in Ulric's employ, but it still felt unnerving. It had all happened so fast. Faster than I had time to process.

Move, a part of me thought. *Make sure she's neutralized.*

I hurried to the corpse and destroyed her gun, then emptied a few more rounds into her chest. I didn't have a disintegration flare—you'd tuck them into bodies to fry nanites and burn the body—but disabling her weapon should protect me somewhat in case she had augments enough to survive the damage.

I doubted she would. Janice had been a low-level flunky. Didn't even have full platings.

I glanced back at Ryan's soldiers. The archers found cover behind some goods dropped by fleeing refugees. Arrows fell around them, arrows that—I noticed—hadn't been turned against me as I'd moved. The enemy archers had seen what I was. They likely didn't want to draw my attention.

Some of our soldiers were fighting the gate guards on the ground, while others returned fire (or whatever you call it with a bow) at Ulric's archers—who were mostly in two groups, one on either side, on the larger platforms along the walls. The enemy had the height advantage and was firing from both directions, while our people were exposed in the middle of the earthen courtyard. Yes, Ryan's plan had been for us to be bait, but—

A typhoon of fury *slammed* into one of the groups of enemy archers, hacking off limbs and sending people falling as he stormed through the middle of them. Ealstan had found his way onto the wall.

I grinned. Then one of the stones near Ealstan exploded. He ducked down as chips sprayed around him.

Damn. That had been gunfire. I tried to trace the sound as another shot nearly hit him, but quiet modern weapons made it difficult. Still, I knew where *I'd* fire from: that building to my left, with the large window.

To test my theory, I fired at the window. My aim was off, and a chunk of the wall sheared away. But the shots on Ealstan stopped.

The large courtyard was now empty save for soldiers, arrows, and bodies. It was incredible how quickly the civilians had vanished. I didn't even see Sefawynn or Thokk. A group of men armed with spears burst into the courtyard from a nearby roadway, and some of our men swapped bows for their axes or swords. The two groups were roughly even in numbers, now that Ealstan had dealt with one of the archer stations.

The man himself stood up, looking concerned as he peered out over the city. I wished he wouldn't present such a great target. That shooter was still nearby.

I put my back to a nearby building and moved away from Janice's corpse, inching toward the building where I thought the shooter was.

"Down the path to your right," a voice like rustling leaves said in my ear. "Between those two buildings. Coming this direction."

"Thanks," I whispered, getting into position. Soon, someone emerged from the small alleyway. I leveled my gun at their head, trigger ready. Then I hesitated.

It was Quinn.

A host of emotions fought for dominance inside me. Squeezing fear, exultant victory, cowering shame. I could remember that day clearly now. I could picture Quinn's smile as he'd stood over me. Victorious. In more ways than one.

Quinn froze in place. "Oh. Uh, hey, Johnny."

"Drop the gun, Quinn," I said.

He tossed his pistol to the side.

"And the one you keep in the leg holster," I said.

He grimaced, then eased the gun out and set it carefully on the ground.

"Other direction, Quinn," I warned.

He obeyed, flipping it so the barrel didn't point toward me. I shot both weapons. The antiplating rounds in my gun essentially vaporized them—and modern ammo was impact stable, so it didn't go off. Guns could respond to voice commands, so it was an extremely poor idea to try to pick up an enemy weapon.

Quinn raised his hands. "What now, Johnny? You gonna shoot me?"

It took only a moment to sort through the emotions and crown a victor. Quinn had let me go earlier. Besides, he was another boxer. We were kin.

"I'm not going to shoot you," I said. "What would Tacy say? Hell, Quinn. You think I'd leave the kids without a dad?"

Quinn visibly relaxed. "So can I . . . ?" He nodded back the way he came.

"Nope," I said. "You're, uh, under arrest."

He gave me a flat stare.

"I'm serious," I said. "I found Ryan. He's going to bring down Ulric. You'll go back through the portal with him."

"With the cop?" Quinn said. "Johnny, you're gonna make me do *time*?"

"Flannagan will get you off," I said. "Come on, Quinn. You'll only do a few months."

"Still," he said. "It's the indignity. If the others find out I got caught by *you*." He glanced at me. "Uh, no offense."

I sighed. Did I tie him up, or what? Ulric's remaining troops were retreating along the wall of the courtyard, heads low. That stupid bell was still ringing loudly, but . . .

Had we won? That quickly? The plan hadn't just worked out; it had gone better than expected.

I shouldn't have been surprised, since it was one of Ryan's plans. But I was uncertain. Should we retreat, or should we press into the city and give him support? Only two people armed with modern weapons had arrived, and I'd managed to neutralize them both. Were there others?

Ealstan was running my direction. Maybe he'd have a suggestion. At the same time, Sefawynn emerged from the alleyway Quinn had come down.

"Runian!" she said, grabbing my arm. "Something's wrong."

"What?" I asked.

"I followed the soldiers running away from the courtyard," she said, her face grim. "They are gathering on the oceanside walls. It's the—"

Ealstan reached us at that moment, panting.

"Hordamen," he said. "They're here."

33

We scrambled up the ladder to reach the wooden path built alongside the top of the city wall, towing Quinn along. We had just enough height to see *hundreds* of ships full of Hordamen gliding out of the fog.

Hundreds.

It took my stunned mind way too long to accept that. They littered the water like debris on the beach after a storm. The first ships had already reached the city, letting out a stream of warriors with axes, shields, and utilitarian helms. Many also had chain shirts or leathers. Damn.

Something flipped in my brain. These weren't the thoughtless barbarians I'd imagined from pop culture stories. They didn't run forward screaming. They formed *ranks*. This was a disciplined, well-maintained, hostile fighting force with a serious technological edge granted by their sailing ships. Fortunately, the docks were beyond the wall, and the gates were closed to—

A blast and a spear of lightning broke the sky. The thunderclap that followed felt like it would lay me flat. I blinked, gaping.

So much for the gates.

"Woden is with them," Sefawynn whispered. "And there are so many . . ."

"Aelv Quinn," Ealstan said, turning to him. I still had my gun pointed his direction, despite the lightning strike. "We must persuade Ulric to put aside our conflict and unite against this greater threat!"

Quinn blinked. "Is he for real?"

"Best I can tell," I said.

"Yeah, whatever," Quinn said. "Johnny, put that gun away. You're not going to shoot me."

I hesitated.

"That's a *hell* of a lotta Vikings, Johnny," he muttered. "*You* can't stop them. Nanites and platings can only do so much. We'll have to bring the rest of the gang through."

"How, though?" I asked.

"Ryan's here, right?" he said. "He'll have brought the beacon. With that, we can get reinforcements."

Wait.

What?

"Johnny, focus!" Quinn said. "Let me go or let the city burn!"

I wanted to argue, but man, the number of Hordamen out there was still breaking my brain. I was in the middle of a full-on war. I lowered the gun.

Quinn ran off. I might have made a mistake, but . . . What had he said? About the beacon?

Ryan was wrong, I realized. *Ulric doesn't have a second beacon. He needs one, though, to get people to this dimension. So he . . .*

The pieces clicked into place. *That* was why Ulric had gone to Stenford to investigate my arrival himself. That was why Quinn had been so excited to take information about Ryan to Ulric. Their only way out of here was *Ryan's beacon.*

Ryan was in danger.

We were *all* in danger. Hell, Sefawynn's entire nation was on the brink of collapse. This was an all-out invasion; those Hordamen would leave the landscape burned and despoiled.

"Ulric will not be able to stop them," Sefawynn whispered. "Woden *brought* the Hordamen here. He's doing this intentionally."

I glanced toward the sky, noting dark thunderheads, crackling with lightning, rolling in supernaturally fast. I wasn't going to second-guess the expert. This was a god's doing.

"Why? Why would he do this?" Sefawynn continued softly. "Why side against us in our own lands? Are we not diligent enough?"

"Woden doesn't reward diligence," Ealstan said. "He never has. He rewards blood offerings, carnage, and conquest."

She squeezed her eyes shut.

"I don't trust Ulric or Quinn," I said to the two of them. "If we're going to stop this, we need the joint efforts of Seattle's finest. Uh, a group of soldiers, from my homeland."

"That would break us," a voice whispered in my ear. "An invasion of a different kind . . ."

Dammit! I didn't have any better answers. "Let's go find Ryan," I said.

Sefawynn still stood with her eyes closed, and Ealstan seemed contemplative. I frowned at him. "What?"

"It might require blood to turn Woden's favor," he explained. "If I die as a sacrifice, it might persuade him. I am no earl, but I am the highest-born blood we have. If my heart's blood is spilled . . . it might help."

I looked to him, finding the words extreme at best—ridiculous at worst. He couldn't *actually* be advocating for something insane, like Wealdsig had done?

No, he was suggesting something worse. In Ealstan's eyes, I found pain. A man pressed up against the wall, desperate. Aging, repeatedly broken. Yes, he'd try something desperate, because he'd given his blood every day for his people.

Now, squeezed dry, his life was the last thing he had to give. He'd try it, because he had no other options.

Or so he thought. "Come with me instead," I said. "We'll find another way. Please. Trust me."

"Runian," he said, "I owe you my life, and the lives of those in Stenford. I will follow you to hell itself if you ask, my friend."

Damn. The earnest way he said it . . . My cynicism tried to find his words sappy or melodramatic, but it got gobbled up and spit back out as gratitude. "Thank you," I said.

"I'm going to the runestone," Sefawynn said, pointing to a jagged chunk of black stone, larger than the others we'd seen, in the near distance.

It wasn't glowing at all.

"The city defenses might stand stronger with my boasts," Sefawynn said. "The wights might help . . ."

I shared a look with Ealstan, who shook his head. He didn't believe that, but neither did he speak up. Ryan's soldiers had already joined the defenses. To them, standing with other Anglo-Saxons—even enemies—was the obvious choice.

I needed to get to Ryan, maybe find a way to get some real weapons here. Except . . . What good would it do to save this land from the Hordamen, only to hand it to people from my world? Ryan wouldn't let this place go, any more than Ulric would.

Two terrible choices. They squeezed the breath out of me as they crushed inward.

But I had to do *something*. "Anyone seen Thokk?" I asked.

The other two glanced knowingly at one another.

"Oh, stop that," I said. "She told me you think she's a witch. She's just been acting up to convince you. I can't figure out what's up with her, but your fear is unfounded."

"As you say, Runian," Ealstan said. "But if we are going to help, we should move quickly. The Hordamen came to pillage. When they're finished, those left dead will be the lucky ones."

We scrambled down the ladder and ran for Ulric's compound. I led the way, using the screenshotted map on my visual overlay. The streets felt hollow, the people all having moved to the defense. I could hear shouts from farther on. Along with the snapping sound of weapons against shields. I didn't know how many soldiers the city had, but the Hordamen would have an incredible upper hand even if every single home were filled with them.

It didn't take long for us to reach the meeting hall Ulric had turned into his operations headquarters. It was a thick, tall structure near the middle of town, not far from the runestone. Sefawynn broke off, running for the center square.

Ealstan and I crouched against the wall of Ulric's base. The windows were all shuttered and locked tight, but I was ready for that. I left a berry on top of one, then had Ealstan look the other direction.

"Really," the voice whispered in my ear. "One berry?"

"You want me to stop Ulric or not?" I hissed back.

"It's the principle as much as anything else." The locks clicked behind us. "Done. Be careful."

I eased open the shutter a crack and peeked into the building. Electric lights—strangely garish to my eyes—illuminated an open room with metal walls reinforcing the wood. The electronic locks on the windows had not been able to stand up to the power of a wight.

Ulric was there with a tied-up Ryan. My earlier suspicions were confirmed—they'd *lured* him here. Ulric grinned and proudly held up the beacon. The room flashed, and three people materialized out of nowhere. Two were outfitted in full-on modern armor with tinted helmets, assault rifles in hand. The third was an unarmored woman with a large backpack. Marta, I thought her name was. Ulric's on-staff dimensional expert.

"Seems like you've been having some trouble, boss," she said to Ulric, unstrapping her large backpack. Probably full of dimensional teleportation equipment. "We came as soon as the beacon came back online. What's up with the portal?"

"Sabotage. Get it set up again," Ulric said. "This dimension is going to be very useful to us, but for now, I'm tired of its stench."

The timeline fell into place. Ulric had come to this dimension a month or two ago to investigate using its probability-altering nature for his gain. He'd set up his base in Maelport. Ryan had been investigating him, though, and had snuck in with an emergency beacon to get himself out. He'd managed to sabotage Ulric's equipment a week ago, leaving Ulric stranded.

But if that were the case, why hadn't Ryan been able to get out? Had Ulric known his enemy would have his own beacon, and jammed it somehow?

No. That's doesn't make sense. But wait. I wonder where Ryan got *that beacon . . .*

Either way, Ulric had anticipated that Ryan would sneak back to finish the sabotage. So Ulric had waited, then grabbed him—and in so doing, won the very thing he needed to escape. Ryan had carried it right to him.

Hot damn, I thought. *He's* not *perfect, is he?*

Ryan Chu, superstar detective, had failed. I squinted at him, sitting slumped on the dimmer side of the room, next to . . . someone else? That must be Ryan's inside man. The one who had let him in the back door and supposedly been in place to help him against Ulric.

It was a woman. I dialed in my visuals, zooming in on her face as she looked up.

It was Jen.

34

Jen was *alive*?

Maybe this was some strange alternate-dimension version of her or something . . .

I slumped down, breathing deeply. I wasn't ready to see her face again. Ealstan took my arm, looking concerned. He didn't dare speak, for fear of warning those inside.

Indeed, it was easy to hear the door slam as someone entered. "Boss!" Quinn said. "We have a *huge* problem. Vikings. Like, a *lot* of Vikings."

"Now?" Ulric said.

"Yeah," Quinn said. "They're straight-up attacking the city. Lightning blew up the gates. It's a full-on invasion."

"Bother," Ulric said. "How long until the portal is ready, Marta?"

"Five or ten minutes," she said.

"Get it done in closer to five unless you want to end up on the wrong end of a Viking's sword," he said, tucking the beacon into his pocket. "Can we send for more soldiers?"

"Not until I get this running," she said. "Information can't be sent via beacons. It's complicated. We had the emergency team ready to come today as scheduled, but—"

"Stop explaining," he said, "and *work*. Quinn, you two, with me."

Then, remarkably, he left. A quick glance showed me Marta working on a circular device—maybe three feet across—she'd set up on the ground. It was just her, Ryan, and . . . and Jen.

I had to know what was going on. I nodded to Ealstan, then the two of us rounded the side of the building, where I had my wight unlock the door. We burst in a second later.

Marta looked up immediately, then relaxed. "Johnny?" she said. "Didn't know you were on this job. Can you hand me that box peeking out of the backpack?"

I glanced at Ealstan, who had his weapon out, seeming confused. "Uh . . . sure." I grabbed the box and handed it to her, then gestured to Ryan and Jen. "Boss wants me to deal with these two."

"Please do it outside," Marta said. "You know how I feel about that nastiness."

"Yeah, of course," I said, walking over to Ryan and Jen. Ealstan cut their ropes, and I made a show of gesturing with my gun for them to walk outside.

"You are friends with many, Runian," Ealstan whispered as we slipped out. "Their affection for you serves you well."

"They don't like me," I said.

"I believe that untrue," he said. "Judging by how few seem afraid of you."

Nah. They all just thought I was harmless. As soon as we closed the doors, Ryan turned toward me and let out a deep breath of relief. "Thanks, Johnny," he said. "They were ready for us, somehow."

"Ulric needed your beacon," I said. "He set this up."

"Impossible," Ryan said. "My beacon didn't work for me. He couldn't have planned for this. He would have assumed I'd send for backup, not come in here alone."

"About that," I said. "Where did you get that beacon, Ryan?"

"Rembrandt," he said. "Quartermaster at the precinct armory."

I groaned. "Ryan, Rembrandt is crooked."

"*What?*"

"He's been working for Ulric for years now," I said.

"Why didn't you say anything?"

"How was I supposed to know that's where you got your tech?" I demanded. "He gave you a locked beacon, probably on Ulric's orders. It didn't work because it was coded to ignore your commands . . ."

I trailed off as I realized other things were far more important. Namely, the woman standing next to Ryan, looking *extremely* embarrassed.

"Uh, hey, Johnny," she said.

Hell. It *was* her.

"Ryan," I said, "you'd better explain this bullshit."

"Oh, uh," he said. "Ulric needed a medievalist, you know? To investigate his dimensions. And Jen had always wanted to visit a place like this. About six months ago, we had her contact him and infiltrate his organization."

"She had her accident six months ago," I said flatly.

She took Ryan's arm for support.

The look in her eyes. In his eyes.

Oh, hell.

"How long?" I asked. "How long were you two cheating on me?"

"From the second week," Jen admitted, looking away.

Our *entire* relationship?

"Why?" I said. "Why would you do that? Why would you say yes to me, if you were going to be with him in secret?"

"You're so sweet," Jen said. "I wanted to see how it worked out."

"I'm not sweet! I'm *literally* a gangster!"

"Look," Ryan said, "perhaps this isn't the best time for—"

"You faked your death," I said, realizing.

"Not exactly," she said. "I was planning to spend several years under cover. I told everyone I was going away. And then Grandma told you I was dead when you texted her. You know how much she hates you . . . It was awkward, but I realized it was easier this way."

"Easier for who?" I demanded. "You could have just broken up with me!"

"I didn't want to hurt your feelings," she said.

"You didn't want to hurt my feelings, so you let me think *you were dead*?"

"Johnny," Ryan said, voice firm, "we needed your connection to Ulric, and the things you might tell Jen."

"I was just the door guard!" I said, waving toward the sky with my gun. "She knew more than I did!"

"Code 1929193," Ryan said. "Reassign back to me."

"Reassigned to Ryan Chu's nanite signature," the gun said. "Currently in hands that cannot operate."

"Oh, *come on*," I said.

"Sorry, Johnny," he said. "Ulric took my rifle. And you're acting a *tad* erratic."

"You think I don't have a reason?" I asked. I glanced at Ealstan, who was standing beside me, face scrunched up, trying to figure this all out.

"I had to take the opportunity, Johnny," Jen told me. "You know how much I wanted to travel to medieval dimensions. Plus, I got to be a double agent. Don't be mad. Please?"

"Oh, well, since you asked nicely," I said, throwing my hands into the air again.

"The gun, Johnny?" Ryan asked.

I tossed it at him. He grabbed it, then slipped back into the bunker, probably to secure the portal.

Jen awkwardly stood there. "Sorry," she finally said. "Johnny . . . you just were always so *intriguing*, you know? Ever since high school."

"We were bad for each other," I said to her. "Always fighting."

"Yeah," she said, then glanced to the side. "But it was never boring. Ryan's great, but . . . You know. He doesn't even butter his toast. Too unhealthy." She smiled at me.

That smile had always worked before. Today . . . nothing. Except some residual anger.

Huh.

The door to the bunker opened a moment later. Marta now sat, bound on the floor—and blue light hovered over the top of the portal.

"Let's go," Ryan said, waving us in. "Jen's compromised. I've set the portal to take us to the PD headquarters to report in."

"You'd leave Ulric here," I said, incredulous.

"What?" Ryan said. "You want to try to stop him on your own? Don't be stupid, Johnny. You're *you*. Besides, didn't you hear? Viking invasion, happening right now. We'll come back later to bring him to justice—if he survives."

The sounds of battle grew louder in the distance.

"Let's move," Ryan said.

Jen immediately hopped into the blue light, vanishing. Ryan grabbed Marta and shoved her through, then paused as I walked up.

"Hey," he said to me, "nice work here today. I'm sure I can get you off, if you're finally willing to testify. You'll do that for me, won't you, bud?"

"Sure. Bud."

He grinned and hopped through the portal.

I flipped the power switch. Ealstan stood behind me like a confused mountain, arms folded, a frown on his bearded face.

"Once again," he said, gesturing to the portal, "those are your *friends*?"

"I thought they were," I said. "I didn't have a good frame of reference, I guess."

"The stories of aelvs may have been exaggerated," Ealstan said. "I think, perhaps, they are not much smarter or better than the rest of us."

"Wise words," I said.

"What do we do?" he asked. "About the Hordamen?"

"I don't know. Ulric still has the beacon—the device that can lead outsiders to this place. Whatever else happens, we need to grab that. Maybe destroy it."

"As you say."

We left, intent on tracking down Ulric. But we stopped just outside the front doors. Hordamen were pouring through the streets to our left, entering the city square, chasing down beleaguered Anglo-Saxon soldiers.

A woman stood in the center of the square. Alone. Unarmed. Between the flood of Hordamen and the city proper.

Sefawynn.

35

She was radiant in the sunlight streaming through a break in the clouds. But damn me, she was going to get *slaughtered*.

And I'd let Ryan take the gun. Hell!

I started forward. My platings could deflect a few axes. I could get her out of the city. I had to—

A hand caught my elbow. Soft, yet unyielding.

"Wait," Thokk said. "Give her a moment."

Ealstan immediately bowed his head to Thokk.

"Where did you come from?" I demanded of her. "This place is dangerous, Thokk! You should run!"

"Oh, *thunders*, you're dense," she muttered. "Give your girl some time, Runian. She might impress us. It's been building in her for long enough . . ."

"Honored One," Ealstan said to her. "Woden is here, serving our *enemies*."

"Yes," Thokk said. "Earlier, you said he only cared about sacrifice and blood. You are wrong. My brother cares only about who is *winning*. He always wants to be on the side that is going to be victorious.

"No amount of blood or sacrifice could have sated him, Ealstan. Woden is frightened. Of the pain these outsiders bring. Of losing control. He *needs* this city to burn, these people to die, so he can pretend it's his punishment for disobedience."

"But we haven't disobeyed, Honored One."

"Not yet," she said.

My brain was chugging along. "Wait. Your *brother*?"

Out in the square, Sefawynn shouted a boast.

> "Of measured meter   I made mastery:
>
> Wove words of Woden   and woke the warriors.

"I . . . I . . ."

She stopped, slumping against the runestone as more Hordamen flooded the square. Though they didn't care about her boast, they gave her some space—attacking a skop seemed to be taboo. Other Hordamen began breaking down doors to nearby homes, and the sounds of panicked women and children rose in the air.

Above it all, I somehow heard Sefawynn.

"Why?" she asked, turning her eyes to the sky. "*Why*? I taught of you. I told your stories and your songs. Why must you have our *blood*?"

"We have to stop this," I said, looking to Ealstan. "We have to . . ."

Do what? I couldn't fight an army.

"Watch," Thokk whispered. "Here, let me improve your sight."

At first, nothing changed. But . . . what were those patches of darkness at the corners of my eyes? I could see the wights, like in the forest—only here, they hid in the shadows of homes. Beneath the eaves of roofs. Hugging close to the buildings.

"They are the protectors of these homes," Thokk said softly, her voice changing, adopting an air of rustling leaves, of blowing wind. Of a forest at night, full of creeping things. "They know Woden is betraying the people of this land. But they are frightened. They need inspiration . . ."

I looked back at the courtyard. Several Hordamen stalked toward Sefawynn, swords out, regardless of the taboo. The sounds of war—no, of a massacre—bombarded me, rattling my soul. Sefawynn bowed her head as the Hordamen loomed. I pulled free of Thokk's grip and dashed into the square, ready to . . .

Sefawynn thrust her hand toward the sky. "I defy you!" she screamed. "Woden! Hear me! I *hate* you! I've always hated you!"

Something changed.

The nearby shadows turned toward her. Their eyes burst alight, pinpricks of white in the otherwise dark, shifting sense of their nebulous forms. Behind Sefawynn, the runestone started to glow.

"I defy you!
I cannot cower   for consequence cost!
I defy you!
I reject in rage   royalty rotten!
I defy you!
I live not for lies   from lame leaders lost!
I defy you!
I will not worship   a worm named Woden!"

Lightning split the sky. Thunder pounded me, making me stop. Around the square, shadows rose up. The city's wights *listened*. When the lead Hordaman raised his sword to strike Sefawynn, a blackness slithered up his legs and wound around his arm in a burst of incredible speed.

His sword fell apart in his fingers. The blade separated from the hilt, and the cross guard fell into three separate pieces.

Sefawynn turned wild eyes, like the heart of a bonfire, upon him. The dark thing slithered inside him. As I'd seen locks disassembled, shoes unwoven, I now saw his *body* unraveled. Bones unhooked, hair fell free, skin disconnected from the layers beneath.

He fell like a bundle of rags, leaking blood and fat out the eye holes. The tide turned in moments. All around the square, weapons failed. Axes left their heads embedded in wood. Armor fell apart, links dropping to the dirt like a sudden rainstorm. Beleaguered Anglo-Saxons found their opponents disarmed—and in some cases, disrobed.

Above it all, Sefawynn shouted her anger toward the heavens.

"*I. Defy. YOU!*"

"Told you," Thokk said, suddenly at my side again.

"What's happening?" I said. "How . . . ?"

"Like I said," she replied, "the wights needed inspiration. They wanted to follow someone who didn't fear him. They needed a strong boast to encourage them."

"*You* were my wight," I said to her. "All along."

"I was the thing you ordered around with a few measly berries," she said. "I *guess* I'll forgive it as ignorance. The trouble you make is novel, Runian. It's been fun." She glanced toward the crackling sky. "But I'm not a wight, and never have been. Surprised you never realized it. I gave enough clues . . ."

Hordamen began screaming and retreating back toward the ocean. But that boiling sky . . .

"He's angry," I said.

"Woden hates losing," Thokk said. "I'll deal with my brother, though. You still need to do your job."

"My job?"

"The poison of your place seeps in here," she said. "If it overwhelms the city, the wights will die. The wyrd will stop functioning. And then . . ."

"The Hordamen win," I whispered.

"I can't touch the machines," she said. "It was painful enough to break that little one you made me take apart in Wellbury. I couldn't reform a body until the next day.

"Outlanders have been here in Maelport for too long. The stink of them brings us all pain . . ." She took a deep breath. "It makes me thin, Runian. Like a plank sanded until you can see light coming through from the other side. I can't stop Ulric. I've tried. My very essence breaks apart near him."

"I'll do it."

"Will you?" she asked, searching my eyes. "Can you?"

"Yes," I said. "I promise."

The old woman—who probably was much more of the "old" and much less of the "woman" than I'd assumed—smiled at me. "Stop wasting time! Go! Scoot! Don't make me regret picking your side. Seriously, I could be getting drunk and castrating giants right now."

I gave her a salute—it felt right—and dashed back past Ealstan, who fell into step with me.

"Did you know?" I demanded of him. "What she was?"

"The goddess Logna?" he asked. "Mother of monsters? Harbinger of the end of the time of gods? Of course. You didn't?"

These people.

At least I had an idea of what to do next. "Remember that round thing on the floor that glowed blue?" I said to Ealstan. "I need to smash it."

I'd need to get ahold of Ulric's beacon to truly cut off access, but a broken portal would slow things down. I'd turned it off, thinking I might need it later, but now I just wanted it in pieces.

We stopped at the door into the bunker. "Make sure nobody enters," I said.

"I will guard this door with my life," he promised.

I slipped back in, and felt like I was stepping forward in time—out of a land of dirt and thatch into a land of steel and electricity. I locked the door, then turned toward the machine. A few punches with my plated fists should render the portal inoperable.

Unfortunately, I wasn't alone. Quinn knelt by the device. He stood and spun toward me. "Johnny," he said. "What did you do to this thing? The coordinates have been altered."

"Step through, Quinn," I said, advancing on him. "Get out of here. The whole city is about to be overrun."

"That's not a problem," he said. "Boss plans to talk to these Vikings. We'll let them have the city, impress them with some future powers, and set up with *them* instead. They're a tougher group—good to have on our side as we conquer this world."

"Go home to Tacy and the kids. Forget about this dimension; pretend it never existed."

He sighed. He stretched one shoulder, then the other. "I told the boss you were in the city," he said. "He sent me back to check on the machine. I see you let Ryan free. Sent him home, I assume?"

I stopped a few feet from Quinn. Ryan would be gathering cops on the other side, but he wouldn't come rushing back to help. He was too careful for that.

And even if he were coming back, I didn't want him to. Not if it would hurt the people here.

"I'm going to destroy the portal, Quinn," I said. "Last chance for you to head home."

"Sorry, Johnny," he said, then put up his fists. "This isn't personal."

"You actually believe that?" I asked.

"Nah," he said. "Every fight is personal. That's just something a fellow says, you know?"

I nodded.

And Quinn came in swinging.

36

Augmented boxing matches are normally about extreme endurance. We hit harder, dodge faster, and can take more punishment than regular boxers. We don't slow, don't get dazed. We don't *break* like regular people do. We don't need gloves, or mouthguards, or rules about where you can get hit. The league had two simple rules: no grappling, no unapproved weapons.

Bouts ended spectacularly, when one of our systems would break, and pain would seep in. A few hits later—full-on system arrest. The result wasn't pretty.

Unfortunately, this wouldn't be a normal fight. I was vulnerable, like I'd been for our last bout. Hell. I was far worse off now, if I was honest. I'd let myself go over the years. Guarding a door and constantly being told you're useless will do that to you.

Still, it felt natural—even comfortable—to put my hands up in the traditional guard position. There had been good days in the ring.

335

The best days. Even if I'd been pretending then, the way I'd pretended when I first entered this dimension.

Quinn came in light and tried three quick jabs. A leftover from the original days of boxing, where a hit like that might do something. These days, it was to pick up the rhythm of the fight. Quick engagements to test your opponent's reflexes.

I pushed his jabs aside and danced back, going onto my toes, falling into the familiar forms. How many times had I imagined a rematch? How often had I *dreamed* of it? Yearned for proof that *I* should have been the one Ulric let win—the one who should have become his right-hand man.

I'd had multiple chances to demand it. But I'd always turned away. Now this fight had been forced upon me, and for higher stakes than I'd ever imagined.

I'd assumed an eventual rematch would be a way to take back my dignity. Turns out, nobody can take that from you. You've got to throw it away.

After the initial clash, and a few moments of circling—each trying to feint or fake the other—Quinn came in with a few real swings. I was quick enough to duck under them, but he immediately followed up with a knee to my chest. Without my platings, I was forced to do a pretty awkward block with my arms.

Plate against plate. A *crunching* sound, unexpected to those who preferred traditional matches.

I grunted, backing away as my system gave me a few warnings. I'd be fine, for now. But a match like this was about endurance. Plating would only prevent damage until your nanites couldn't keep up with the hits.

I took a few hits along my arms—which I'd pulled in tight to protect my ribs. The platings along my back should be enough to protect my sides, something I was forced to test out as I took a few solid strikes there.

During the barrage, I also took one jab to the face. His strength augments, like mine, were minimal. One hit to the face wasn't enough to break my skull, but *hell*. I was *not* going to last long in this fight.

For now, I was forced onto the defensive, dodging, blocking, backing away using methods that would have gotten me booed in the ring.

"You're vulnerable, Johnny," Quinn said. "Still no plating on your chest or head?"

"Never managed to guess the password," I said with a grunt, putting the portal machine between us. "Don't suppose you'd throw it my way to even up this fight?"

"Oh, Johnny," he said, rounding the machine, his eyes on me. "You think we saved that code?"

"What?"

"Boss just hit a bunch of random numbers," Quinn said with a shrug. "Why would he care to remember what he'd typed? It made him laugh to think of you trying different combinations all these years, though."

As soon as Quinn said it, I knew it was true. Why would Ulric bother remembering the password? When you cut off a man's hand, you didn't keep it around to be sewn back on.

The weight of this final realization almost dropped me, right there. Because I *knew*.

I was never getting my platings back. I'd been hoping for something impossible.

Quinn came for me again, and *damn*—he was fast. I parried the blows, until one hit a little too far forward on my side. I grunted, taking most of the blow in my chest. A rib cracked, and the memories flooded in. Taking the fall. Being broken. Bloodied.

Quinn pressed the attack, but I shouted and got in my first good blow—a solid kick to his side. That earned a grunt. Problem was, with all the extra augments, every hit you landed did some damage to you too. It was best to connect with sensitive areas—which the system would have to work harder to protect and repair—but still, every blow weakened you.

Quinn advanced, controlling the fight. I tried to stop that with another kick, but he shoved me to the side, and I went down. A rain of shots at my face followed, which I blocked, letting him hit me in the chest again. My nanites were going crazy, and I'd certainly taken some real damage from that hit. Fortunately, my instincts kicked in. I rolled to the side and hurled myself to my feet, blocking his kick to my head with my forearm.

I stumbled away, warnings on my visual overlay telling me I was risking damage to my internal organs. I managed to put my hands back up to guard, keeping my distance.

I'd always been a close-quarters power boxer. I favored heavy-duty hits to the body in succession over jabs to the face or kicks, though I could do both if needed. But I was slow. I'd always been slow. I—

Something slammed against the door outside. We paused, glancing over as the reinforced structure shook. I heard shouts outside. Ealstan.

"Boss must be back," Quinn said, staying on his toes. "He has Marshal and Byungho. Give up. If they walk in here and see us fighting, they *will* shoot you."

I attacked. Maybe if I could land a few solid body shots, I could win. I did connect once, but took a blow to the face in return. My readout told me that my nose broke on that one. My weakened nanite system was in a full panic, judging by the error messages.

The door kept rattling. I advanced, striking again—but Quinn dodged, which threw me off. I reoriented, but not before he body-checked me against the wall. That left me without room to maneuver as he backed up one step, then came in swinging, forcing me to block. I wasn't finished yet—my nanites were rerouting my blood vessels and generally keeping me going. But since I'd taken so much damage to sensitive areas, they were overwhelmed. My platings were losing the energy that let them redirect force.

The skin of my arms split, and blood seeped through my shirt. I stumbled away from the wall.

Damn. So this was how the rematch went.

What was I doing here? I couldn't beat Quinn. I'd never been able to beat Quinn. I'd failed before; I'd failed today. Because that's what I did. So much for all those dreams. *Washed-up boxer barely gives an effort,* I thought. *One-star performance. At least he bleeds well.*

I dodged. Ryan could clean up this mess. Could I get through the portal, grab Ryan and reinforcements, then come back? I gave a good showing with my next few feints, but I was really looking for a way to run away.

Again.

Embarrassed by my art, I'd cut my losses and run. Overwhelmed by my classes in the police academy—and tired of the mockery from the other cadets—I looked for loopholes that let me get kicked out.

Then, the league. I'd imagined a long run, a title bout, and a successful retirement. I'd ended up with a forced fall and a laughingstock of a life. And it was my fault. When Ulric had told me to fall, I'd obeyed. Because even then, I'd wanted a way out, worried that I'd start losing anyway.

Always looking for an out. That was Johnny.

I glanced at the portal machine.

And thought of Ealstan, who'd been ready to race home, knowing he'd die fighting Vikings in an attempt to save his family and people. I thought of Sefawynn, standing before the enemy horde, screaming her defiance to a vengeful god. I thought of their lives, full of impossible fights.

And I thought . . .

My life had been worthless. But . . . maybe my death could be worth something.

I gritted my teeth, then spun and dashed to the portal machine. As Quinn cursed at me, I slammed my fist into the control panel, cracking it in half, mangling the buttons. I got one more hit in before Quinn tackled me.

We rolled, and he came up above me. I got my arms over my face as he started pummeling me. He mostly struck my arms, but that didn't matter much at this point. The nanites—now too busy just trying to keep me alive—stopped preventing the pain.

Agony washed across my body.

Just before I was finished, Quinn paused and glanced toward the door. I blinked, dismissing the current crop of error messages, groaning softly. My arms throbbed, my broken nose was bitingly painful, and every breath was spiked with agony. Through the pain, I managed to make out Ulric—built like a wall with a face—standing in the doorway. Behind him, Marshal knelt over Ealstan's bloodied body. I felt a little stab of pride that Ealstan had managed to stand for so long against augmented soldiers.

Ulric closed the door, then frowned, looking at the dimensional portal.

"What's this?" Ulric said.

"Sorry, boss," Quinn said. He got to his feet but kept an eye on me. "He got a swing in on the control panel. I . . ."

"No matter," Ulric said. "Another rescue team will come."

Right. He still had the beacon. As long as it was active with Ulric's code, his teams could get here—but Ryan's couldn't. My fight had been meaningless. I'd failed again.

"Something is wrong outside, Quinn," Ulric said. "The Vikings have been pushed *back*, somehow. They're regrouping on the docks, and some insane woman is running around writing runes on the doors."

"I thought they didn't write," Quinn said.

"So did I," Ulric said.

No. Breaking the machine hadn't been meaningless.

None of this was meaningless.

For once, it meant everything.

I crawled to my feet and put my fists up. "Hey Quinn," I said, tasting blood. "Ready when you are."

Quinn hesitated, then glanced at the holster on Ulric's hip. The boss folded his arms.

"Go ahead," Ulric said. He'd always enjoyed a good boxing match.

Quinn sighed. "Don't make me do this to you again, Johnny," he said softly as he approached. "You let me go earlier. Lie down, take the fall."

Then he lurched at me and swung. I managed to block, so he tried again, a little reckless. I slammed my fist into his stomach, earning an *oof* and a widening of his eyes.

He danced back, frowning.

"You know something, Quinn?" I said, spitting blood to the side. "A friend of mine, she said . . . said I didn't really throw that fight. Because I didn't have a choice. I *did*, because I agreed. Still, it has me wondering . . ."

Quinn growled, more careful on his next attack. Our exchange let me get a knee into his chest—but it also let him hit me in the side a few more times. Each one caused a flash of pain that shook my vision. I was at the edge of what my body could take.

But the thing was, for the first time, I had *no way out*.

"Makes me wonder," I hissed, shoving him back. "Why did you two take my platings away, when I'd agreed to the fall? You said you wanted extra blood, to make it extra real. But that risked making it look less real. Too much blood. Too much injury."

He came in, and I started *pounding* on him, one fist, then the other, back and forth into his sides. I took a few blows. Alarms went off.

No running, I thought.

I shoved him back against the wall and kept hitting.

No escape.

He broke away, but not before I landed another kick on his side. He was probably seeing some of his own warnings by now. Low system power. Low nanite density. Soon, they'd have to start letting the pain through too.

"Come on, Quinn," Ulric said. "It's only *Johnny*."

"Only Johnny," I said, meeting Ulric's eyes. "You wanted me to break, didn't you? When you demanded I take the fall? I was doing *well*. For once in my life, I was succeeding. So you had to break me."

Ulric didn't disagree. Quinn forced himself forward again, and we danced, trading jabs and half-blocked kicks. I saw something in

Quinn. Those wide eyes, those jerky movements, those increasingly desperate attacks.

Was that . . . fear?

I remembered what he'd said earlier. *If the others find out I got caught by you . . .*

As I landed another blow, I saw him flinch. He was feeling the pain now.

Ulric clicked his tongue in disapproval as he inspected the mangled portal controls. Quinn threw a wild punch. I dodged to the side, then came in and hit him right in the kidneys—the force of my blow going straight through his platings.

He danced back with a grunted curse. I was on my last legs, though I was trying not to show it. Exhausted, in agony, bleeding from multiple cuts across my arms, I needed an edge.

Hey . . .

Boxing wasn't the only thing I'd ever been good at.

What if . . .

"Ulric," I said as Quinn and I rounded one another. "Quinn told me you hit a bunch of random keys for the passcode for my platings. Something you immediately forgot. Is that true?"

"Yes," Ulric said, barely watching the two of us. "You were washed up, Johnny. I couldn't remember that code if I wanted."

"Yeah, but there's a thing about this dimension," I said, calling up the password entry screen for my platings. "Something about probability. And numbers. And statistics."

Quinn hesitated. Even Ulric turned toward me again, curious.

"What are the chances," I said, "that I'll get the same code you put in if I hit a bunch of numbers in here? Think I'll unlock my powers again?"

343

Both were silent. I hit a string of numbers.

Password denied, the overlay said. But they couldn't see that.

I stood up straighter. I shook my hands, then grinned wickedly as I fell into an aggressive boxing stance.

"Now look at that," I said softly, with as much malice as I could summon. "Look at *that*."

I was a failed artist, a pitiful excuse for a cop, and a passable boxer.

But I was a *great* liar.

Quinn went on the defensive, believing I'd just been renewed.

A little pebble starts an avalanche.

I got my hands around his head, then kneed him right in the face. He stumbled back, and started bleeding. The nanites were no longer preventing incidental blood flow.

You lose a little—and that makes you wonder if you deserve to lose.

I swung again and again. I remembered the gang's forced laughter as Ulric mocked me.

So you lose some more.

Quinn hit the wall, and I got him in the stomach, dropping him. I remembered him on that day when I'd dropped. In that memory of his face, I saw something I'd missed in my own agony.

Relief. He'd been worried that he'd lose, even with my augments disabled. Even though I'd agreed to throw the bout.

He'd known, all those years ago, that I'd been the better boxer.

And it all compounds.

My body knew what to do next. I bashed his face again and again.

You're behind, no matter how you scramble to stop it.

I froze as he whimpered, beaten, broken on the floor.

You're too far gone.

I looked at him, then over at Ulric, who flipped something on the base of the portal. The blue light activated. "Manual override," he noted, taking out the beacon and hooking it to a bit on the side of the machine. He dusted his hands off before glancing at us. "Ah, Quinn. You're such a disappointment."

That's what he'd always said to me.

Hell. How had I never seen? Humiliating me hadn't been about punishing me specifically. It had been about holding on to his power. Ulric had knocked me down at my prime to remind the others what he could do to us.

Work this, I thought. *Fix it.* Ealstan had died for this. I couldn't let that mean nothing.

It all came down to me. Following through.

"I *told* you I could beat him," I said, grabbing Quinn by the front of his shirt. "I *told* you I should have been the one to win that bout! *He* should have taken the fall."

Ulric studied me for a moment. He wasn't stupid. But he also thought he understood me. Thought he knew who I was.

He was working from outdated information.

"I suppose I should have let you prove it, Johnny."

I dragged Quinn past Ulric, who stepped back, wisely not trusting me. But he also didn't shoot me.

"I think you might have a new door guard," I said.

Ulric snorted, then I pulled Quinn close. "Give my best to Tacy," I whispered to him. "You did right by me, Quinn. When you get out of prison, do me a favor. Start a new life. You're worth the effort."

He looked at me through bloodstained eyes as I winked at him, then tossed him through the portal. That would deposit him right in the police station. If something was dangerously wrong with his system, they'd save him.

Ulric *really* shouldn't have let me get close to the machine. I stamped my boot on the manual override switch, heard the thing crunch. The light went out as I snatched the beacon away.

Ulric shot me.

The round hit me right in the chest. Blood began spurting from my cuts as I collapsed to the ground, my nanites scrambling to keep me alive.

Ulric stepped up. "So, you lied. No plating on the chest, I see. Presumably not the head either." He pointed the weapon square at my forehead.

But . . . the beacon . . . was still in my fingers . . . I forced all available power to the augments in my hand.

"Johnny," he said. "Drop it."

"Sorry, Ulric," I whispered. "I've learned to fear someone else more than I do you."

He frowned. "Who?"

"The man . . . I used to be."

I squeezed, crushing the beacon.

A shot sounded.

Ulric gasped, a gaping hole in his chest.

The next shot vaporized his head. No nanites were going to keep him alive through that.

The headless corpse slumped to the side, and I looked past it to the now-open front door. Where Ealstan leaned against the frame, bloodied from what looked like a hundred cuts. He held a gun and a *severed arm*, the finger still curled around the trigger.

Two corpses in riot gear lay in the courtyard behind him.

What in the *ever-loving* hell?

"How?" I said. "How did you beat two fully armed and moderately plated modern soldiers!"

"They didn't have bows," Ealstan said, then sank down beside the doorframe, giving me a tired grin.

I couldn't help but return it.

THE WIZARD'S BURDEN

The following is an excerpt from *My Lives: An Autobiography of Cecil G. Bagsworth III, The First Interdimensional Wizard™*. (Frugal Wizard™ Press, 2102, $39.99. Signed editions available to Frugal Fans™ subscription club members.)

The life of a wizard is a strangely lonely one.

I don't write this to depress or discourage. Traveling the dimensions has been among the most thrilling experiences of my (exceptional by any definition) life. Ever since scientists identified the perimeter of the universe itself, we have been asking ourselves what lies beyond. Is there more than this bubble we live in?

Yes, there is more. Just as there is no end to human ingenuity, there is no end to reality itself. Wherever we go, there is another horizon.

Earth was only the beginning. You can explore, discover, travel to places no person (of our substance level) has ever traveled. The infinite highway lies before you.

But once you've traveled as I have, you may begin to feel a regretful sense of solitude. So many dimensions, full of countless people with no idea that anything exists outside their little villages. People with no *concept* of the *breadth* of reality. It feels quaint, seeing them in their little homes, with their little families, thinking that somehow that is the center of the universe.

You bear a burden. For you know.

Again, I do not speak of this to depress or discourage—but perhaps to warn. Prepare yourself for this feeling. The burden of knowledge shall come upon you, bringing with it this inevitable solitude.

You can have no equal. And so, you can know no peer.

You are a wizard.

37

A few hours later, I sat on the docks of Maelport, looking out over the ocean, the Hordamen's fleeing ships no longer visible on the horizon. A tired Sefawynn leaned against me, holding on to me as much as I held to her. My emergency system had patched me up enough to move, but I had a massive scab on my side, and my face . . .

"You're *sure* facial scars are fashionable here?" I asked.

"If you're not going to wear a beard, then yes," she said. "Scars will look nice."

I didn't tell her that my nanites would heal them eventually. Perhaps I could order them not to? There had to be a setting for that.

Except . . . I wasn't going to be here long enough, was I?

"I'm sorry about the aelv ring," she said, referring to the portal. Apparently, rings of mushrooms or rocks in the forest were said to lead to the world of the aelvs. She thought that's what the portal had been.

And why not? It had been close enough.

I'd have to find another way out. The damage I'd done to both the portal and the beacon was extensive. Maybe someone smarter could have repaired them, but not me. But first, I wanted to hold Sefawynn a little longer. She was so *warm*. I hadn't realized my nanites prevented me from feeling warmth from others. In regulating my system, the stupid things stole something basic about human connection.

"What you did back there was amazing," I whispered. "All of Weswara will be protected now. Because of you."

"Until Woden strikes me down."

"If he hasn't yet, he won't."

She didn't seem convinced, but a grin fought through her fatigue. She kissed me, and her breath on my face, her lips on mine—that felt warm too.

When we broke apart, she whispered, "I want to learn all of the writing you know. The words of your world. The words of all lands, all people."

I smiled, though it broke my heart to know what came next.

"You," I whispered, "are the most wonderful thing that has ever happened to me. Thank you for being amazing."

"Well, *you* have misled me," she said. "You're not the lowest of aelvs, are you, Runian?"

"No," I said. "No, I'm not."

And I believed it.

"In fact," I said, "I'm pretty incredible. Good with women, you know. It's always been one of my talents."

Her smile widened. "Oh, look," she said. "Normal clouds. How nice."

I took her by the chin, gently tipping her head back down to meet my eyes. Then I kissed her again.

"Not that I mind," a voice said behind us. "In fact, I enjoy watching. But you two *really* should be more respectful in my presence. It's traditional."

We spun to find Thokk—Logna—standing on the dock. Still in the form of a short old woman with a bundle of sticks on her back.

We scrambled to our feet. "Goddess," Sefawynn said—but didn't bow or show subservience. "How is Ealstan?"

"Still breathing," she said. "He will likely continue that way for a while. I haven't broken it to him yet that Ulric killed the earl. He'll take it hard."

"We'll need a new earl, then," Sefawynn said.

"Fortunately, you have a good candidate."

Sefawynn hesitated, and glanced at me. I slowly grinned.

"I meant Ealstan, you aers!" Logna said.

"Oh," Sefawynn said. "Of course."

"Yeah," I said. "Much better choice."

"You're both idiots," Logna said. "But I suppose you're my idiots."

"Pardon, Goddess," Sefawynn said, her chin still up. "But we are *our own* idiots."

Logna grunted. "Go check on Ealstan, child," she said to Sefawynn. "And get some food. I need to talk to the aelv."

Sefawynn looked at me.

"Go," I said. "With my love."

She grinned, kissed me, then walked up the steps to the city. A powerful glow shimmered in the center of town—the new runestone, inscribed with liquid-looking letters Sefawynn had carved.

I watched her until she vanished into the city. The docks had been mostly cleaned of blood. It was peaceful here, with the sun setting out in the west, the waters shivering softly over the sea.

"I know why Woden discarded this people," I said to Logna.

"Oh, so you've gotten smart all of a sudden?"

I nodded. "He wanted to use this city—this people—as an example. He's been doing it for years. Beating them down, so others who worship him would be afraid of what he might do to *them*."

Woden was basically Ulric with a priesthood.

"Guess you are a *little* smart," she said. "I'm not going to do your bidding anymore, by the way. That was a temporary thing, so I could hide myself from prying eyes. Your aura has an interesting effect on my kind."

"That's fine," I said. "I won't be here to hurt you much longer anyway."

I looked back over the ocean. With my nanites at dangerously low levels, they wouldn't be able to activate the antisuicide protocols or keep me alive once the water filled my lungs.

Not being able to swim was a bonus, this time. But I couldn't wait until the system came back. Time to *follow through.*

"Thunders," Logna said. "What idiocy are you contemplating, Runian?"

"My kind ruins the protections on this land," I whispered. "My existence unravels Sefawynn's magic. If I stay, this land dies. And with it, everyone I love. So . . . thank you. For helping me find myself. It was nice to know him for a few days."

I stepped off the dock.

Then sat up a moment later.

"It's only about two feet deep here," Logna said. "Dullard. You realize that's why the wooden pier extends so far out, right? You'd need to walk out much farther to get to the deep part."

"Right, then," I said, standing up. I turned toward the ocean to start walking.

"That's very brave of you," Logna said. "So brave. Stupidly, amazingly, *ridiculously* brave."

I turned and glared at her. "Can't you let me do this with dignity?"

"You tried to drown yourself in knee-deep water," she said. "The chance for dignity has passed."

I sighed. Why had I ended up in the dimension with the *annoying* gods?

"You're right, though," Logna said. "Your poison . . . your substance . . . *will* work against the power of the boasts. It will ferment and undo the runes in any place you remain. For longer than about a month."

I hesitated. "A month?"

"Yup," she said. "That's how long Ulric stayed here, which is what prevented me from doing anything about him. Stay in one place too long, and sure, you'll poison the land. Keep moving, and it won't really matter. You're only one man. But off with you. Noble death. Very warrior-like. Too bad Sefawynn won't have your protection anymore."

"Wait. My protection?"

"Sure," Logna said. "You think I can stand up to Woden by myself? Kid, if I could do that, I'd have stepped in *ages* ago. It was only when you people arrived and disrupted his power that I saw an opening.

"If you keep her close, you should be able to keep him from touching her. My brother *hates* being reminded that—despite being a god—he'll someday die. Pain drives him away, and the pain your presence causes is just enough.

"If you were to, say, keep moving—traveling from town to town— you could protect Sefawynn with your presence *and* prevent your poison from killing any wights or disrupting the runes. But then there'd be no noble warrior's death for you. So, off with you! When my skops tell the story, we'll leave out the part where you belly flopped into a puddle."

I glared at her. Then felt an almost electric warmth.

I could stay?

I could STAY!

She offered her hand, and had a surprisingly firm grip as she hauled me out of the water. Guess that was part of the whole god thing.

"Thank you," I said to her.

"Eh," she said. "I'm just in it for the stories. You have no idea how boring eternity gets. Particularly when your remaining kin are idiots. Have you heard about the thing with the tree?"

"Yeah," I said.

"Then you know the kind of geniuses I'm dealing with," she said. "Go, Runian. Get some food, have a feast, and stop being so glum. Kiss the girl. You did something great here. *With help.* You deserve to enjoy being a person you like—for longer than a few days, at least."

I grinned. "What are they fixing for dinner anyway?"

"Fish."

"I think I'll . . . seize a few, eh?"

She actually grinned at that. As if it were actually funny. Well, hot damn. I turned back toward the city, and my mind—being the ridiculous piece of work it was—searched for a rating I could give this entire experience.

I settled on no rating. The whole point of those had been to figure out what I wanted in life. Now that I had it, well, maybe I would need to rethink the system entirely.

(. . . five out of five. You served me well, rating system. Enjoy your retirement.)

With a whoop of joy, I ran to meet up with Sefawynn and Ealstan. Turns out, even a coward can save the world. So long as you leave him with no other options.

THE END OF PART FOUR

Epilogue

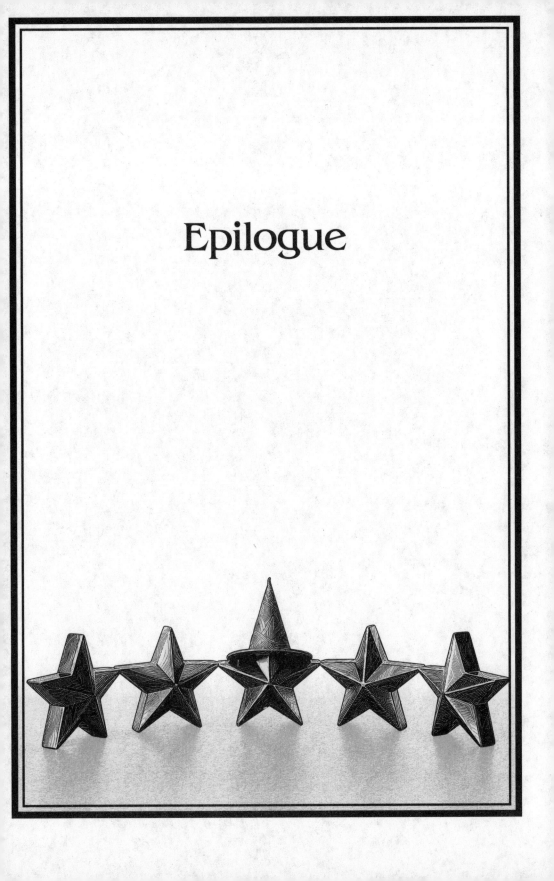

A few months later, Logna watched—unseen—as the skop and her outlander husband spun the tale of the defense of Mael-port to the people of Treewall. Sefawynn spoke the words, and Runian acted it out through something he called a puppet show.

Logna approved. Not only were there ample amounts of silly voices, Woden's puppet was cross-eyed. At first, many of the people in this town were uncertain, hostile. Yet, over the course of the story, they began to lean forward. They began to understand. They began to *believe*.

Sefawynn was not as good of a storyteller as Logna, mind you, but one did not earn a recitation from a goddess without great merit. Technically, saving the world counted—but they hadn't asked, so that was that. Either way, she was pleased to have an acolyte with some modicum of skill. Logna had spent decades hunting for a skop with the spine to stand up to Woden. To have one finally do it, *and* to have the woman actually know how to spin a boast . . .

Well, it would do.

Her kin would regret abandoning these people. Woden could keep his Hordamen. He always had been too easily infatuated with shiny new toys. But it was the builders, not just the takers, who changed the world. Logna knew that for certain now.

Runian made the Woden puppet hide in tandem with Sefawynn's words. He used his strange abilities to create sound effects, so Logna didn't need to add any thunder or anything. That was nice. Thunder wasn't really her thing. She did flare the fire when her part in the story came up again.

He, she thought to herself, *was a particularly good choice.*

Not that she'd *chosen* him, really. She'd sent numbers to him when he'd come looking. A . . . beacon, one might say. Wyrd affected even gods. She hadn't known who he was, or what it would do, or even that her interference would make him enter the world where he did. She'd only known that these were actions she'd needed to take. That was enough.

She did know the codes for his platings. He'd messed that part up. He should have asked for a wight to choose the right symbols, rather than typing them himself. Perhaps she'd deliver them to him someday. If he was nice.

As the story neared its end, the people grew excited, encouraged. Yes, this was the part that got them all. The story of the brave new earl, the aelv-slayer. Logna hadn't mentioned how she'd briefly disrupted the little machines in the blood of the outlanders he'd fought at the doorway. It hadn't been easy. She'd been sick for weeks after that.

But Ealstan had earned his victory, nonetheless. He'd been properly out-numbered and out-weaponed. She'd simply slipped a little grain onto the scales to help them balance.

She could see the people discarding their worries. They would let Sefawynn restore their runestone, then perhaps send a daughter or two—or some sons, Logna wasn't as picky as people thought—to Maelport for training as skops.

Soon, talk of Woden would change. From their hero to the god of their enemies. Which was fair. He had *always* been their enemy.

Logna slipped into the private chamber the people had given Runian and Sefawynn to use during their stay in the village. Here, the two had set up bedrolls and a few curious items. Wires trailed down from the solar panels on the roof to the laptop they'd recovered from the equipment Ryan left in the woods.

On the device, Runian was writing his memoirs. She checked on his progress each day to make certain he was representing her part well. He hadn't been able to open any of the encrypted files Ryan had left, as he didn't know the passwords. Logna did, of course. She could steal any word. It was one of her things. One of those files was a full textual encyclopedia Ryan had downloaded before going on his mission. No big deal. It was only the sum total of human knowledge in his realm.

She formed herself a body—a slender young man, this time—and settled back with the laptop. She could vaguely remember a time before . . . Coming to this land from deep, deep, deep beyond. From the depths of distant places—other beyonds, other times, other *realities*. Swimming upstream as far as they could go, to this place. But then, a wall of pain. They could go no farther.

At least, so far as any of them knew.

She opened the locked files, wincing as the touch of the machine burned her fingertips. She pressed on, however, and picked up reading where she'd stopped the night before.

In a section titled "Dimensional Portals: Mechanical Schematics and Repairs."

THE END

POSTSCRIPT

So where on Earth did this book come from?

This is the odd man out in the group of secret projects I wrote in 2020 and 2021. It's not in the Cosmere, it's in first person, and it's more science fiction than fantasy.

I can trace the original idea back to a story I told myself at night sometime in 2019. You see, as I'm going to bed each night, I tend to imagine a story. Like telling myself a bedtime story. This is how my brain works. If I close my eyes, movies start playing. The one I told myself then wasn't what you're holding—but it was similar. It was the story of someone on a game show where you go back in time and try to stop the *Titanic* from sinking.

I kind of loved the idea, particularly since I hit on the concept of an alternate dimension rather than actual time travel. This let me play with how going "back in time" wouldn't change the future, and how you could actually have a game show that did this—even with multiple seasons and different groups of contestants. That spun me onto the idea of purchasing an alternate dimension.

The fake author of the book, Cecil G. Bagsworth III, is a character that has shown up before in books I've written. (He's the in-world editor of the Alcatraz series.) He's shared by me and my friend Dan Wells, as we dreamed him up back in college: an interdimensional adventurer and writer. Like Indiana Jones if he worked in publishing instead of archaeology. He looks, by pure coincidence, exactly like my brother Jordan. (Jordan is now officially a professional model: We licensed his likeness for the picture of Cecil in the book.) As I first started noodling on the idea of writing this book, it involved Cecil in some capacity.

Back in the early 2010s, I'd actually come up with a cool-sounding title: *The Frugal Wizard's Guide to London*. It felt a tad too Harry Potter, so I shelved it, but as I started getting serious about this book I realized having inserts from the guide would be a fun way to do world-building and insert some levity into what could be a dreary story if handled differently.

I changed it from the *Titanic* because I felt that was, first, a little overplayed, and second, a historical event I don't actually know that much about. Since these secret projects were primarily written for me and my wife, I wanted to have fun with them—and I'm a big fan of Anglo-Saxon England. (It's a mark of pride to me that Michael, my historical expert, didn't have to change *too* much to get me straight on a lot of the facts. The ones I didn't make up, that is.)

The last piece to fall into place was making this what I call a white-room story, where a character wakes up with no memory and has to figure out who they are along with the reader. I've never done one of these in novel form, and I've always wanted to, ever since I read *The Bourne Identity* long, long ago. (*Project Hail Mary* by Andy Weir is another excellent example of this trope done brilliantly—and it certainly had an influence on my decision to use the concept in this book.)

All of that together, stirred up in a pot, became the book you've just read!